SAM CRESCENT

EVERNIGHT PUBLISHING ®

www.evernightpublishing.com

Copyright© 2021

Sam Crescent

Editor: Audrey Bobak

Cover Artist: Jay Aheer

ISBN: 978-0-3695-0397-8

SAM CRESCENT

Sam Crescent

Copyright © 2021

Chapter One

Ava Sinclaire stared into her shot glass. Tequila wasn't her drink of choice but tonight she was celebrating. The divorce had finally come through. She was a free agent from that lying, cheating scumbag.

"You okay there, sweetheart?" the bartender, Ryan, asked. He'd told her his name the moment she sat at the bar.

"I'm perfectly fine."

"I haven't seen you around here before."

"I'm kind of new." She offered him a smile. Totally new. Three months new. After moving to Fort Clover, Ava had set up her bakery in town and was doing quite well. Her first official day of opening turned a small crowd, which she loved. Everyone in town was so nice to her. They all wanted to know more about her, but the moment she told them all she was in the process of getting a divorce, everyone seemed to accept that.

"You sticking around?"

"Yep. Have you heard of the baker called Ava's?

It's mine."

"No shit. I had one of the nicest cream pies from there just last week. You made them?"

"Yep, that was me."

"Wow, shit. You do good. I hear you only work three days a week, though, right?"

"Yes, right."

Someone hollered his name, and within seconds, she was alone again.

Yep, she had her bakery three days a week. Her parents had left her a small fortune that Derek had tried to get from her, but thanks to the prenup her lawyer demanded he sign, she'd been saved from handing over half of her parents' money.

She rarely used it, or at least had rarely used it until she moved towns and bought herself a small house. It was on the edge of town. Just a small place. Two bedrooms, a nice garden. A space for her to enjoy and relax. After all the drama her ex had put her through, she wanted it.

At thirty years old, she knew it was lame to just want peace and quiet, but she was done with men. Done with all the drama they seemed to entail.

Ryan came back, filled her glass with more tequila, and she thanked him. She didn't even know if Fort Clover had a cab company. She was way past her limit.

When the bar suddenly went silent, she frowned and turned around to see what the problem was. In the doorway stood not one, but six, or maybe it was three, or perhaps twelve angry-looking bikers. She must be seeing something, or the tequila had gone straight to her head.

The realtor had warned her there was a local motorcycle club hanging around. There had been one close by in the last town she lived in, and that hadn't been much of a problem.

Spinning back to the bar, she stared down at her shot, wondering why the hell she was even celebrating anyway. Yes, she was finally rid of Derek, but why celebrate that? He'd been wrong for her from the start.

Before he'd entered her life, she had friends, a great job, fun. Her ex had turned her into a woman who slowly stopped seeing friends, stopped going out, and just lived for his approval, only to never get it. He'd chipped away at her armor until she walked in on him fucking his secretary, right in their bedroom. The moment she saw him, it was like a switch had gone off inside her head, and she'd flipped right back to who she was. Only now, she was all alone and ten years older. No kids. No marriage. Fuck all but a nice house, her bakery, and her parents' money still safely belonging to her.

A large, sexy-looking man took a seat right beside her. The leather cut didn't have any sleeves and his heavily inked, muscular arms were on full display. She also caught sight of his knuckles. *Hell's* was written across them with the apostrophe in the divot between the *l* and the *s*.

She'd never gotten any tattoos. It was on her bucket list.

Thank you, lame-ass Derek. Fucking loser.

She lifted her glass into the air and knocked it back, nearly choking on it.

"Wow, what are we drinking to, pretty lady?"

His gruff voice went straight to her core. No man should ever be able to turn a woman on with just the sound of his voice. She turned her head to her little neighbor and stared at him. To her surprise, he glanced from her face down to her ass, then back up, lingering for a few seconds on her tits.

She wasn't a slender woman. Big tits, huge hips,

massive thighs, and she didn't give a flying fuck about it either. After ten years of being told how ugly she was and how she didn't measure up to Derek, she'd made a vow to never allow a man to see her as small. She'd tossed out every single item of clothing and bought herself a whole new wardrobe.

This move was about her. Not about a single man.

"Wouldn't you like to know," she said.

"Are you a regular?"

She shook her head.

"Just passing through?"

She shook her head again. "If you want to know who I am, just ask."

"And you'd give me an honest answer?"

"I've got no reason to lie to you." She glanced at his leather cut, seeing the label marking him as *President*. "And why would I lie to the boss?"

He held out his hand. "The name's Smokey."

"Ava." She shook his hand. "I've just moved here."

He turned her hand left and right. "No ring."

She chuckled. "Single, and I'm totally off men. I hate every last one of them."

"A woman scorned?"

"Nah, a woman sick and tired of them and all the bullshit that comes with them." She didn't miss Derek. There was no pain or sadness. Just an overwhelming anger she didn't even know she possessed. All her life, she'd been the calm one. The sweet one. The person to never make any waves and to always find the good in people. She was done with being a doormat. "To be scorned, I'd have to have actually cared what he did."

Smokey's hand lingered on hers, and she waited for him to say more. "I detect a mark where a ring should be." His thumb grazed over her finger. "Recently divorced?"

"You got it."

"And you say you're not scorned?"

"Nope. It was the wake-up call I needed."

"What did the bastard do?" he asked.

She chuckled. "What makes you think he did something?"

"You're new here. You've got this ... thing about you. I don't know. It says you're the one moving on, not him."

Ava pulled her hand away from him, running a finger across her lip. Maybe it was the alcohol or just the fact she was finally free to do and say whatever she wanted, which was why she blurted out her next part. "I went home to discover my husband anally fucking another woman. Our sex had been completely lackluster. No spark. No nothing. It was just nothing. Let's just say I'm well shot of him. He was the worst thing I ever did."

Ryan came back and filled her glass. "What can I get you, Smokey?"

"The usual."

"So, you visit this bar frequently?" she asked.

"Only when I hear there is a pretty lady sitting here all on her own."

Ava snorted. "Please, I wasn't born yesterday." The drink was going to her head and her mouth. She needed to stop speaking. She pushed the drink away as Ryan put a beer down in front of Smokey. "Do you know of any cab company that will take me home?"

"Not this late, sweetheart. The only guy who does that is sitting right over there." Ryan pointed toward the corner.

"Oh, crap. Looks like I'm walking." She opened her purse, put down several bills, and got to her feet. "Pleasure to meet you, Ryan." Then she put a hand on

Smokey's arm. He was rock hard. Pure muscle. "And you, Smokey. See you both around." She turned on her heel and left the bar.

The tension between the two men was clear, and she had no interest in getting involved in whatever the hell that was. She just wanted some peace and quiet in her own little world.

Holding her purse tight, she began the trek back to her home. She'd have no choice but to make the same trek back to grab her car. This was just like her. Finally experiencing freedom, and look where it got her. All alone and having no choice but to walk home. Next time, she'd plan a little better. After three months in a brand-new place, she really should have her bearings about her now.

Running fingers through her hair, she glanced up at the dark, star-filled sky and took a deep breath.

The divorce from Derek had been stressful because multiple times, he'd tried to find ways to reconcile or any loopholes surrounding the prenup. Fortunately, her parents had been sure to steer her in the direction of a good lawyer. One who had been in the family for a long time.

"Ava."

She stopped at the sound of her name.

"Ava."

She must have drunk way too much if she was starting to imagine people shouting her name.

Tucking her hair behind her ears, she glanced behind her and was surprised to see Smokey heading her way. His long strides captured her attention.

"What's up?" she asked.

"There's no way a pretty woman like you should be walking all alone by herself."

She groaned. "You really don't have to do this.

Honestly, I'm super fine."

"Well, let me take your super-fine ass home."

Ava rolled her eyes. "Seriously? I'm not going to have sex with you."

Smokey smiled, and it nearly knocked her right off her feet. "Now that I wasn't expecting. I'm not after sex, sweetheart. I just want to know you got home safely. I'm being a gentleman." He frowned.

"Not used to the feeling?"

"I'm not used to a woman turning me down."

She laughed and reached out to stroke his leather cut. "It must be the jacket. Do you get cold in the winter?"

"It's not the only cut I wear."

"Ah, I see."

"You seem to know your way around a biker."

She wrinkled her nose. "Not really. Kind of hard not to understand it. President, boss. It's leather and all your BFFs back there were wearing one." She shrugged. "Not hard to deduce."

"Are you always this adorable?"

"Nope." She made the *p* pop. "It's the drink."

"Now that's a shame. Let me walk you home."

"And you're not expecting sex?" she asked.

"Not everything is about sex."

No, not with her. "I get it." She started to walk again, pushing some of her hair off her face. No matter how much time she spent trying to tame her blonde locks, they always had a mind of their own. She more often than not just pulled it back into a ponytail or a messy bun. Right now, she was frustrated with it.

"What do you get?"

"I saw the way some of the other single women at the bar were looking at you. The way they were dressed. Sex with them would be far more enjoyable." She licked her lips as Smokey grabbed her arm and spun her around to face him.

"I'm sensing this asshole of an ex did a number on you," Smokey said.

"What makes you think that?"

"It's a hunch. I've never met a woman who would so willingly put herself down."

"You've got that all wrong, biker boy. I'm not putting myself down. I'm a realist, and it's what we do. I'm not the kind of person men think of having sex with. Not the dirty kind anyway." She shrugged. "It's a fact."

"Really?"

"Really." She offered him a smile. "I'm not offended." She began to walk again.

"Then please tell me, Ava, why it is that my dick has been hard as fucking rock since I saw you at the bar? And I've wanted you from that moment."

She stopped and turned toward him, shocked. There was no way she'd heard that.

****

Hunter had wanted fresh meat. It was the only reason Smokey had decided to go to Ryan's Place. There was plenty of free, willing pussy of all ages back at the clubhouse. He hadn't been out for a short time, and with Ugly Beast spending more time at home with Abriana and the baby, and the shit that went down with the mafia, he was bored.

He needed something to excite him.

No new deals had come through for him. He'd only gotten a single phone call from Sebastian Drago about a possible meetup with the head of the mafia, but he'd so far declined.

His club didn't need the money, nor the heat. They made their money in several different ways.

The moment he'd entered the bar, he'd checked

out the blonde sitting on her own. Her hair was fucking wild with so much curl to it. Instantly, he'd wanted the locks spread across his pillow. Once he sat beside her and caught sight of her pretty face, he'd wanted to fuck her.

Every single part of her body called to him. Fat, juicy tits, hips he could hold on to, and those thighs. He wanted them wrapped around his waist as he pounded her cunt.

In fact, he wanted it all.

Rather than say that, he'd gotten talking. Now, he'd never been a jealous man, but whatever her ex-husband had done to her, Smokey wanted retribution. This woman had no reason to be saying the shit she was.

"Is this supposed to get me into bed?" she asked.

"I'm not trying to get you into bed." He closed the distance between them. Ava stood firm, not shrinking back, and he found that incredibly hot. Grasping her hand, he tugged hard until she fell into him. He placed her hand right over his dick.

"We're out in the open."

"Do I look like I give a fuck what people think?" he asked. With her hand directly over his cock, he smiled. "Now, do you question what I want?" he asked.

She licked her lips, and he couldn't help but groan.

"That mouth would look good wrapped around my dick."

"You're saying this stuff to distract me."

"No. I'm saying what I think. It's a habit." He reached out, cupped her cheek, and ran his thumb across her bottom lip. "You really have no clue the kind of things I want to do with you."

"This is crazy. You don't know me."

"Don't need to know a person to want them,

Ava." He tilted her head back. "I'm guessing your ex-husband didn't teach you that."

Instantly, she shut down. She removed her hand and stepped back. "I need to get home."

"Do you love your ex?" he asked.

She stopped and turned toward him. "No. I don't."

"Did you ever?"

"What is with the twenty questions?" she asked. "I don't know. You shouldn't be putting my hand on a body part, or asking so many personal questions. It's rude."

"It's how I get to know a person."

"Then you really do need help. I'm not the one to help you."

She started to walk again, and for a few seconds, he admired her round ass. After a few seconds, he fell into step beside her.

"You don't need to do this."

"I think it's time we establish something here, babe. I do whatever the hell I like when I like. No one tells me what to do."

"Must be nice to have that kind of power."

He smiled. "Anyone can have it."

She folded her arms and didn't ask him any question. The minutes ticked on by and all he got was more and more curious about her.

The divorce. The asshole ex-husband.

"What's your full name?" he asked.

"Not happening. You think I haven't seen those horror movies where the girl gives away all the dirty details?" She shook her head. "Not happening. I'm not that stupid."

He laughed. "I didn't say you were."

"You've got my first name. That's more than

enough."

"I'm going to go out on a limb here and say you're not used to being hit on." He watched her reaction. She merely stayed looking straight ahead. "With the imprint of the ring, you've been married for some time. You're a sweet-looking kind of woman. I'm guessing your first real relationship ended in marriage."

This made her stop. "What's your point?"

"You didn't get used to men flirting with you. You don't think you've got it in you for men to want to flirt with you."

"You don't know what you're talking about."

"No? Then how many men have you fucked?"

She burst out laughing. "You really think I'm going to tell an absolute stranger?"

"I know people. I've gotten to where I am today by knowing what people are thinking. What's going on in their head at every single moment. I know you, Ava."

"No, Smokey. You don't know me at all. I just want to walk home in peace and quiet, and you're not giving me that."

"How old are you?" he asked.

"A woman never tells."

"I'm guessing late twenties."

"You're close."

"Thirty."

She nodded.

"So, you're a thirty-year-old woman. Moved to a small town. Recently divorced because you caught your ex cheating on you. You don't have much experience with men, and you're nervous around them."

She began laughing again. "I'm not nervous around you."

"Exactly."

This made her stop and frown. "You're not

making any sense. You know that, right?"

"A woman who knows men would know to steer well clear of me. Instead, you talked to me at the bar as if it's a regular thing between the two of us."

Ava stared at him. Her face a complete blank.

He couldn't read her, and he wanted to know what was going on in that head of hers.

"If this is your way of trying to warn me away from you, you're doing a really bad job of it," she said.

"On the contrary. I'm trying to fuck you, Ava," he said.

She didn't stop walking. He stayed beside her, step by step.

The silence stretched on, the minutes gradually building.

They were getting close to some houses, and he saw them coming even closer, which would mean he'd have to part with her if that was where she lived. He didn't like the thought of leaving her alone.

"Is that all you want?" she asked. "Sex?"

"Is that a deal-breaker?"

She came to a stop. Her hand went to her forehead as she shook her head left and right. "I'm so confused right now. We're talking in riddles. It must be the alcohol, but I'm not going to agree to anything." She smiled at him. "It was a pleasure to meet you."

Her speed picked up, and he found her so utterly adorable. The way she moved and talked. He liked it.

Every woman he'd come across either gave him a withering stare or thrust their tits in his face. He was used to more women throwing themselves at him, begging for his mark. They wanted the bragging rights to have taken the president of the Hell's Bastards MC. It was fun until it had stopped.

Now he used women to scratch an itch. He had a

feeling Abriana was to blame—the woman he'd arranged to marry one of his men. She'd distracted him. He wasn't attracted to her in any way. It was what she represented to the club, to Ugly Beast. The brother with the ugliest-looking face had been able to find true love. They now had a newborn daughter and every time he saw them, he witnessed a whole new lot of possibilities. Did he want that? Women had yet to prove they were worth his time. All he'd ever been was disappointed in them and by them.

They walked toward one of the few houses on the outskirts of town. It explained why she didn't mind the walk. It wasn't too far to the bar.

She stopped at the gate of a sweet-looking house. Small, but it just screamed hers.

Ava turned toward him. "Thank you for the walk home."

"Can I see you again?"

"I don't even know if I'm going to remember this conversation, Smokey. It was nice to meet you." She held her hand out and he frowned.

Taking hers within his own, he shook her hand. She smiled at him. Her eyes were a beautiful, bright green. Her lips begged to be kissed.

He was never the kind of man to let an opportunity pass him by. Pulling her close, he gripped the back of her head and slammed his lips down on hers. She gasped, parting for him, and he plundered inside.

She moaned as he deepened the kiss.

Running his hand down her back, he cupped her generous ass. He knew it would be the perfect fit for him. Her body was made for him and him alone, and damn it, he wanted to fuck her, hard. To consume every single part of her.

This went against everything he stood for.

Smokey stepped back. "Good night," he said.

Her lips were swollen, and she didn't say a word. She turned on her heel and walked up to her home. He saw her hand raise to her lips as she fit the key into her lock. After she looked back one last time, she was inside her house.

He waited until he heard the locks click into place, which they did.

Spinning on his heel, he saw Hunter waiting for him.

"We were going to the bar for me? Why is it you got the pussy, as did Brick and Kinky?"

"You're becoming way too picky."

"Oh, bite me. You know as well as I do you took the best fucking pickings." Hunter looked back at the house. "You willing to share?"

"Hell the fuck no."

He'd shared women with Hunter in the past, but with Ava, he didn't even want to consider it.

"Whatever. One hot woman and you won't even share. When did you get so spoiled?"

He chuckled. "I guess having a club work their asses off for me."

Hunter rolled his eyes. "Who is she?"

The kiss had been good for two things. One, he got to feel those plump lips on his, which was more than fine by him. He wanted to kiss her a hell of a lot more. Two, distracted from the kiss, she'd forgotten all about her purse.

A gentleman wouldn't look inside. But Ava wouldn't tell him her full name.

Walking beside Hunter, he opened the purse and flicked it open.

Hunter had his cell phone out with the flashlight.

Ava Sinclaire. Well, he was going to get to know

everything there was to know about this woman.

"Club pussy or just some fun?" Hunter asked.

"Time will tell."

Pocketing her purse, he listened to Hunter bitch and moan all the way back to Ryan's Place.

Several of the cars had already disappeared from the parking lot. The club's presence had a tendency to do just that. They had the power to send people running. Load of pussies.

Entering the bar, he saw Ryan cleaning a couple of glasses.

"You know why I'm here," he said.

Ryan put the glasses down. "I know, and I got everything for you in the back."

Kinky was already rounding the bar, grabbing Ryan by the scruff of his neck. "Then why don't you show us?"

The rest of the clientele left. Rumors would be running rife, but if everyone knew what was good for them, they'd keep all the real details private.

Chapter Two

Ava wouldn't panic.

She'd keep the smile on her face and pretend everything was fine.

Women lost their purses all the freaking time. It was no big deal.

The purse had her driver's license. Bank cards. She'd even written down a couple of passwords because she hadn't had the time to memorize them yet. All of that was now in the hands of a potential thief.

Just keep smiling.

She'd gone to the bakery, and it was only as she was looking through her bag for the keys that she realized her purse was missing.

Damn it.

The details of last night were a little hazy to her. She hadn't drunk a lot. Tequila wasn't even a drink she'd enjoyed in the past, but last night had been special.

Now, she was cursing everything.

Smokey.

He was the only person she remembered from last night. She didn't know if their conversation actually happened, or if she made it up, which fucking sucked.

She handed out fresh cream cakes, lemon pies, and cookies. Her gingerbread men were pretty special, and kids loved them.

Decorating was something she'd been learning for many years. All those hours of being stuck home alone, waiting for her ex to arrive, she'd taken all that time to learn how to bake and decorate cakes.

A couple of builders from the local construction yard came in for their sandwiches. She was a bakery that offered sweet and savory treats. With the breakfast wave over, she leaned back as the oven pinged to let her know the fresh batch of cookies was done. It always surprised her how much sweet stuff she sold in a morning.

Her little bakery was proving to be a treat she hadn't seen coming.

Still, no matter how often she thought about her success, it didn't detract from the fact her purse was still missing.

She'd have to go to the bank, cancel all of her cards. Who the hell did she need to alert about a missing driver's license?

So much to do.

She was never visiting Ryan's Place again. The tequila was great, but the morning after was proving to be something to juggle. This was supposed to be stress-free.

This was anything but stress-free.

With the cookies cooling, she returned to the main store.

Several items had already disappeared off the shelf, and she quickly rearranged, removing the cards to neaten it up.

The morning continued to be busy, leaving her only short ten-minutes spots of no customers. She really did love staying busy.

However, she was close to tearing her hair out just before the lunch rush. She was going to have to close the shop to go to the bank. She couldn't handle the pressure of not knowing where her purse was.

She was about to find the closed sign when the doorbell rang. "I'll be out in a second," she said.

She didn't have the patience to find the sign. She wrote *Closed! Back Soon* on a piece of paper. Grabbing the sticky tape, she headed to the main desk only to come to a stop.

Smokey stood on the other side of the counter, a

smile on his face, with two of his men from last night.

"Hi," she said.

"Well, hello. This is a small world."

She looked at his men who were glancing at the goodies on offer. "What can I do for you?" She frowned. "Did I tell you I owned a bakery?"

"No. You didn't, and I have to wonder why. Everything looks so good."

She smiled, feeling her cheeks heat. Were the compliments he'd paid her last night real? She wasn't used to men saying nice things to her or about her.

"Er, thank you. I hate to ask you to leave but I really need to get to the…" She stopped as Smokey held up her purse for her.

"Missing this?"

"You … how?"

"You dropped it last night. You'd already gone into your house, and well, I didn't want to send it through the mail when I could see you in person."

"You wanted to see me in person?" she asked.

"What do you think?" He still held her purse.

Her heart had stopped pounding.

She put down the sign she'd written and reached out to take the purse. "Thank you. I've been freaking out about this all morning. I didn't know where it was, and yeah, thank you." She held on to it and smiled. "Can I get you anything? On the house. I don't know if that's the right term for baked goods."

"What do you have in mind?"

Ava pointed at the displays. "Have a look and tell me what you want. I'll be right back." She rushed toward her small office. Pushing the purse into the bag, she glanced at herself in the mirror. With baking, she had to put her hair into a net, but once all the baking was finished, she needed to serve customers. Hygiene was very important to her. Did she want her hair down?

No, she wasn't going to go crazy for a man she barely knew.

As she stepped back into the main shop, Smokey's gaze followed her.

"Did you decide?"

"He hasn't decided, but I have," a large man said from the right. "Three of those cookies, please."

"Coming right up."

"Hunter's paying," Smokey said.

"Dude, she said it was free."

"No, she said what I'm having is free. You pay, Hunter. As do you, Kinky."

She looked at the disappointment on the men's faces. "Er, if they want..." Smokey looked at her. "Or not."

"They can pay their way. You don't need to be out of pocket for them."

The guilt was there though.

The freebies were on offer for Smokey, but she didn't mind extending it to his friends. "I honestly don't mind."

"You're running a business, Ava. They will pay their way."

"Lady, it's sweet, but you don't want to argue with the boss."

She didn't know who was who, so she merely smiled and rung up their purchases, being sure to put a discount on them, ignoring Smokey's stare as she did. He could attempt to boss her around all he wanted to, but she wasn't going to let him get away with it.

Single.

Independent.

And loving every second of it.

His men left the store, but she noted they didn't

go far. They stood right outside the door.

"They're going to scare off my customers."

"This won't take long."

"I haven't been here long. I don't want them to ruin this."

Smokey smiled. "It'll take more than them to steer them clear of this place. I'd heard of it before I even realized this was yours."

Her cheeks heated. "You're just throwing a compliment at me. You don't mean that."

"Sweetheart, you're going to realize one day that I don't say shit I don't mean," he said. "Which is why I'm asking you to come to a party."

"A party?"

"Yeah. At the clubhouse. Tomorrow night. I know where you live. I'll pick you up. I'll take a muffin."

She held her hand up. "I haven't said I was agreeing to go with you."

"Why wouldn't you want to come?"

Ava couldn't think of a single reason why.

"I'm still waiting, darling."

"My name's Ava."

"I remember."

"Then use it."

Smokey smirked. "Can't take some sweet names?"

"They're empty names. You probably say them to everyone." She rubbed at her temple. "I don't think going to a party is a good idea."

"Why not?"

"I'm not the party kind of girl."

"What kind of girl are you exactly?" he asked.

She stared at him. No words came to her. She was a complete and total blank. "I don't know."

"Then don't you think it will be fun to explore exactly who you are?"

Blowing out a breath, she shrugged. "You're right. I don't know. Sure. Who else will be at this party?"

"People."

She rolled her eyes. "Is it a theme?"

"Wear something sexy. Now, how about that muffin?"

"What kind?" she asked.

"I'll take a chocolate chip. Do you have a thing for chocolate?"

"Love it." She wrapped up his muffin. "I hope you enjoy it, and thank you for returning my purse."

"Do you get drunk like that often?"

"Hell, no. It was a one-off."

"The divorce?"

"Yeah."

"And where is Derek nowadays?"

Ava looked at Smokey. "I never told you my ex's name."

"You must have."

She didn't believe him. "I don't know what Derek is doing, and to be quite frank, I don't care. I moved on. I'll see you tomorrow night."

"You sure will, Ava Sinclaire," he said.

She watched him leave the shop.

Three women paused outside her shop. One look at the angry-looking bikers and they continued to walk. She also noticed they continued to ogle all the men.

Shaking her head, she went back to checking on the remaining baked goods. She didn't have time to think about her encounter with Smokey straight away as the lunch rush was chaotic.

She sold out of everything and had no choice but to close the shop early.

More often than not, she didn't stay open for dinner. With the shelves empty, she cleaned up, set about the doughs to make her life easier in a couple of days' time, locked up, and arranged for a cab to take her to Ryan's Place.

She hadn't gotten her car yet, and now that she had her purse, she was even happier.

Arriving at the bar, she paid the driver, climbed out, and saw her car was the only one in the parking lot. She also happened to notice the bar was completely closed. Like dead.

Curiosity got the better of her as she walked up to the main door, and sure enough, stuck on the front was a notice of being closed until further notice.

"What?"

It wasn't any of her business, so she climbed into her car, started up the engine, and smiled as it purred to life. This was the life. Securing her seat belt, she pulled onto the road and drove the short distance back to her house. With her car parked in her driveway, she grabbed her bag and walked into her home.

The scent of lemon greeted her, such a divine smell. She was a sucker for anything lemon or chocolate.

After locking the door behind her, she placed her bag on the hook, along with her jacket. Reaching inside her bag, she grabbed her purse and took it out. She walked into her kitchen, taking some water from the fridge, and sat at her small table.

She opened her purse and saw everything was as it should be. The money was all still there. Her bank cards and her driver's license.

Not that she thought Smokey would steal anything. No. It was his knowing her ex-husband's first name. She hadn't said *Derek* aloud. She was sure of it. Even with tequila inside her.

Alcohol wouldn't have made her that vocal. It just wasn't possible.

Running a finger across her lip, she tried to think, and there was no way he could have known. Not unless he got all the information from looking into her. People could do that, couldn't they? Look into people they were interested in? Find out every single little minute detail?

Why would Smokey look into her?

Did she even care that he'd done some kind of background check on her?

She closed her purse and sipped at her water.

Smokey wasn't a man she was used to. He was powerful, dangerous, and he clearly was used to getting whatever the hell he wanted, no matter what.

"Oh, stop worrying, Ava. Nothing is going to happen. So, he checked you out. Big deal. Get over it and move on." She finished her water, got to her feet, and ignored the niggling feeling working its way inside her.

****

Smokey knocked on his date's door and waited.

He wasn't going to take no for an answer. She'd love one of these parties, he was sure of it. If not, he'd get his answer about the kind of woman she was. He didn't want a fucking prude, and no matter how badly he wanted to fuck her, there would be limits to what he was willing to do to get her in his bed.

Like now.

He wanted to party.

The brothers were all back at the clubhouse enjoying good food, sex, and beer. Probably all in that order.

It had been a trying couple of weeks for the club, especially as the Italian mafia picked a new Boss, not to mention the waves that had been caused with the Twisted Bastards MC. The fact Ryan had allowed some of the fuckers into his bar a couple of weeks ago, and was known to have been doing business with them, pissed him off.

He'd been too distracted by shit going on at home to look at the bigger picture. That shit wouldn't happen again, which was why he'd arranged a meeting with the Twisted Bastards MC President, Creed. Tonight, he wanted to spend time with Ava. The curvy baker had gotten under his skin, and the only way for him to work it off was to fuck her.

Ava opened the door. A fresh smile on her face, and she wore the cutest black dress he'd ever seen. It molded to her curves and flared out at her thighs, giving it a *whoosh* effect.

"Damn," he said.

"I'm being frank here. I don't know what kind of sexy we're going for. This is the closest I've got." She wrinkled her nose. "I know it's not great."

He wrapped his arm around her waist and pulled her close. "Who says it's not great?"

"I did."

Smokey ran his hand down to the curve of her ass. "I like it."

"Good."

He stepped back to reveal his bike.

"Hell, no," she said.

"Excuse me?"

"I'll take my car to your clubhouse. There's no way I'm getting on the back of a bike."

"Babe, get your ass on the bike."

"Er, no. This babe doesn't get told what to do and obey." She walked to her car. "I'll drive. It'll be good this way. I can come home without having to stop you from having fun."

"You're doing this to piss me off," he said.

"Why would I do that?" She gave him a little chuckle, but she'd already climbed into her car.

Two could play at this game. Straddling his bike, exceedingly disappointed in the fact she wasn't seated behind him, he reeved his engine and glared at the offending car. Most chicks wanted to be on the back of his bike.

Ava was … totally different, and he was going to have to get used to that.

Still, he liked that she didn't back down. Ava wasn't a doormat. However, if she thought she was going to get away from his party easily, she was very much mistaken.

Smokey took the lead, driving with her following him. The guys were going to laugh their asses off when they saw him, but he didn't care. He'd have the prettiest girl at the club.

Riding to the clubhouse, he'd hoped to use the vibrations of the machine to turn her on and to get as close to her as humanly possible. That wasn't going to happen.

Arriving at the clubhouse, he cut the engine as Ava picked a spot. A couple of the guys were already drinking. The scent of barbeque was heavy in the air, and music covered any wave of laughter.

Ava climbed out and he took her hand holding the keys.

"Hey, what are you doing?" she asked.

"I'm making sure you don't run off from me tonight. You need these keys back, you've got to ask nicely."

He put the keys into his jeans pocket.

"You're not playing fair."

"Neither are you." He pressed his lips to hers. "But you don't see me complaining."

"I barely know you."

"And you think I know a lot more about you?"

She glared at him. "Are you telling me you didn't run some kind of background check on me?"

He paused as he looked at her.

"Yeah, you think I'm stupid? Suddenly knowing where I work. My ex. All topics I'm pretty sure I didn't cover." She smiled at him. "I also happened to notice Ryan's Place is closed until further notice and your knuckles are bloody, like they hit someone. Am I getting hot so far?"

He had no idea an intelligent, observant woman could turn him on so much. Most of the women he knew turned a blind eye to the happenings within the club. Ava took it all in.

"Did you like what you found?" she asked, hand on hip.

"Do you think you'd be here if I didn't?"

"Fair enough. I need a drink. Are we going to get this party started or are we going to stand outside and chat about how unfair you are?"

He smiled and invaded her space, pressing her up against her car. "You know, I've hurt men for less. I don't like being disrespected."

Ava put her hands on his shoulders. He liked her touch a little too much. "And I don't like having my privacy invaded."

"You would've given up your personal details so easily?"

"In time. I'd have shared anything, including my ex's name. Seeing as you know all about me, I think it's unfair. I need to know more about you, besides the fact you're an arrogant asshole."

"Believe me, that's one of my better qualities."

"I have no doubt. Drink or not?" she asked.

He pressed his body against hers, seeing the flare in her gaze. "How about I take you up to my room?"

"How about I get a drink first and you're nice to me?" she asked. "You want a girl to fuck, I'm sure there are plenty of willing women around."

He put his hands on her hips, letting her feel how aroused he was. "Let's get one thing straight, Ava. You can give me lip all you want. I like it, but you and me, it's a sure thing."

"Not if you're an asshole." She took him by surprise, pressing her lips against his. It wasn't a deep kiss or even a long one. Just a single peck on the lips. "Drink?" She brushed past him, and he grabbed her hand.

He wouldn't allow her to shake him off. The dress wasn't the skimpiest thing that would be worn. He guaranteed there were women wearing absolutely nothing. What he didn't want was any of the brothers to think she was an easy ride.

She belonged to him. Every single part of her.

He wanted her so badly. His time in her bed would come.

Until then, he was going to have fun exploring this woman. He'd gotten used to the club whores throwing themselves at him. He couldn't remember a time he actually had to do anything but snap his fingers.

They entered the bar, and Ava came to a complete stop. There were three completely naked women dancing across the bar. Two were kissing as the other one danced. The bar was high enough that as she went down and spread her knees, they got a clear sight of her pussy.

"Oh," Ava said.

"You can handle this, right?" he asked.

She glanced over her shoulder. "Your party is one big orgy?"

"No, my party is a bunch of guys having a whole lot of fun." He pressed a kiss to her cheek. "Come on."

He moved through the crowd, going to the bar and ordering her a beer.

"I'll just have a soda."

Smokey pressed the beer into her hand and took a swig of his own.

He spotted a couple of the guys checking her out, and he pulled her close to his side, putting a hand on her ass for good measure. They all backed off. There were a lot of benefits to being the president of the club. This was one of them.

He took her hand, swigging the beer and moving her away from the crowd. They were stopped on the dance floor by a topless woman.

"Hey, Smokey, I'm so wet for you." She ran her finger down his chest.

He shoved her away.

"Hey, that wasn't nice," Ava said.

Pressing her against the wall with his body, he stared down into her eyes. She was a lot smaller than him.

"These women need to learn their place."

"You don't have to be mean about it."

He smiled. "Yeah, I do. You don't understand this world, but that's okay. In time, you'll come to see what it's all about."

Smokey noticed she started to take small swigs of her beer as they watched the room. Guys were playing pool, men and women were making out.

They'd come back into the main clubhouse. He took her outside where couples were eating and dancing. The loud music inside could still be heard from a short distance.

A couple of fires had been built in trash cans.

Night had already fallen.

Ava finished her beer and he pulled her into his arms.

"What are you doing?" she asked.

"Dancing. It's what you do at a party."

"I'm pretty sure naked girls flashing their personals is not all that happens at a party."

The sound of a moan filled the air. Smokey glanced over Ava's shoulder to see Kinky was once again not caring where he was to get his dick wet.

One of the girls who worked for them in the porn films, Swallow, he believed she'd named herself, was completely naked with Kinky behind her, pounding her.

"Yes, yes, fuck yes," she said.

"Now that's a different party," Smokey said.

He spun Ava in his arms to see where his gaze was. The moment she caught sight of the couple, she tensed in his arms. He put his hands to her stomach, drawing her back against his body.

"Smokey?"

"Don't panic. Nothing bad is going to happen. I promise you," he whispered against her ear. She let out a gasp. "She works for us. Swallow is used to people watching. She gets off on it."

"You don't think she's faking it?" Ava asked.

"I'm sure there are times she does. Women do it all the time, but right now, look at her. Look at her face and the way she's fucking back against Kinky. She loves it. She loves having a cock in her pussy." He slowly glided his hand up toward her breast. His thumb skimmed the side and she tensed up again.

He held perfectly still.

Kinky pulled out of Swallow, removed his condom, and came all over her face.

It wasn't exactly the ending Smokey was hoping

for.

"I need another beer," Ava said. She pulled out of his arms, and he wanted to go and beat the living shit out of Kinky. Women didn't want to have cum all over their faces.

Damn it. That was the last time he was ever going to trust Kinky.

He followed Ava back into the clubhouse, only she didn't stay at the bar. She took one look around, shook her head, and stepped right on out. She walked to the car and clearly forgot he had the keys.

When she spun around, he was already there, waiting.

"Can I have my keys?"

"What's going on, Ava?" he asked.

"Do you really need to ask that?" She shook her head. "I can't compete with that. There's no way that's a normal party."

"At the clubhouse, it kind of is."

"Why did you invite me, Smokey? I don't get it." She looked past his shoulder. "You know my history. I bet you know every single little detail about me. Still, you bring me here. I don't know if you're trying to laugh at me, or..."

"I'm not laughing," he said.

"What is this?" she asked.

"I wanted you to have fun. You're right. I know everything about you. Every single little detail you can get on a piece of paper. I even looked into your ex and I can already form a picture. The lonely housewife. Left alone, passed over by your ex. He's fucking everything in sight and you're at home, wondering what the hell you did wrong."

"You don't have a clue what you're talking about."

"That's where you're wrong. I know what I'm talking about," he said. "You're not angry or offended by what you see here." He advanced toward her. "You're fucking envious."

"You don't know everything. You've got it all wrong!"

"No?" He pressed his hand between her thighs and found exactly what he expected. "You're soaking wet, baby. That can only mean one thing—you're very much aroused." He removed his hand. "Now, when you remove that stick from your ass, maybe we can talk. Until then, have a nice life." He slammed the keys into her hand, turned on his heel, and left.

Chapter Three

Ava couldn't remember a time she'd been so … pissed. Was that even a strong enough word? She let out a growl as she pounded her fists into the dough. Over and over, she beat it until she had no choice but to let the dough attempt to proof.

She stepped back, removed the gloves she'd been using, and washed her hands.

Ever since she'd left the party last night, she'd been angry. There were no other words or explanation for it. She was so incredibly angry. At herself, at Smokey, at Derek.

She folded her arms across her chest and closed her eyes. Counting to ten didn't work, nor twenty.

Even the enjoyment she got from baking and serving customers didn't cut it.

She didn't know what the hell Smokey had done to her, but it had pissed her off. The door opened, and she felt tears fill her eyes. She wafted her face in an attempt to get herself back under control and headed out to go serve.

Two women stood side by side. One with long, intense, raven-black hair, the other long and brown.

"Hello, welcome to Ava's. What can I get for you?" she asked.

She'd spent a long time staring at the mirror, trying to figure out the best way to offer a welcome at her bakery.

"Wow, you are pretty," the raven-haired one said.

"Do I know you?" she asked.

The woman spun around, showing off her leather cut that proclaimed her to be a Hell's Bastards MC member.

"Are you Smokey's daughter?" Ava asked.

The woman burst out laughing. "I'm so going to be telling the big man that one. Wow, hell, no. I'm not his daughter. It's rare to happen, but I'm a member of the club. Earned my patch some time ago."

"Oh." She frowned and then groaned. "Oh, crap. I'm so sorry. I didn't mean to offend you."

"No offense. You should see the way it throws men off. They think they stand a chance with a daddy's princess, but when they get to know me…"

"Right," Ava said, chuckling. "What can I get you two ladies?"

"Ladies. I've been called many things."

The brunette chuckled. "Don't mind her. I'm Abriana, this is Raven."

"It's nice to meet you. I'm Ava." She held her hand out and they all shook hands. "What can I get you?"

"I'll take whatever is your best thing," Raven said. "I came to check out the woman who has our president in an awful mood."

"Raven, don't."

"Smokey's upset?" Ava asked.

"Smokey's pissed off. Barking orders. I mean, he's usually like that anyway, but he sometimes has a bit more tact, you know?"

The truth was she didn't have a clue, and so she merely smiled, nodded, and just left it at that.

"So, when are you stopping by?" Raven asked. "I caught sight of you and the boss himself last night. You can't tell me you don't want to tap that."

"My best friend has yet to develop a filter," Abriana said.

"He's rough around the edges and an asshole, but come on, you're not intrigued by how this is going to go?" Raven asked.

The two women began to have a conversation

between themselves. Ava picked out a couple of baked items, rang them up, and then told them the amount.

"So, what do you say?" Raven asked.

"What do I say to what?"

"You get that stick out of your ass and you give Smokey a chance?" Raven held out some money. Ava took it and counted out the change, wondering if Smokey had asked Raven to approach her.

"You were married, right? Bad husband and all that deal."

"Forgive my friend. She is usually much better at being tactful," Abriana said.

"Oh, please, I'm not. This is who I am."

"Well, it was nice to meet you both," Ava said.

"Come on. Her husband was a grade-A asshole. You heard it," Raven said. "I bet the asshole never considered her, even in the bedroom."

"Raven, we're not talking about this."

The two women left the shop, and Ava stood at her counter, confused. There wasn't even a lunch rush yet and already, she felt exhausted.

Men.

They were … confusing.

Smokey was strange. What exactly did he want from her? It wasn't like he was giving her a whole list of things he wanted.

She rubbed at her temple.

The lunch rush took it right out of her. Fortunately, she had another sold-out day. She cleaned, put everything away, and left her shop. She made sure to lock it up tight. Now she got to enjoy a couple of days of experimenting, maybe put her feet up, enjoy some hot cocoa or a good book. She hadn't decided yet which one she wanted to do. Either option was fun for her.

She climbed into her car, but rather than start the

engine, she sat back and thought.

Raven was right. Her ex had never been great in bed. Their sex life had consisted of missionary position until he found his release, and she was always left wanting. For five years, that was her married sex life. Then one day out of the blue, she picked up a book, and from start to end, it was pure sex. Hot, undeniable, no-holds-barred sex. The kind of sex she thought about but figured didn't exist.

Then some searches helped her to discover there was a whole load of people out there enjoying lots of good sex. She just wasn't one of them. Would never be one of them.

After her research, she tried to get Derek to do more. She'd bought sexy lingerie. Toys. Spent lots of time practicing how to approach. One night, when she did, it was like Derek realized she wasn't an idiot anymore.

He'd gotten mean. Cruel even. Telling her the reason he only did missionary. How he couldn't stand to see her naked. The sight of her sickened him.

"Stop it, Ava. You're a beautiful, kind, woman. No man has this power over you." Still, the tears welled up. She pressed her lips together to calm herself.

The traitors fell. She refused to cry because of Derek. He shouldn't have any more power over her. She wouldn't let him. Yet, here she sat in her car. Emotional.

Smokey had offered her a chance, and he'd shut her down.

Frowning, she put the key into the ignition, fired her machine up, and took off. She remembered the route from the previous night, and it didn't take her too long to get there. She'd pushed her foot to the gas, and now, as she arrived, her heart pounded. Rather than stop, she kept on going.

She parked the car, climbed out, and walked toward the main door.

One of the guys she remembered from her shop sat at the bar, rubbing at his head.

"Hey," she said. "I'm looking for Smokey. Do you know where I can find him?"

The guy looked up. "Oh, it's you. He's in his office." He waved her off.

She followed his direction and without thinking about what was going to happen, she stepped into Smokey's office.

Ava had expected him to already have a woman screwing him. He sat in his office, hunched over the table, reading.

When the door closed, he looked up. "Ava," he said.

She held her hand out. After closing the door and locking it, she turned back toward him. "I need you to sit right there. You're not going to do anything." She dropped her bag to the floor. "I'm thirty years old. I got married at twenty. I knew Derek since I was eighteen. He was my one and only boyfriend. For a good portion of our marriage, I didn't realize sex could be had without the light on, or that we could do it any other way than with me on my back."

She began to remove her jacket. Her hands shook. "Of course, I found out you can do a lot more. I tried to spice things up with Derek. I did. I was bored. I hated sex. I hated the way he got on, did his thing, and then I was left with nothing. We didn't even cuddle, let alone kiss."

She got to her shirt and pulled it over her head. "However, when I tried to spice it up, he told me how ugly I was. How loathsome. That he loved me, but he didn't find me attractive. He couldn't stand my big tits, jelly legs, slobby stomach, and disgusting hips. He had a lot more inventive, colorful names for my body." She stripped down until she stood before Smokey in her black lace lingerie.

It was beautiful. The model who'd worn it enhanced the colors, and she'd wanted it. Ordered it that night.

"I … I don't know what I'm doing. The sex I'm accustomed to is for me to lie down and wait for it to be over. I don't know what real arousal is unless I'm watching some kind of porn or reading a book." Tears filled her eyes. "I don't think I've experienced a real orgasm. I think I've enjoyed a release, but not an orgasm."

She pressed her lips together, counted to ten as he still sat there, saying nothing. "I moved here to start over. To not have my ex dominate everything, but here I am, pushing you away because of that. I don't know if I can be what you need. Not after what I saw last night. This is all I am. If you don't find me attractive, tell me now."

Smokey put his pen down and leaned back in his chair. "Turn around."

"What?"

"Turn around."

She clenched her hands into fists but did as he asked, turning for him to see every single part of her.

This is not embarrassing.

You're the one who came here and stripped down naked.

She turned full circle and Smokey stood. He rounded his desk and leaned against it. "Take off your underwear."

Ava flicked the catch at the back of her bra, letting her tits spring free. She dropped it to the floor and stepped out, so inelegantly out of her panties. This wasn't a striptease.

Now she stood in front of Smokey completely naked.

This had to be the worst idea of her life. There was no way she could justify why she'd done this. Pushing some hair off her face, she waited.

"Your ex was an asshole." Smokey moved from the desk and stood in front of her. He touched her waist, and she felt on fire from that contact alone. "You're all woman, Ava, and he wasn't a man." He tugged her close. "But I am, and I know exactly what you need."

****

The information he'd gotten on Ava's husband had given him enough details to know the man was a bastard. A fucking piece of scum of the highest order. What pieces of paper didn't give him were actual accounts of what the asshole had done to Ava. The abuse she'd taken at her ex's hands. It sickened him. No, it infuriated him. He wanted to kill the fucker, slowly and painfully. He was good at torturing. In the last few years, he'd become a master at it. Hearing men scream was something he relished.

He pushed all those thoughts aside because he didn't want to be thinking about them while he had his woman so close to him.

Stroking her cheek, he pushed her hair back. The hold he had on her waist moved down to cup her generous ass. He let the cheek go and slapped it.

"Now do you want to know how a real man treats a woman?" he asked.

"Yes."

He lifted her in his arms. She let out a squeal. Her arms circled his neck and he chuckled. He didn't go far. After shoving all the papers he'd been working on to the floor, he dropped her butt down on his desk and spread her legs wide. He stepped between them. "I'm willing to offer you a deal, Ava," he said.

"What?"

"I'll show you how it is between a man and woman, and in return, you give yourself to me. Completely. You're not allowed to be with anyone else. You're all mine to do with as I please," he said.

"You won't hurt me?"

"I have no reason to hurt you, do I?"

She licked her lips and nodded. "I agree."

He put his hand on her chest, pushing her down on the desk. "Hold on."

She tried to grab the desk, and he sat down in his chair. He took her feet, placing them on his knees.

Touching her ankles, he traced up her calves, hearing her gasp. The fucker hadn't even taken the time to touch Ava. She was deprived of so much, but he had no problem with that because he was going to make up for it.

He stroked up to her knee, then down again, taking his time before he went to her knee. This time, he used his mouth, kissing inside her knee and trailing his lips up toward her core.

Smokey slid his hands beneath her ass and dragged her back against him. He pressed his face against her pussy, sliding his tongue through her slit. Ava cried out, arching her back.

She begged and moaned for more as he flicked his tongue across her clit. Back and forth, working her pussy until she shook beneath his hold.

He let go of her ass and took the lips of her pussy in his hands, spreading her wide with one hand, and with the other, he pressed a single finger inside. She was so tight but soaking wet.

In and out, he worked a single digit, then added a

second.

She thrust her pelvis up, trying to get him to take more.

He pumped inside her, wanting it to be his cock, but for now, he was going to show her the kind of pleasure that could be had with just his fingers and mouth.

Smokey took her clit into his mouth, sucking on the bud, driving her wild as he finger-fucked her pussy. Her cunt tightened around his fingers, and he turned, pressing against her G-spot, stroking her there, setting a fire that had her wild.

This time, he didn't stop.

There was so much for Ava to learn, and he was more than happy to be the one to teach her. She'd already given herself to him. He wasn't going to back out. What he did plan was for Ava to enjoy the pleasure of his cock, repeatedly, multiple times a day.

She came on his tongue. Her release coated his fingers as he worked her pussy. She shook, and she was so wet some of her orgasm spilled onto his desk.

When it seemed she couldn't take it anymore, she lifted up on his desk and cupped his face, kissing him.

He eased his fingers from her pussy, placing them on her thigh as he stood up. Breaking the kiss, he tilted her head back and pressed his fingers to her mouth. "Open."

She did so and he slid them into her mouth.

"Taste yourself. You've got the most delicious pussy I've ever eaten."

She sucked her cream off his fingers, and he gripped a fistful of her hair, keeping her head at the right angle to kiss her hard. He gave her a kiss she deserved. One that told her she was a fucking sexy piece of ass that deserved to be fucked, to be taken.

She gripped his hips, tugging him close.

"We have an oral contract, Ava. There's no backing down. You're a businesswoman. You know the terms."

"We didn't iron out the terms."

He chuckled. "You, me, sex. It's an open-ended topic. Nothing is off-limits. The only thing I can't do is hurt you." He kissed the tip of her nose. "And I have no intention of doing so."

"That was ... wow," she said. "You really find me attractive?"

Smokey pressed a thumb to the frown between her brows. "You really need to stop questioning everything I do." He kissed her lips again. Putting his hands on her thighs, he gave them a squeeze.

"I just ... I guess after ten years of being told you don't measure up, you start to believe it."

"Now you need to understand he's the one that didn't measure up. Not you. Him."

"I get it. I do."

He didn't believe her.

"Don't look at me like that. I do understand. I knew he was just using me." She glanced at him. "You know why."

"Your parents' inheritance."

"Wow, you really do have a good PI, don't you?"

"The very best."

She smiled. "I had a good lawyer. He saw right through Derek's games."

He stroked across her thighs. "Are you still hung up on your ex?"

"No. I wasn't sad about the divorce. Angry mostly. I've wasted so much time."

"And that asshole was your first?" he asked.

She nodded.

"And he only ever had you on your back, fucking you in the dark."

She winced. "Do we have to describe the exact details?"

"I only want to know so I can make up for lost time."

"I certainly wasn't splayed across a desk completely naked. This is new. He also never brought me to orgasm. Can we please not talk about this? It's really embarrassing."

Smokey stood, pressing his face close to hers. "Babe, you saw one of our parties, and that shit was tame. You've got a lot to get used to."

"That was tame?" she asked, pointing behind her.

"You're adorable."

She wrinkled her nose. "Anything but that. Kids are adorable. So are puppies."

"And I can add you to the list of what I find adorable, but that doesn't mean I don't find you sexy, hot, and fuckable." He grabbed her hair, tilting her head back and slamming his lips down on hers. She wrapped her arms around his neck, pressing her body against his, and fuck, he wanted inside her tight little cunt so badly.

A knock at the door interrupted him.

He broke the kiss to yell across the room. "What?"

"We're needed out at the shack," Hunter said. "Ugly Beast said it's urgent."

"Ugly Beast?" Ava asked.

Smokey shrugged. "You'd understand it if you got to know him. I'll be out in a minute."

"I met Raven today," she said. "She was with a brunette."

"Sweet woman?" Smokey asked.

She nodded.

"That's Ugly Beast's woman. Raven's club. We'll protect her, but Abriana is property, just like you."

"I'm not anyone's property."

"You're mine." He kissed her. "Sorry to cut this short, but I've got business to tend to."

"No problem."

She moved off his desk, and when she looked back, she gasped. Her juices had smeared right on the desk. "Holy crap, I'm so sorry."

Bent over his desk, she reached down to grab some tissues that had fallen. Smokey stood back so he could admire the curves of her ass. He'd be spreading them wide and fucking her puckered anus very soon. His cock was so fucking hard. He hadn't given himself the pleasure today, but soon, he'd be inside her pussy.

Ava wiped his desk and quickly rushed toward her clothing.

"Before you go, I know the ground rules we set out was nothing was off-limits," he said.

"Have you changed your mind?"

He'd never seen anyone get changed so fucking fast. Rubbing at his chin, he brought his focus back to her. "No. Look, I know how women get when it comes to sex. This is plain and simple fucking, Ava. I'm not going to marry you. I'm never going to be the guy who will remember an anniversary or a birthday. I don't do shit like that. I'm all about the club. This place, my boys, Raven, they're what comes first. This between us is fun. You're not club."

"Okay."

"I'm not going to change my mind."

"Smokey, I get that a lot of women mix feelings in with sex. I've just gotten out of a ten-year bad relationship. Believe me, I'm going to be using you for your body and what you can do for me. Not the other way around. I don't want love. I don't want commitment. I'm happy with just sex. It's all I want." She was dressed, and Smokey didn't like how easy this was for her.

This was the kind of arrangement he wanted. What he actually needed, and yet, knowing Ava didn't want anything from him but sex bothered him. "You're sure?"

"I'm sure. No commitments."

"You can't have any other man."

She nodded and clicked her tongue. "All right. The same goes for you. I don't want any sloppy seconds." She pulled in the corner of her lip, let it go with a smile. "I guess I'll see you around, Smokey. You know where to find me."

He watched her turn on her heel and leave the office.

Seconds later, Hunter turned up.

"Wow, she left with a smile on her face," Hunter said.

"Shut the fuck up. What could possibly be going wrong at the shack?" he asked. The shack was a large warehouse where their porn gig was set up. Men and women worked for them. Occasionally, the boys would step in to have some fun, but for the most part, it was people they employed.

"A couple of girls arguing about their paycheck. They're holding up Bill, and a couple of the girls have had no choice but to go home early," Hunter said.

"For fuck's sake, save me from drama queens. Anyone would think they're actual celebrities." He rolled up his sleeves and took off out of his office.

"Do you want to talk about the new piece of ass?" Hunter asked, following behind him.

"No."

"Don't you think with the mafia breathing down

our neck and the Twisted Bastards meeting that you should be taking it easy? The bitch could be a spy."

Smokey grabbed Hunter's jacket. "What the fuck are you talking about?"

"You think it hasn't happened before? Women working for different clubs? It happens all the time."

"Ava's not a damn spy."

"She could be."

"Hunter, enough. I know what the fuck I'm doing." He glared at his VP as he climbed on his bike.

Ava wasn't a threat. He was sure of it.

Chapter Four

Ava glanced over at the bubbling sauce. The peppers, onions, and tomatoes along with several herbs, and a lot of garlic, smelled so amazing. She grabbed a spoon, dipped it into the sauce, and had a quick taste. Closing her eyes, she smiled. Perfect.

She reduced the sauce to a simmer before salting the pasta water. Next, she didn't care it was an entire packet of spaghetti, it was what she wanted. Ever since she'd gotten home, all she'd been thinking about was that kiss. Not just the kiss, but also the way his lips had felt on hers. The touch, the texture. The very thought of it aroused her even more. She wanted more of his kisses, more of his touches.

In fact, she just wanted more.

In all her adult years, she'd never felt this way about anyone. Not even her ex.

"It's not love."

She'd meant every single word she'd said. This wasn't about love, and she didn't care for it to be either. All she wanted was sex. Lots and lots of sex. Her pussy throbbed at the memory of his face between her thighs. She'd read about it, seen it, but never experienced it. The orgasms she'd produced at her own hands were mediocre at best.

"Get your head in the game." She tried to shake off the memory and just focus on the pasta, but each second, she recalled Smokey's face and the way he touched her. It meant something to her. It was crazy. She didn't consider it love. It wasn't that, but it was something.

"Focus, Ava. Just focus." There was no way she was going to behave like a schoolgirl in front of him.

Smiling, she checked the pasta. It was almost

cooked.

She quickly prepared the sink so she could drain it. After turning off the sauce, she checked her pasta again, perfectly cooked. She reserved some water and drained the pasta, returning it to the pot.

Ava was adding the sauce and sprinkling in some cheese when her doorbell rang. She paused with a frown.

Leaving her pasta and sauce, she went to the front door, forgetting to check who it was before she opened the door.

Smokey stood on the doorstep.

"Hey," she said.

"Hi, yourself." He stepped forward, banding an arm around her waist and pulling her close. His lips brushed across hers.

"Your business ended early?"

He winked at her. "I got it done as quickly as I could because I knew I was coming here." He kissed her again. "Something smells really good."

"That's dinner."

"Care to share?" he asked. "I'm starving. I haven't had anything to eat."

"Sure. I've got plenty." She didn't like to make small portions, so more often than not, it ended up in the freezer or as leftovers, which was another reason she rarely used meat in her food.

Smokey let her go and closed her front door. She returned to the kitchen and finished preparing their food. She served two generous portions for them. There was a place setting for her. She gave it to Smokey, sitting opposite him, and grabbed herself a knife and fork.

Pushing some hair off her face, she sat down. "Enjoy."

"Can I ask you a question?" Smokey asked, looking almost hesitant.

"Sure."

"Can you actually cook?"

She chuckled. "You've got proof right in front of you. I don't understand."

"It's not that. It's just, I know a woman who is trying so hard to learn to cook, and she's fucking awful. The woman has nearly given me food poisoning more times than I can count."

Ava laughed. "I can cook. I haven't had any complaints." It was the one area Derek couldn't moan about. Meals were always good. "Just try it. I won't be offended if you find it disgusting. I know peppers aren't to everyone's taste."

He tentatively took a bite.

She tried not to laugh. "Does this woman know she's scarred you?"

"She's a sweet woman. It's Abriana. You met her."

"Oh, right. The one that didn't talk all that much." She didn't want to feel jealous. He'd said the woman was married, but that didn't have to mean anything, did it?

"Before you ask, she can't bake for shit."

"That is awful. She made meals for you, and you're still complaining." She shook her head. "It's mean."

"I tell you what, the next time Ugly Beast invites me over for dinner, you're coming."

"It's a date," she said. "I won't be mean."

"Woman, you've yet to try this woman's food."

She twirled some spaghetti on her fork and looked over at him. He'd already taken three more mouthfuls of her dinner. "Is it really that bad?"

"I didn't think it was possible, but the woman can burn a chicken without it being cooked on the inside."

"That can happen?"

"I didn't think so, but she is the master of fucking up in the kitchen. She tries so hard though. We're all rooting for her to get it right."

She laughed. "You're so mean."

"I'm being nice."

"Well, I don't ever want to be on your bad side."

"I doubt that will happen."

Silence fell between them, but it wasn't awkward. She enjoyed it. It was fun eating with someone. She hadn't done this in such a long time. Even before her divorce from her ex. They'd stopped sharing meals together long before then.

"I did happen to make a small chocolate cake," she said after dinner.

"Care to share?"

"Love to."

"Good." She took their empty plates. Smokey had enjoyed seconds, which she loved. Feeding him had given her so much pleasure. She put the dishes in the sink and went to the fridge. Chocolate was one of her favorite things in the world, then peanut butter. The two were the best.

"Do you have a peanut allergy?"

"No, babe, I don't."

"Phew, good." She laughed. She took the cake to the table. It was only a small cake, but it was heavily frosted. Peanut butter frosting on the inside layer. Dark chocolate on the outside.

"Fuck, that looks good."

She served him a slice, then cut one for herself. Before she took a bite, she sat and watched him.

On the first bite, he closed his eyes and leaned back. "Now that is fucking delicious."

She couldn't stop smiling.

Enjoying her own slice, she watched as Smokey ate his. He had an additional two slices, and the cake was nearly gone. She returned the last remaining slice to the fridge and quickly did the dishes, surprised when Smokey helped her.

"You're one fine cook. The boys are going to be so pissed."

She put away the last of the dishes when Smokey came up behind her. "Why are they going to be pissed?"

"Because I found the hottest woman who can cook. You've got the most perfect ass." He cupped her ass and drew her back against him. "I've been thinking about you all day."

One of his hands moved between her thighs, and she moaned.

Within seconds, he spun her around and had her pressed up against the fridge. "Do you have any idea what you do to me?" he asked. "No woman has made me want her the way I want you, and I've only tasted your fucking pussy. I haven't taken it."

His other hand grabbed her neck, drawing her back. His lips bit down on her pulse.

She cried out at the instant hit of pleasure. It was amazing. The way he rubbed her pussy, held her captive to him. Any other man she'd have been terrified. With Smokey, she felt safe within his arms.

"Babe, I'm going to fuck you right now, hard, and it's not going to be gentle. You've got to tell me now if you need gentle because I don't have it in me to do that tonight."

"I want it, Smokey, please."

He flipped up her dress and tore at her panties. The sound of the tear should have woken her up, but it only served to turn her on even more. Glancing behind her, she watched as he pulled down his zipper. He was already rolling a condom over his cock.

The head of him pressed against her core, and he moved her so she was bent over the counter.

She waited with just the head of his cock within her. Pleasure rushed through her body. Need unlike anything else consumed her. She wanted everything he could give her. For him to not stop. To fuck her. Ava didn't want him to hold back. All her life she'd been holding back, making do. It was time to live life to the fullest.

He slammed to the hilt within her, and she cried out at the intense pleasure and pain it caused. He was long, hard, big, and thick.

His grip on her hips tightened and he growled. "Fuck. I knew you'd be tight."

Smokey didn't give her a chance to get accustomed to his length. He held on to her and fucked her, pounding his large cock deep inside her, hitting all the right spots.

"Touch your pussy. Make yourself come all over my dick."

She didn't want to. Any orgasm she gave herself was always so boring. Afterward, she'd wonder why the hell women were even given sex organs. At Smokey's command, she couldn't deny him. Sliding a hand between her thighs, she stroked her pussy to bring herself to an orgasm. Her eyes closed as the pleasure took over.

It was incredible. The way he held her in place as he took her.

Even her clit felt sensitive to the touch. His hands moved from her hips, capturing her tits. He gripped them tightly, using them to pound inside her.

Flesh hitting flesh filled the air, along with their groans. It was a sound Ava loved. "Come for me, Ava. Let me hear you. Let me feel you come all over my cock."

His rough voice and commands drove her wild. He stopped gripping her tits and stroked her nipples, pinching them to the point of pain, and that sent her over the edge. She came hard, screaming his name.

Smokey let her tits go, returned to her hips, and took her even harder than before. She didn't think it was possible, but the speed and depth of his penetration prolonged her release.

He joined her, slamming in deep, and she felt his cock jerk and pulse within her. Wave upon wave of his release filled the condom.

They were both panting when Smokey pulled out of her. She struggled to keep herself upright. Out of the corner of her eye, she watched as he removed the condom, tied it up, and threw it in the trash.

She let out a yelp as he picked her up, and before long, he carried her toward her sitting room. He sat down on the sofa with her across his lap. Then he moved some pillows behind her head and stroked her hair back from her face.

Neither of them spoke.

She basked in the glow of her orgasm.

Smokey twirled a finger around her hair. "Is this real?" he asked.

"Yes, it's real." She chuckled. "I wouldn't spend time trying to dye my hair. Are we really discussing hair color right now?"

"What would you like to talk about?"

"I don't know. Anything. How was your day?"

"Good."

"You're not going to tell me about the parts I'm not in?"

"It's club business, babe. It's nothing to do with you."

"Wow, okay."

"Don't be offended."

"I'm not. I'm guessing it's all top-secret," she said. "I'm not offended. Like you said, the club comes first."

"It doesn't mean I will always want it to be that way. I've got to make sure I can trust you," he said.

She took a deep breath. "You can trust me. I won't break it. I promise. You don't know me, but maybe one day, if you give yourself time, you can trust me."

****

Smokey shook his head. "Strip."

"I have to open my shop today."

"Not today. You're the boss. Strip."

Ava moved toward him and shook her head. "I want to, but I do have other commitments. If the club called you right now, you'd go."

"Your bakery is not club."

"But my bakery is club to me. It's my own little piece of heaven."

"You think my club is my own peace of heaven?" he asked.

"Isn't it?"

It was on the tip of his tongue to deny it. There was no way he'd see the club as a peaceful place. "You're right."

"That's a sentence you're going to have to get used to saying." She moved toward the bed and cupped his cheek. "I want to spend all day in bed with you, but this is fun. I don't want to run the risk of losing my clientele."

Smokey stroked another of her curls. He loved her hair. It was so soft, but also blonde in a way he didn't think he'd care for. It was almost white.

"The bakery means a lot to you?"

She smiled. "Yes. I know some girls have dreams of becoming a princess or marrying a rich billionaire. Being a doctor or a lawyer. I didn't. From a young age, I loved to bake. My mom was amazing at it. There was nothing she couldn't do."

"What was she like?"

"I look a little like her, but she was a slender woman. An amazing cook. I used to get annoyed because she was the kind of woman who could eat her heart out in calories and fats and not gain any weight."

"Did she not like you?" Smokey asked.

"No, of course not. My mom loved me. She was the one who told me to embrace who I was. Whenever I was sad or feeling anything but happy, she'd go into the kitchen and I'd watch her cook. She'd make chocolate chip cookies if I was upset. With her hot cocoa, they were amazing. Cheese and onion pies to chase away the horrible days. A quiche. She was pretty good at them as well. I never liked them, but hers were something special."

"She sounds lovely."

"She was. Losing them was the hardest thing of all."

"A car crash?"

"Yes. A car crash. Took both of them instantly."

"Is she the reason you wanted to own a bakery?" he asked.

"I wanted to help people the way she did me. It's probably silly and childish. I tried to think of owning a bakery when I was married, but my ex was dead-set against it."

"You worked as an accountant," he said.

"Yeah. Nine-to-five. Absolutely hated it. I spent a lot of time baking. People in the office always complimented me on my cooking." She shrugged. "So, my bakery is getting rid of a whole lot of bad memories."

"You're a good person, Ava."

She smiled. "Don't sound so surprised. If you gave yourself the chance to get to know people, you'd see there is a lot more of us around. We're not some strange species."

"You'd be surprised."

"Because of the club?"

He tensed up.

She held her hands in surrender. "I'm not fishing for information, but when you're not around, I watched this program and a few other things."

Smokey laughed. "It's not like it's in the movies."

"No, I get it. This stuff is real." She looked down at her hands. "I hope one day you can learn to trust me."

"Club information can get people killed, Ava. I have enemies. I have a whole lot of problems."

"Is that why you're not married?" she asked. "You don't want to put anyone at risk?"

"I haven't gotten married because there's no woman good enough. My boys put their lives in my hands every single day. I'm not going to put it at risk for a woman."

"Okay."

"Have I offended you?"

"No. I think it's going to take a lot more than that to offend me. I get it. You're from a different world than me. It doesn't mean I can't cross over into yours, Smokey. I'm not ... I don't even know how to say this. I'm not a goody-two-shoes. I think." She shrugged. "I've got to go. You can let yourself out?"

"Yeah, I can do that, babe." He tugged her down and kissed her lips.

She gave a chuckle. "I'll see you later?"

"We'll see."

She smiled at him and turned on her heel to leave. He watched her go, fucking curious about this woman.

Ava was sweet and kind, and yet, at the same time, she was so much more. He ran a hand down his face as he heard the door close. He got to his feet, headed to the window, and watched as she pulled out of the drive to go into town.

What was it about her?

Why was she so different?

He hadn't known about the relationship she had with her parents. That kind of shit was never talked about in black and white. He did know her father invested in stocks and shares. So much so that Ava didn't need to work ever again. From his digging, he'd also discovered she rarely used the money her parents had left her.

She had someone occasionally invest back into the market, and so far, she'd gotten a massive return. Yet, she lived modestly. A small house. A used car.

The only real luxury was her bakery, which she didn't need because she was set up for life.

Some of the women back at the clubhouse would be drooling for the money she had. Yet, when it came to the club, she never pushed. All she wanted from him was his trust.

He didn't buy it, but until he'd gotten her from under his skin, he was going to keep on using her pussy.

Alone in her home, he started to look through her stuff. Opening drawers, trying to find anything that would give way to the woman he was fucking.

There was nothing. There were receipts in her office. All pertaining to her business. Some warranties on stuff she bought. Everything was all neatly packed away. Her books were organized by title, he noted.

Her kitchen was probably the most lived-in part of the house. He opened cupboards and they were cluttered, but he realized they were in an organized kind of mess. She had a baking cupboard, which spread into three of the kitchen.

Two drawers were for spices. She had a separate pantry with tinned goods, pasta, rice, and other shit he'd never heard of.

His woman seemed pretty damn genuine, and that fucking baffled him.

Ryan had said that the head of the Twisted Bastards MC was going to meet someone at his bar. That was it. Since then, Smokey had been trying to figure out who it was.

Who better to infiltrate the Hell's Bastards MC than a woman who was completely different and would stand out to him?

He wasn't used to picking women up in a bar, certainly not a civilian.

His cell phone rang, and he took Hunter's call. "Talk to me."

"Ryan's done a runner," Hunter said. "All his shit is cleared out. Our guy gave me the heads-up that nearly ten grand was deposited into his account last night."

Smokey cursed. "Where was our prospect?" He rubbed at his temple. "Fucking Hanson. Where was he?"

"He's in the hospital. He was stabbed three times in the chest. He's holding on."

"Fuck!" Smokey clenched his hand into a fist. Hanson was nineteen years old and had come to them the day he'd graduated. All he wanted was to be a brother, a fully patched-in member.

The kid was loyal. A little slow at times, but one of the meanest motherfuckers he'd ever seen, and considering Hanson's age, that was a compliment. The kid had a lot of rage, but it was directed at their enemies. The boy knew a lot about controlling his temper.

"Ryan didn't pack everything. We've got some pictures here. You might want to come and take a look."

"I'm on it." Smokey hung up the call. He'd spent all night enjoying Ava's pussy, and now he was pissed off.

Leaving her house, he locked it up and kept the key. He went to his bike, straddled his trusty machine, and took off, heading toward the bar. Ryan lived directly above it.

The ride was quick and with it, his temper went to an all-time high.

Kinky was outside smoking a joint as he arrived. "Hunter's inside."

He headed to the back of the bar, following the stairs that led up to the office.

Hunter sported a black eye and a split lip. "Do I want to know what the fuck that is?"

"If you want to know what happened to the guy who gave it to me, he's pissing blood."

"Why?"

"He came home early as I was fucking his hot wife. He didn't take too kindly to me breaking in her ass virginity, or whatever kids are calling it these days."

"You've got to stop chasing married women," Smokey said. One day, he was going to get a call to tell him someone had killed his VP. The dude just couldn't keep his hands off married women.

"They're fun. They're a challenge."

"We've got club whores for your games."

"But they don't play hard to get and I love the chase. There's always something more rewarding when you fuck pussy you work for." Hunter held out two pictures. "I don't like the look of these."

He took the pictures and stared down at them. They were of the clubhouses. One was of him, the other of Raven.

"What the fuck has Raven got to do with this?" he asked.

"Beats me, but we better find out if she's shacking up with anyone. I haven't seen her screwing around. You?"

"Nope." Smokey wasn't sure who Raven was into. He'd watched her kiss men and women. He couldn't recall any of the guys bragging about fucking her. She was a loyal woman. Giving her a patch had gone against everything he believed in. She was the only woman he'd ever trusted.

"You think this has to do with the Twisted?"

"I think it has something to do with us. That's all I can tell you."

"You don't think the mafia's coming back for another taste?" Hunter asked.

"Everything has been quiet. Drago's dealt with it."

"What if Drago's made an arrangement to get rid of us to take the job as Boss?"

Smokey looked toward Hunter. "Then we need to call in Ugly Beast. We need another meet."

"Ugly's not going to like it," Hunter said.

"Do I look like I give a flying fuck what Ugly likes? He'll do as he's told. What's the update on Hanson?" he asked.

"So far, he's stable, but it could go either way."

"We're going to find Ryan. I want to know everyone who has been near this fucking place. I know Ryan had security feeds. Get them. I want to go over them as soon as you do. Hanson is going to have his justice." Smokey folded the pictures, sliding them back into his jacket.

Heading back out, he ignored Kinky and the boys. Climbing back on his bike, he took off toward the hospital. He fucking hated hospitals more than anything else in the world. They were sterile and filled with the sick. He'd been in them way too many times, and now that a prospect was there, he was going to have to figure out who was trying to come after them, and more importantly, why.

Chapter Five

Ava hadn't heard from Smokey all day.

She hadn't needed to open the bakery, but she'd gotten the call about her delivery arriving a day early, so she'd gone in to deal with that. Seeing as she was already in the shop, she'd decided to open up.

Sales had been good.

She hadn't sold out, and she'd taken the leftovers over to the preschool for the kids. Rather than go home, she'd headed to the grocery store.

As she rounded the vegetable section, she spotted Raven. She had a list in front of her.

"Hi," she said, smiling.

Raven ignored her.

Ava didn't want to be rude, so she grabbed the vegetables she needed as Raven growled and looked up.

"Smokey's lady," she said.

"Ava."

"Do you know what the fuck this says? I swear Ugly Beast does this to me on purpose to make me feel like a child." Raven held out a piece of paper.

Ava took it and glanced over the scrawl. It looked like a child had written it. "Which item?"

"That one." Raven pointed to the third one down.

After looking at it for some time, she smiled. "Onions."

"Really? What the fuck?" Raven took the list back and shook her head. "This is what happens when you take his wife and get her drunk. He makes you pay by shopping for him."

"Well, I wish you luck. That is one intense list."

"Wait, you understood this shit though, right?"

"I did." She nodded.

"You want to be shopping buddies?"

Ava chuckled. "Sure. Why not?" She followed Raven around the store, grabbing her own groceries while also helping her to decipher the list. It was pretty hard. She couldn't wait to meet Ugly Beast. He seemed like an interesting person.

Still, by the time they came to the checkout, Raven had talked her ear off about everything from the latest movie she'd watched, to babysitting, and then to shopping.

On the way out, she was surprised to see she'd parked right next to Raven.

"What a coincidence," Raven said. "How come you don't like parking near the store?"

"It's really silly."

"Try me?"

"Er, I parked close to a store once, and it ended in a confrontation with a pregnant woman. I got slapped. Fat shamed and made to feel like the lowest form of a human being. I had only just parked and was going to jump right back in my car and move. Instead, I went to a different store."

"Holy shit, that happened?" Raven asked.

"Yep."

"I'd have slapped that woman."

"She was pregnant."

"So, if I didn't slap her, I'd have found another way to shut her mouth. You can't have people talking to you like you're crap. You allow one person, all of them will."

"Oh."

Raven slammed her car trunk down. "You're not from around here, are you?"

"No."

"Are you looking for a friend?"

"I … think so." This seemed like really dangerous

territory. "I know you're club and Smokey has said himself that I'm not part of the club. I get it."

Raven started to laugh. "And you're still giving it to him?"

Her cheeks began to heat. "I don't know how to answer that." Any way seemed bad.

Raven snorted as she laughed. "Honey, I need to teach you how to talk to these guys. Smokey's going to walk all over you if you keep being the quaint woman."

"I'm not looking for trouble."

Raven shook her head. "It's no trouble. Do you want people taking the piss out of you?"

"No." She spoke slowly, not exactly sure how to answer anything with this woman.

"Girl, you need me as a friend. It's quite pitiful to see this."

She laughed. "Okay, fine. I'm Ava Sinclaire."

"Raven." There was no last name. "How about you come with me and I'll give you a proper introduction to Abriana and Ugly Beast. My girl will like you. I think she finds my attitude a little too brass. She's a mafia chick, so she's still adjusting after all this time to the MC life."

"I'm not part of the MC life."

"Not yet, but you've kept Smokey's attention for a week. Now that's a world record in his book."

"Oh." One week. They'd been having sex one day. He'd licked her pussy the other day. It wasn't even a whole week. This wasn't good. Was Smokey the kind of guy who moved on when he got bored? What made him bored?

"Do you do that often?" Raven asked.

"What?"

"Look like you're having a million thoughts at one time."

"Kind of, yeah. I'll follow you, okay?"

"Fine by me."

Raven climbed into the driver's side and Ava got into her own car. After turning over the ignition, she stared straight ahead as she pulled out, following behind Raven. The other woman seemed nice. A little talkative, which she liked. She also loved Raven's attitude.

Ava didn't pay attention to her surroundings, just focused on the car in front. She pulled in behind Raven and was thankful she hadn't purchased any items for the fridge or freezer. She grabbed her bag, slinging it over her shoulder as she rushed to help Raven unload the car.

The door to the house opened, and seconds later, they were joined by a very large, heavily inked, scarred man who took Ava's breath away. He wasn't ugly in the slightest, but the scars told a story.

Her mother had always taught her to not stare. To see past people's imperfections and to want to get to know the person within. She offered Ugly Beast a smile.

"Who the fuck are you?" he asked.

"We've talked about this, Ugly," Abriana said, coming out of the house with a baby on her hip.

"I don't know who she is."

"I'm Ava," she said, holding her hand out.

"Who the fuck is she, Raven? Another stray?"

"Don't start. I don't pick up strays. You're just pissed that I know someone you don't." Raven growled at him. An actual growl. "This is Smokey's piece."

Ugly Beast turned his gaze on her, and she tensed up. He looked her up and down.

"Ugly, don't," Abriana said. "They're all very protective of their president."

"I can see that." She offered Ugly Beast another smile, but he didn't return one.

After a few seconds, he clearly decided she

wasn't worth his time as he grabbed the bags of groceries from Raven's car, turned on his heel, and left.

"Don't mind him. He's an asshole."

"I can hear that."

"It's nice of you to stop by, Ava. You want a drink?" Abriana asked.

Ava was captivated by the young girl in her arms.

"She's so cute, isn't she? She's my daughter. Little Bella. Say hi." The baby didn't say anything, but Ava was smitten.

"She's adorable."

"Do you not have kids?"

"No, I don't." She'd wanted them, but again another control Derek had over her. "I don't want to intrude. I don't think your husband likes me very much."

"Don't take it personally. Ugly asshole doesn't like anyone," Raven said.

Abriana chuckled. "Don't mind him. He has a hard time trusting people."

"I have a hard time because most people can't be trusted," Ugly Beast said, coming up behind Abriana.

"And you've already decided I'm not trustworthy?"

"I don't know you."

"I don't know you either, but I'm not judging you. I'd rather not impose. It was nice to see you, Raven."

"Don't be a dick, Ugly. She helped me decipher your handwriting. When are you going to grow up and start acting like an actual adult?" Raven asked.

"Fuck off. Don't you have someone else to go and bug?"

"Nope. It's my night with my best buddy." Raven slung her arm across Abriana's shoulders, reaching over to little Bella and tickling her feet.

Once again, Ava knew she didn't belong. "Have a wonderful night," she said. She was the person who hadn't been around. She didn't blame them for not wanting her to be part of their group.

She headed back to the car.

"Stay," Ugly Beast said.

She turned to see all three and the baby were watching her. "It's fine, really?"

"My wife wants you to stay. She gets what she wants."

"I'd like you to come and enjoy some tea or coffee. I've got beer."

"I'll take a coffee," Ava said. She didn't want to appear rude. After closing her door, she locked the car and walked up the steps. She followed them into Abriana's house. Holding her bag, she put her keys inside.

Ugly Beast didn't linger. He took Bella and left them alone.

"I don't know what you do to make him disappear," Abriana said.

"It's my charming personality. I think you take way too much crap from him."

"I don't take any crap and you know it."

Raven snorted. "Do you remember the time you were this sweet little mafia princess?"

Abriana rolled her eyes. "Don't mind her."

"Tell us about how good it is to fuck Smokey," Raven said.

"Raven!"

"What? Come on, aren't you curious? Until Miss Baker here turned up, Smokey seemed to be taking a break from any kind of fun. All fun, actually. Sex being the biggest one."

"How do you hear this?" Abriana asked.

"Club bitches talk, babe. That's how I get to know as much about the guys as I do. They need to learn to keep their mouths shut. So, do you like Smokey?"

"I like him," Ava said.

"That's all? You like him?"

"We're not exactly, I mean, it's, I, it's complicated."

Raven stared at her for several seconds as Abriana began to put the groceries away. Ava hated being under Raven's scrutiny and got to her feet, immediately helping to put everything away. She hated sitting down while other people worked, and she really had to do something with her hands.

"At least you like him."

"Yep, I do." She offered a smile, but Raven didn't return it.

"Don't mind her. She's being club again."

"Club?"

"Raven takes her role was being the only female club member seriously."

"I went through hell to earn my patch." She tilted her head toward Ava. "You ever been around an MC before?"

"No." She had helped to put away the groceries. "I've heard of MCs, but never been close to one."

"And you still bought a house near a town with one?" Raven asked. "Are you fucking stupid?"

"Damn it, Raven, enough," Abriana said.

This had both women looking toward Abriana.

"When did you grow a set of balls?" Raven asked.

"Since she is clearly a nice woman and bakes the most delicious cookies and muffins. If you want to keep her around because you've been drooling after her baked goods as much as everyone else in town, stop being a first-class bitch. She doesn't deserve it." Abriana shook her head. "She's really nice when you get to know her."

"I think I miss your timid approach. Since you gave birth to Bella, you've grown a spine."

Abriana stuck her tongue out. "Have you ever thought that it's your influence?"

"Please, I'm a saint."

Ava sat back down in her seat. She didn't know if she'd rather face off with Ugly Beast more. Raven had a spiteful edge to her tone. She understood it. Smokey was her leader. She was looking out for him.

Abriana and Raven continued to banter with each other. Rather than leave, Ava sat, enjoyed a cup of coffee, and when the time was right, she made her escape.

The club was intense. No doubt about it.

If they were all like Raven, she had no doubt it was going to be difficult to be in Smokey's world.

She drove home, unloaded her car, and the empty house that greeted her wasn't a blessing. Seeing Abriana with her baby tonight had stirred up all kinds of feelings. She had tried to forget what it was like to want a child and a big family. Being an only child, her parents had been unable to have more children, even though it was exactly what they wanted. Her mother had been amazing with kids. She wanted a huge family. During the few times she'd seen Smokey around his club, she'd seen a closeness that could only be described as family.

Her lonely house only served to make her realize how little she had.

****

Hanson was stable for now, but Smokey hadn't been able to talk to him for very long because the drugs they had him on made him very woozy.

He headed back to the clubhouse with Hunter

calling ahead to arrange a church meeting. They didn't have a lot to go on, but the brothers needed to be informed of what he had discovered so far.

Arriving at the clubhouse, he took note of all the bikes and cars in residence. Women in skimpy clothing were hanging outside, smoking cigarettes and joints. He ignored them, heading straight inside and taking his place at the head of the table. As with all the brothers, they handed in their cell phones and weapons at the door. The church was their sacred place, their patch their main link. They were all united as one.

"How's Hanson?" Ugly Beast asked.

"He's doing good. The doctor believes he'll be home in a couple of weeks. Nothing was severely damaged. Were you able to get any kind of surveillance?" He turned toward Hunter.

"Nope. Everything from that night has been taken or wiped. Not a single security tape. They were all useless. All we've got to go on is Hanson when he wakes up," Hunter said.

"I want round-the-clock security on him, starting now."

Kinky got up. "I'm on it. Whoever takes over from me can give me the rundown." He turned on his heel and left.

"I think you need to postpone your meeting with the asshole," Vice said.

He looked toward the brother in the corner. Vice rarely said anything at these meetings. "Why?"

"We can't rule him or his club out."

"It's settled then," Ugly Beast said. "You don't go."

"We haven't taken a vote." Smokey wasn't going to be a coward. "You think not turning up to meet him will help our situation?"

"I think if you turn up, it could be a bloodbath," Elijah said, leaning forward. Brick, Hunter, and several other brothers agreed.

"This meeting is arranged," Demon said. "It's a certified trap. We all know it."

Smokey sat back, not in the best of moods. "I don't like this."

"We're not going to get you killed," Hunter said. "I don't give a fuck what they think of us. Let them claim us to be pussies. They'll be the ones in the fucking wrong. Not us. I'm not having you go out there and get yourself killed."

"I always knew you loved my ass." Smokey blew Hunter a kiss. "I already called off the meeting. Any time I meet up with the asshole of the Twisted Bastards MC, it's going to be a surprise one so he doesn't see me coming. I haven't been running this show for them to take the fucking piss. You all should know that by now." He shook his head.

"Have you considered your piece could be a plant?" Ugly Beast.

"Ava is no plant."

"Is that because you're sticking your dick in her?" Ugly glared right back at him.

Smokey's hands clenched into fists. Anger rushed through his body, but rather than let it spill forth, he stayed perfectly still and stared right at him. "My judgment isn't impaired. You worry about your wife. Why not knock her up again? It will only help to cement more ties to the mafia."

"We're out of the mafia, and you know it."

"With a little declaration, you'll be right back in."

"Enough," Hunter said. "Ava's been checked out."

"Yeah, well, until we're sure where her loyalties

lie, I don't want her hanging out with my wife."

"Ava's a good person," Raven said, finally speaking up.

All this time, it had surprised him she hadn't said something sooner. Raven wasn't exactly known for keeping her mouth shut. She liked to be involved. Even though she was a patched-in member, he sometimes believed she tried to make up for the fact she had tits and a pussy rather than a dick.

"And you think you can make a judgment call?" Ugly Beast asked.

"What gives you the right to question my judgment?" Raven asked, stepping away from the wall.

Ugly Beast stood. "Since your judgment call got my woman hurt. Think hard, Raven. If you hadn't sent her off with a prospect that wasn't even one of ours, my wife wouldn't have lost our first child. She wouldn't have had a concussion, and she wouldn't wake up screaming some nights, terrified."

"One mistake that anyone could have made."

"Yeah, but it was you who made it. No one else."

"You fucking prick."

"Enough!" Smokey slammed his hand down on the table.

Ugly Beast and Raven still glared at one another.

"Ava's not up for discussion. She's not part of the club. She's a woman I'm fucking. Nothing else."

"Wow, does Ava know that?" Raven asked.

"Ava knows what she needs to, and I don't need you sniffing in my business. Sit the fuck down."

Raven stepped back and Ugly Beast sat down.

He had to wonder how Raven was friends with Abriana. The woman was like a puppy in comparison to Raven.

"I hate to take sides, but Ugly Beast is right. It's a

little suspicious how Ryan does a runner, our boy gets hurt, and Ava arrived in town."

"She's been in town longer than a couple of weeks. They've been raving about her baked goods for months," Raven said.

Smokey ran a hand down his face. This was getting them nowhere.

"For now, the Twisted Bastards meetup is off the table." He looked at Ugly. "I need a word with Drago. Arrange it."

Ugly nodded his head but didn't look happy. Smokey didn't give a flying fuck about making his boys happy. "Until then, I want you all to keep an eye on everything. Don't turn your backs on anyone. Stay fucking alert. Do I make myself clear?" he asked.

They all nodded. "Let's move out." He slammed his gavel on the table, and everyone got up, to leave.

As he knew she would, Raven stayed behind.

"If you've come to do some feminist crap, I'm not interested."

Raven held her hands up. "I'm not here to make waves."

"Then why are you still here?"

"I don't know her, and like Ugly Beast said, I made a mistake, but she doesn't seem like the kind of woman to just enjoy a random hookup."

Smokey snorted. "Are you trying to warn me away from her?"

"No, I'm worried about you," she said. "I get that you're the one in charge and your word is law and all that crap, but ... what if she is the one?"

Now Smokey burst out laughing. "I don't believe in that shit. You know that?"

"Look how happy Ugly Beast is. Don't you want that?"

"What Ugly has is once-in-a-lifetime. I'm not going to get that, ever. I have the club. That's all that matters. Now, get the fuck out before I call for your patch."

Raven rolled her eyes but didn't say another word.

Running a hand down his face, he left the church room and made his way outside into the warm air. He took several deep breaths. Someone was after them. Whoever it was, he was going to find them and kill every fucking person who posed a threat. The shit that went down with the mafia should have ended all of this. He got his end of the deal, and in return, he got more ground.

Lewis and Verge, the two other presidents of the Hell's Bastards MC around the country, hadn't reported shit to him in weeks, which meant he was the primary target.

This left his current enemies, the Twisted Bastards MC, and his good old friends the mafia.

He needed to find Ryan, and fast, to get the answers he needed. Turning on his heel, he went back inside the clubhouse, going to the one man who would find anyone: Big Dick.

The man himself was bent over the pool table, about to pot a ball. Smokey picked it up as Big Dick made his shot.

"What the fuck, man? That shit is cold."

"I need you to find Ryan."

"I thought we already had feelers out for his ass," Big Dick said.

"We do, but I need you on it. I want him found today."

Big Dick smirked. "Boss, I got a whole lot of talent, but even I have my limits."

"I'm not laughing. Go."

His man shook his head, threw his pool stick on the table, and muttered all the way out of the room.

Staring at the ball, he thought of Ava. He had his own suspicions with regards to the woman, but he knew they were completely unfounded. She'd never done anything to him to warrant the suspicion.

Even still, she was a woman, and to him, that made her a problem.

He placed the ball on the pool table, turned on his heel, and went out to his bike. No one stopped him as he straddled his machine and took off, heading toward town.

The open road did nothing to calm his thoughts. In the back of his mind, he knew he should be backing off. Ava wasn't part of the club. Her place wasn't with him. He sped up, pressing on the gas to get to his woman as fast as he could.

Not once did he turn back, even though he knew he should.

She wasn't club.

She wasn't a slut.

But she belonged to him.

No other man at the club would know how tight her hot little pussy was. No one would feel her tits against him, or see how fucking glorious they were when they bounced right in front of his face.

He ached for her.

After parking his bike, he headed down her front yard path. The door opened. Ava was there, a smile on her lips. Her long, blonde hair fell around her in luscious waves.

The moment he was close, he banded an arm around her waist and pulled her close. Slamming his lips down on hers, he walked into her house, ravishing her mouth as he kicked the door closed.

He spun them around so she was pressed against

the door. He held her hands up above her head, keeping her in place.

"Hello to you too," she said the moment he broke the kiss and trailed his lips down her neck, going straight to her tits.

He pushed her shirt up to beneath her neck and groaned, cupping the large mounds. Flicking the catch of her bra, he watched mesmerized as they sprang free. He held them up as if they were an offering. Large nipples begging for his mouth. He took one nipple between his teeth, biting down. He heard her gasp. He didn't care if it was too hard. Moving to her next one, he devoted the same attention to it, loving the sounds she made.

His dick was rock-hard and ready to fuck.

"Please, Smokey."

"You want my cock?" he asked.

"Yes."

He pressed down on her shoulders and she went to her knees before him. Staring into her eyes, he released the belt and the button of his pants, He opened it up enough for his cock, and once he had himself released, he worked from the root up to the tip, then back down again.

"Open your mouth."

She opened her lips.

"Do you want my cock?" he asked.

"Yes."

He moved forward and pressed the tip of his cock to her lips. The moment her tongue came out and teased the head, he groaned.

Ava jerked back. "I'm bad at this."

"What?"

"I'm ... I don't have a lot of experience." She winced.

"Babe, let me be the one to tell you if this is good

or not. Open your mouth."

"I just wanted you to know in case there's something I might be good at."

He chuckled. "Your ex really did a number on you." His cock hadn't softened, and he stared at her, waiting.

She spread her lips for him and he pressed the tip of his cock to her mouth. She opened her hot little mouth for him, and he slid in several inches. He groaned. "Suck." She did and fuck, it was perfect.

Reaching out, he grabbed a fistful of her hair for something to hold on to. In and out, he fucked her face, taking his time, letting her become accustomed to the sheer size of him.

All he wanted to do was come down her throat, but watching her now, he was in rapture. He knew her lips would look good around his dick, he just didn't realize how good. She was perfection. Her inexperience was a massive turn-on.

There was no way in hell he was going share her with any other of the club brothers. With Ava, he was going to be selfish and keep her all to himself. He'd always put the club first. Never saved anything for himself.

Ava was different though.

"When I hit the back of your throat, relax. Take all of me." He eased into her mouth, but rather than withdraw when he hit a certain depth, he went a little deeper. Her eyes went slightly wider, and he groaned at the feel of her mouth around him.

He pulled out. Saliva coated his entire length. He guided her mouth over him and she bobbed her head to his pace until he couldn't stand it anymore.

"Fuck!" He pulled out of her mouth, grasped his length, and aimed at her full tits. His cum decorated the glorious mounds as he came on her, milking every single last drop.

Afterward, he collapsed back against the door, a little taken aback by the sight of her.

She nibbled on her lip, and he saw the nerves in her eyes.

"Your ex was an asshole. You're fucking incredible."

And she'd just guaranteed her life and body belonged to him and him alone.

Chapter Six

"Lie on the bed. Spread your legs wide. I want to see your juicy cunt."

Ava couldn't ever recall a time in her life where she'd been this aroused. Smokey wasn't even in the room yet, and she was ready to come. He hadn't left for two days. Tomorrow, she promised herself she was going to open the bakery.

Since the night he arrived at her house and she'd sucked his cock, he hadn't left. He took phone calls as she'd watched him. She expected him to leave, but he hadn't.

Instead, he'd spent the entire time either fucking or feeding her. She'd been the one to do all the cooking while he'd been sure to put it to good use.

She never knew chocolate could taste so good as he'd drizzled it on his cock and she sucked him until he'd come in her mouth. She loved watching Smokey lose control, especially when she took him in her mouth.

The sheer power was exhilarating.

What she loved more was when he didn't turn the light off, and so far, they hadn't had sex in the missionary position either.

Nope, it had been so many different possibilities. She particularly loved it when he spread her out on the dining room table. Hers wasn't very big, but the way he described wanting to take her on the one at the clubhouse, she doubted it would ever happen. Her curiosity was piqued though.

"You better be naked or I'm smacking that sexy ass."

She never knew a spanking could be so erotic. He'd slapped her ass a few times during sex, or even as he passed. She loved the attention.

Ava looked down the room and smiled as Smokey stood in the doorway. He was completely naked. Every inch of his muscular, inked body on display. He could be a male model. He was sexy, dangerous, and had an air of mystery about him.

She didn't even know his real name. Just Smokey. No other name.

She liked it.

"Reach down, spread those pussy lips. Let me see your juicy cunt." Smokey made no move to enter the bedroom even as she did as he asked. He groaned.

His cock was already hard, and he wrapped his fingers around the length. "Now that is a sight every man fucking loves." He stepped into the room. "Tonight, I want you to touch yourself."

"Smokey?"

"I need to know you can take care of yourself. I'm not going to be available twenty-four seven when you need a good fucking. Do this for me." There was a short pause. "Please."

It was the *please* that did it.

She let go of her pussy and lifted up on her elbows. "You want me to play with myself."

"I want to make sure you're doing it right."

She chuckled. "Why?"

"I've seen the way you are, Ava. You've never sucked a cock before, and your ex, he hasn't helped you with anything. I'm going to make up for it."

"I don't need that."

"But what about me?" he asked, climbing on the bed. His hands went to her knees, holding them open.

"What do you mean? I'll always be available." I hope that doesn't make me sound like some kind of slut.

"And there are going to be times that I'm not available. I'm going to want to hear you play with yourself."

The way Smokey talked, it sounded like he was looking at them being together long-term. Ava refused to get her hopes up. There was no reason to. This was for sex only. They hadn't known each other long enough for her to want more.

"Now, touch yourself. Let me see how you do it."

Her cheeks were on fire as she slid her hand down, feeling a little self-conscious as he watched her. She used a single finger to stroke her pussy. Her clit was there, and she stared up at the ceiling.

Smokey clucked his tongue. "That won't do," he said. "Are you afraid of getting dirty?"

She sucked in her bottom lip. "Tell me how you want it."

"Start with two fingers. Dip them into your pussy. I want you to hold them up to me so I can see they're nice and wet. Don't fucking tell me you're not soaked. I know your cunt better than you do, and I know you want me. You want my cock."

She used two fingers and went to her pussy, sliding them inside. She was soaking. When it came to Smokey, he aroused her so easily. Closing her eyes, she gasped.

"No, you look at me. When you play with yourself, I want you to remember me."

She opened her eyes and stared at him.

Smokey had his fingers wrapped around his cock, working from the base up to the tip, and back down again.

Up and down, he worked his length, and she couldn't take her gaze off him.

"You like what you see?" he asked.

"Yes."

"Well, you're going to come for me, and then I'm

going to fuck you." He held his cock in his hand. "This is your reward."

She worked her pussy, sliding her fingers in and out of her pussy.

"Now, touch your clit."

She used both fingers and stroked her pussy, watching him.

"Fuck, that is a pretty sight. How does it feel?" he asked.

"So good."

"Yeah, you're right, it's so good. But you need to do it more. Work that pussy."

She watched him as he continued to play with his cock. The sight of him alone was enough to set her own orgasm blazing. She cried out his name as she came, stroking herself through the pleasure.

Smokey's hands went to her knees to hold her open and he grinned. "That was good, but I know you can do better." He pressed his cock to her entrance, and she gasped as he began to tease her.

"We're not using a condom," she said.

"I'm clean, and I know you are. Don't worry. I'll pull out."

She giggled. "That's not protection."

"I'm not going to stop." He groaned. "Fuck, your pussy is tight." He kept hold of her knees as he worked inside her, taking his time.

She watched him, mesmerized as he teased her. He pulled out and slid his cock between her slit, bumping her clit.

Each touch had her moaning for more.

"Please," she said.

"You want my big, fat cock?" he asked.

"Yes."

"Beg for it."

"Please, Smokey, I need you."

"Who does this pussy belong to?"

"You."

"That's right. It's fucking mine." He pounded inside her. One of his hands slid up to rest around her neck. She gasped, loving when he did this, holding her in place as he took his pleasure. He didn't squeeze or hurt her.

She moaned his name, not wanting him to stop, and he didn't. He fucked her harder, and she met each of his thrusts until she couldn't think straight.

"Fuck!" He growled the word and suddenly jerked out of her.

She stayed still as he pumped his release all over her pussy and stomach.

After the last of his cum had finished, he collapsed against her.

"That was close," she said.

"Yeah, it was." He cupped her face. "But your pussy feels so fucking good. You need to get on the pill."

She wrinkled her nose. "They make me kind of sick. I don't do well with them."

"Fuck. I guess it's back to condoms."

"They can't be that bad," she said.

"It feels even better being inside you without anything between us."

"I'll make a doctor's appointment. See if there's anything else I can do."

"You do that, baby." He kissed her lips, and she was on cloud nine.

****

Two weeks later

Hanson was able to leave the hospital. Smokey had decided to decorate the whole clubhouse.

He wanted the prospect to know that he was part

of the club. The young kid had earned his patch. He'd been attacked from behind. Knocked unconscious and stabbed for the effort.

When he'd gone to question Hanson at the hospital, the kid had looked distraught, not knowing who'd attacked him as they had come out of nowhere. Hanson had thought he was going to get kicked out of the club.

Far from it.

Smokey looked out of his office window to see Ava at the buffet table. She'd offered to cook all the food needed for the party, and he didn't see a reason to stop her. She was a damn good cook and it saved him money.

Abriana and Raven were there. The club whores were keeping their distance, but it was at his request.

"Hanson's due to arrive any minute," Hunter said, coming into the room. "Kinky's bringing him in with Brick."

"Good." On a normal patch celebration, Verge and Lewis would be present, but seeing as they had to keep an eye on their clubs, this was going to be a more personal celebration.

"Do you think it's wise to have her here?" Hunter asked.

"Ava doesn't pose a threat to anyone." None of the men were giving her the time of day even though they'd fallen in love with her food.

Raven was constantly making stops at Ava's bakery for a resupply of food.

"We don't know her."

"She offered to make the food. Enjoy it." He turned on his heel, brushing past Hunter on the way out of the office and the main club building.

Abriana let out a moan and Smokey caught sight of Ugly Beast watching them. Bella, their daughter, was in Abriana's arms.

"Why is she here?" Ugly Beast asked. "She's not club."

"She's mine." Smokey grabbed a beer and ignored the looks his men gave him.

He'd never staked his claim on any woman, and he didn't intend to start now, but with the way the brothers were acting around Ava, she wasn't going to stick around.

Smokey wanted her around as long as it took to fuck her right out of his system, and that was it.

"And you think I act irrationally." Ugly Beast shook his head.

"Get used to her."

He'd been fucking her for nearly three weeks now and rather than be bored by her, he was more fucking enraptured by her. The way she smiled, the softness of her laugh. It was all getting to him.

There was no doubt she drove him crazy with need. He thought about her every single day, and that was bad news. He should be cutting her out of his life, not finding reasons to keep her in it. He loved that she didn't have any other experience. Her ex had done a number on her, and well, he loved showing her everything she could have. She was an amazing student.

With a beer in hand, he left the brothers who were staring at him as if he'd gone insane, and made his way over to her.

The moment she saw him, her smile grew even wider.

He banded an arm around her and took possession of her mouth. The entire club was there to see it.

"You did good, babe," he said.

"It all looks good, but I guess it would have to

depend on what people thought." She rested her arm on his shoulder. "I hope I didn't go overboard."

"People will love it."

"He's here," one of the club women said, bringing silence to them.

They all made their way around the clubhouse to the main parking lot.

Kinky had taken the van.

The passenger door opened up, and cheers erupted all around.

"Are you sure he should be leaving the hospital?" Ava asked. "He looks so bad."

"He'll be fine soon." He nodded at Hanson.

Hunter came out and handed him the jacket.

Smokey let Ava go and made his way toward Hanson, who stood next to the truck. His face was bright red.

"I'm sorry all the brothers couldn't be here to see this, but you earned this." He opened up the jacket and he watched as Hanson struggled to contain his joy. He handed the leather cut to him, gripping the back of his neck. "Welcome, brother."

Hanson shook his hand and slapped him on the back.

He watched for a few seconds as the club pulled Hanson in, hugging, shaking hands, slapping him on the shoulder.

Smokey watched as Ava smiled. She looked happy.

"You know the kid?" Smokey asked.

"No. I don't know him, but it's not exactly hard to see that he was so thrilled to earn his cut."

"He did a good job."

"He looks happy. I'm so thrilled for him."

It wasn't long before music fired up and the party

started. Smokey took Ava in his arms, danced with her, drank, and it was only an hour into the party, but he saw the way his woman kept on glancing over at the buffet table.

No one had touched the food.

His club was known for eating shit loads at events like this.

"I'm just going to go to the bathroom," she said.

Smokey nodded, and as soon as she left, he turned to the brothers. "Why aren't you eating?"

"We don't know her. Ugly Beast made a valid point. It's one thing for you to fuck her. It's quite another thing to allow her to cook for us," Brick said.

"Oh, fuck this shit. You're all happy to eat her baked goods." Raven climbed off the wall where she'd been sitting and went to the table.

Smokey watched as Raven took a slice of bread and dipped it into another bowl. She scooped out a generous amount and took a bite.

"Oh, fuck," she said. "This is good."

Before anyone could take one to try, she picked up the dip and the bread, and moved away.

"Hey!" one of the brothers called out.

"You losers were too lame to try the food. This is mine."

Smokey smiled as the club descended on the table.

This was what Ava saw when she came out of the clubhouse.

She stopped and watched them all at the table. "They finally got hungry?" she asked.

"They did. All it takes is one person." He winked at her.

"Did you do this?" She put her hand to his chest.

"Nah, I don't do any kind of shit like that."

"I was worried that no one liked what I picked, and I did research what goes well at a picnic."

He kissed her forehead. "Stop frowning. The club knows you're an easy target. They'll get used to you. You've just got to stop letting them get to you."

"Thank you," she said.

"What for?"

"For making them eat it."

"Babe, I can't make them do anything. Is there anything *you* can't do?" he asked. She could cook, bake, keep house, fuck. So far, she was the perfect woman.

Was that why he couldn't keep away from her?

He wanted her.

She wasn't like the whores who stuck around hoping for any cock to notice them. Ava didn't look toward any of his brothers. Her gaze was always on him.

"There's a lot I can't do." She smiled. "I just hope you don't find out what it is."

Chapter Seven

"You don't think this looks stupid?" Ava asked, turning left and right for him to see.

"Hell, no, it doesn't." Smokey let out a whistle.

Tonight, Smokey had invited her to a club party. The only warning he'd given her was that it wasn't going to be tame.

The men were going to play, and he wanted her to join him.

She didn't have any party clothes and told him so. In response, he'd turned up to her house tonight complete with the appropriate attire. Staring down the length of her body, though, she had to wonder. The skirt went above the knee, and it was way too indecent to go out in.

The bra and shirt he'd purchased for her, well, her tits were squeezed together so tightly it gave the word *cleavage* a whole new meaning. She was so far out of her comfort zone it wasn't even funny. She gave a little wriggle and Smokey chuckled.

"What is it?"

"I don't know. You don't think it's too revealing?"

"That's its purpose. I want to be able to see you."

"I don't know. This feels … strange," she said. "Look."

Smokey stepped away from the doorframe and moved toward her. His hands went to her hips. "What are you finding difficult with how you look?"

"You're going to have club women there."

"So?"

"And I … look at me. I'm thirty years old. I don't equal them. I never will. I should just stay home tonight." She pulled out of his arms and collapsed to the bed.

There were moments late at night when his arms

were wrapped around her that she could allow herself to dream and imagine that he belonged to her. They hadn't changed the dynamic of their relationship.

It was still sex. Great sex.

Smokey was teaching her stuff she'd never even heard of, let alone seen.

He'd awakened her body, but he'd also opened up her heart. She hadn't been looking for love, far from it. After Derek, she'd sworn off all men. They were all rat bastards, but Smokey was different.

It didn't matter, though.

There was no way in hell she intended to bring up the possibilities of a relationship. The club wasn't exactly warming to her, even though she adored them all. She loved stopping by with extra baked goods, or listening to them talk about nothing. They treated her as if she was a nobody, and that was fine.

She got it. To them, she wasn't anyone important.

"I'm not going to this party without you. I've been looking forward to it all week. I even broke my rules for you. I promised myself no matter what, I wouldn't shop for a chick. I did all of that for you." He grabbed her arm and she followed his tug as he moved her in front of the mirror. "Now I don't know what shit is going on in your brain and quite frankly, I really don't give a shit. I love what I see."

He wrapped his arms around her waist and pressed his chin against her shoulder. "We're going to that party, and you're going to have fun. Do I need to threaten to put you over my knee?"

She snorted and rolled her eyes. "Fine, but if they all laugh at me, we're coming right back here, watching a movie and drinking cocoa. Deal?"

"Deal."

He took her hand and walked her out of the

house. She groaned when she saw his bike waiting for them.

A couple of times now, she'd ridden on the back of it. Each time, she'd ended up screaming and begging him to stop. So embarrassing.

"It'll be fine."

"Seriously? Couldn't we, like, walk?"

"In those heels?"

She glanced down at her feet. He'd purchased a pair of stiletto heels. They were quite high, and she felt a little dizzy just glancing down at the floor.

"Fine. It seems you're winning all the arguments tonight."

"It doesn't take me long to do." He winked at her.

He climbed onto his bike and waited for her.

She threw her leg over the bike and climbed on, trying not to jostle her weight or show him how heavy she was. The women at the clubhouse were slender. Each woman, apart from Abriana and Raven, had been sure to tell her how easy it was to diet and how important it was to count calories.

Ava got the message big time. They were slim, she was not. Big deal.

She held on to Smokey as he started up the bike and took them off into the night. A small scream escaped her, and she held on even tighter to Smokey, not wanting to let him go for even a second.

"I've got you, babe. You just got to have a little faith."

She closed her eyes when she felt the panic rise up inside her. They were going to crash. In the back of her mind, she knew it wasn't possible because of how good of a driver Smokey was, but she couldn't stop herself.

"You're doing good, babe. Not long to go now."

Still with her eyes firmly shut, she squeezed Smokey even tighter, praying for the ride to end. When it did, her fingers ached from the tight hold she had.

Slowly, she opened one eye, then the other as the clubhouse parking lot surrounded them.

The desire to climb off and kiss the pavement was strong. She held herself in check, settling on just getting off the bike in the most elegant way possible. It wasn't easy. She struggled with it, but fortunately, she achieved it and she felt so happy.

Smokey chuckled. "Damn, you've got a firm grip."

She winced. "I didn't hurt you, did I?"

"Nope, but I love having you at my back." He cupped her face and kissed her. "You're going to have to get used to it."

Ava didn't want to get her hopes up, but each time he said something like that, she found herself on the cusp of believing this was more than just sex. Rather than ask him, she simply smiled and followed behind him when he took her hand.

They were heading toward the main clubhouse, but the loud, hard music could be heard outside.

She heard a couple of women giggling, but rather than look toward them, she kept her focus on Smokey's hand.

Once inside the clubhouse, she looked past his shoulder, and wow. There was no other word for it as naked women danced on tables, the bar, and she even caught sight of a naked woman on the makeshift dance floor. If it could really be called that.

Women in many different states of undress were everywhere.

She'd never noticed so many brothers in one place.

"We've got two different chapters in tonight," Smokey said. "It's a party."

Ava couldn't deny that.

There surely was a lot of nakedness going on.

Smokey didn't stay in the sanctuary of the entrance for long. He held her hand even tighter as they moved through the circles of people. She smiled at any familiar faces, but other than that, she stayed perfectly content.

They made it toward the bar where Smokey ordered them both a couple of beers. Ava was distracted as she noticed Kinky sitting in the corner. It wasn't the man himself that captured her attention, but what he was doing. He had a woman on her knees before him, worshipping his cock.

Ava saw the way Kinky had wrapped the woman's hair in a fist and used the grip he had to control her.

Both of her hands were on his knees and Kinky guided his cock in deep. She noticed he slowed as the woman began to gag but that didn't seem to stop him. He took his time and stared at the woman. A communication clearly happening between the two that she wasn't privy to.

"He wants her to swallow his entire dick," Smokey said.

She whirled around. "He does?"

"You're looking a little flustered there."

She looked at Kinky then back at Smokey. "But she's ... gagging." She leaned in to whisper the last part.

"And it what makes it all the more fun." Smokey winked at her. "You're like a virgin, did you know that?"

Ava shook her head. "I'm not."

"No, I've taken care of it, but you act like you've never seen a good blowjob."

"I've seen them. Never in person, but on the internet." She waved her hand in the air trying to brush the subject over, but Smokey wasn't having any of it.

"You've watched porn?"

"Don't, Smokey. Come on. You know I have. Don't embarrass me."

He chuckled, and with his hand still on hers, he tugged her close until she had no choice but to be body-to-body to him. He placed her hand over the back of his neck. "I have no intention of doing that, but you see, knowing my woman loves to watch porn. It turns me on."

"I haven't watched it since we … you know."

"Fucked."

"Yes."

"You can say the words, babe. It's not a bad thing." The hand on her ass had her heart rate speeding up. The bar, the couples, the blatant sex that was going on around her, it all faded away until all that remained was the two of them.

"Fuck," she said.

"I shouldn't like that as much as I do." He took possession of her lips, and she closed her eyes. The hand on her ass moved down until it grazed the bottom of her skirt. She let him go to release a moan.

"We need to get ourselves a seat," he said.

Before too long, he'd grabbed both of their beers and led her across the main room. There was a spare seat in the corner, and Smokey took it. She was about to sit opposite him, but he grabbed her hand, tugging her so she had no choice but to collapse against him.

"People will see," she said, seeing his intention.

"Do I look like a man who gives a fuck?" He tugged her a little harder and she had no choice but to follow, moving her thighs to either side of his as he gripped her hips tightly. The skirt she wore rode up, and she quickly pressed her face against his shoulder. Smokey wasn't having any of that.

He wrapped his hand around her hair and gave it a tug, forcing her to lift up, which she did.

"I want to see your face."

"Smokey?"

"I've got you. The club doesn't give a fuck, and if they do, they can look away or blow themselves. I don't care. This is a party, and I want my woman seated on my dick. Is that so hard?" He circled his finger. "This doesn't matter. Forget about all of them. It's me you should be focused on. No one else."

She cried out as his hands returned to her hips and he thrust up. His cock was close to her pussy. The flimsy panties she wore provided zero protection above his denim-covered cock.

"That's right. You know you want me, Ava. Stop fighting it."

She wasn't fighting it, but as he broke down her walls, she no longer cared when his hand touched her pussy. At first, he rubbed her across the fabric of her panties, then he slid a finger beneath and started to work on her clit. She whimpered as he took her clit between his fingers and gave it a squeeze before using both fingers to massage on either side. She sank her teeth into her lip as the moans threatened to erupt from inside her.

He wasn't happy with that as he moved down to plunder inside her.

"Please," she said.

"I don't want you to be silent, babe. Give it all to me. Forget the club. Only focus on me. It's what I want."

He slammed two fingers knuckles deep within her, making her cry out from the sheer pleasure of his touch. Smokey made her forget everything. She loved being with him. He didn't put any controls on either of them. They were both free.

Ava knew she was falling for the man, but she also didn't care. He was everything she ever wanted and then some more.

****

Smokey didn't really care for exhibitionism, but when it came to Ava, he couldn't help but feel the desire to push her. Her ex had kept her trapped in the same toxic cycle for ten years. Even though she wasn't a virgin, she certainly acted like it.

He wanted to break down her walls, to show her the desirable woman she was beneath. How she didn't need her husband or anyone else to tell her how to live her life or how to be. All she needed was to enjoy fucking.

Nothing was off the table for him. She could have everything her heart desired. Especially when she chose to use him to get it.

He added a third finger, spreading her pussy wide, and she gasped. Her eyes closed, and this time, he allowed it as her attention was on him.

In and out, he worked her cunt, using his thumb to graze across her clit. The music for the most part drowned out everything that was happening in the club. She didn't get to see the woman spread out on the pool table, with a line of men.

Smokey didn't care what she thought as she rode his fingers.

When he knew she was close, he pulled his fingers from her core, and her eyes opened. With her gaze on him, he took each digit into his mouth and sucked her cream right off. "So delicious."

"Why did you stop?" she asked.

"I want my cock inside you when you come."

She glanced behind his back and he pinched her nipple, drawing her gaze. "Ouch."

"Me. That's who you have to look at. Just me."

She nodded her head. The nipple he pinched was hard.

Over the white shirt, he took her bud into his mouth, sucking hard.

"Please."

He eased back from her and released the zip of his jeans. Pulling out his erect cock without hurting himself took some patience, but he got it done. He moved Ava over him, and with her panties to one side, he ran the tip through her slit, coating the head of his cock in her arousal.

Gripping the cheek of her ass, he moved her until she was right over his length. As he stared into her eyes, he slowly got her to lower herself down until she began to take him, inch by inch.

Fuck!

He loved it when he wasn't wearing a condom. Ava was so tight and her pussy was so wet. She was a woman designed for taking cock, and he relished it. Craved it. She moaned his name, and when there was enough of his length inside her, he grabbed both of her hips and tugged her down until he was balls deep inside her.

Her hands went to his shoulders and he smiled.

"Now that is a fucking party," he said.

Ava went to look behind her, and he captured her face. "No, not what is happening there. What is happening between us." He thrust up inside her and she cried out. "See. Fucking perfection."

He went from her hips to the curves of her ass. Lifting her up, he began to rock her on his cock, getting her to take more of him.

The way she moaned his name was so fucking perfect.

"Show me your tits, Ava," he said.

Her hands went to the front of her shirt and started to work the buttons open. The white lace bra he'd gotten her to wear made his cock pulse even deeper, which had her moaning for more.

"That's right, babe. Now, slide the cups beneath your tits."

She was such a good girl, doing as she was told. He moved one of his hands to the back of her neck, pulling her down to kiss her lips. She cupped his face as he slammed up inside her pussy.

Ava started to work on his cock, and he broke the kiss, lifting her up so that he could suck on one of her perfect nipples. Taking one into his mouth, he held her in place with his hands, keeping her still as he devoted a good amount of time to one tit, then moving onto the next. He pushed them both together and proceeded to bite each one, loving her gasps and the sounds she made.

His balls ached.

Smokey let go of her breasts, showing her a pace and rhythm that brought them both pleasure. Up and down, dancing on his dick as he worked himself inside her.

She moaned his name and he felt his own orgasm close.

He used all of his force, drawing her down on his length until with one final thrust, he closed his eyes and spilled every single drop of his cum within her. He didn't have the energy to pull out, and the truth was, he didn't want to. They were both clean, and pregnancy was a risk, but at that moment, he really didn't give a fuck.

All he cared about was coming deeply. Marking her as his own in front of the entire club.

He was aware women looked at her with envy. How the guys were shocked. He rarely took a woman in front of anyone, especially not like this. Any of the club pussy were free game to his men.

Ava was off-limits.

No one could see anything. It was why he'd been careful in picking this spot and the clothes he'd purchased for her.

He wanted everything to be perfect, and when it came to Ava, she was turning into everything. His men still doubted her integrity, but he didn't. He knew this woman. She was sweet, kind, and cared about everyone but herself. He'd even seen the way she'd been with the club. They weren't giving her an easy time of it, but she wasn't doing anything for herself.

Knowing everything he did about her in the short amount of time he'd actually known her, she'd found a family she'd been searching for in him and the club.

Ava wasn't going to like this life.

In time, he was going to have to cut her loose. Each time he planned to, he'd look at her smiling face and the truth was, he didn't want to. The club had to come first. It was the motto he lived by. It was why no one challenged his leadership. But that didn't stop him from wanting Ava.

Many nights in her bed, he'd lain awake just watching her. It was messed up. He never shared a bed with a woman. In the past, before Ava, he'd kicked them right out as he had no interest in them being there.

Ava was different. She was the kind of woman he wanted.

He slid out of her pussy, returning the fabric of her panties over.

"My cum is going to be spilling out of your cunt, baby," he said. He leaned in close and brushed his lips across hers. He eased his cock back inside his jeans. "Let's dance."

Ava had already put her shirt back to right.

Her face was bright red as he sipped his beer. She did the same and then he took her hand, leading her onto the dance floor.

He pulled her into his arms, and she rested her head against his chest. Smokey wrapped both arms around her, resting his face on the top of her head. Even with the heels she wore, she wasn't as tall as him.

He held her still against him. Stroking his fingers in her hair, he kissed the top of her head.

Brothers were watching him as if he'd lost his mind. He didn't give a flying fuck what any of them thought.

With Ava draped over him, he felt complete, and he didn't know what that was all about. Women were to be used, not enjoyed like this. Ava had blown his world apart, and he loved it.

Ava lifted her head. "The woman on the pool table. Does she enjoy it?"

Smokey didn't bother pretending he didn't know what she was talking about. "She wouldn't be there if she didn't. The women here want to fuck as many men as possible. It's what they want. In the morning, you'll hear them bragging about how many patches they took."

She nibbled on her lip. "I only want yours."

He smiled. "Babe, I'll kill any man that comes near you. That's a fucking promise."

She rested her head back on his shoulder and he kissed the top of her head. Glancing across the club, he caught sight of Ugly Beast, who raised his beer glass in his direction. He nodded but didn't say or do anything else.

They stayed for several dances, a couple more

beers, and a round of pool. He'd laughed when she'd wriggled her nose at the thought of playing on the same table people had fucked on. The club knew the rules. They could fuck anywhere, but clean it all up after. He didn't need to have dirty cum drops on his table. Finally, after several hours of partying, and her meeting a couple of the guys from different chapters, he took her to his bedroom in the clubhouse.

He slept on the main floor right in the back. Whenever there was a problem, he wanted to be the first on the scene.

Within seconds, he had her clothes off and bent over the desk. He spread her ass and stared down at her tight little asshole.

Cupping her pussy, he felt his cum inside her, and it only served to arouse him more. As he gripped his cock, he didn't see a need to put on a condom after filling her pussy for a second time. He held her hips within his grasp and slid in long and deep. They both cried out at the out-of-this-world pleasure.

Her tight cunt fluttered around his dick, and once he was as deep as he could go, he closed his eyes, relishing the pleasure for a few short seconds.

Then, he began to move, watching her take all of him. He spread her asshole and teased between the globes of her ass, working her anus. She let out a gasp, but he wasn't done with her.

He pressed against her asshole. She wasn't wet enough, and leaning over, he released a trail of saliva across her anus, coating his fingers in it and pushing his finger into her asshole. She tensed up, and to help distract her, he pounded inside her, hearing her startled gasp. So pretty.

"Let me inside, babe," he said.

He worked his finger into her ass, then used a

second one to stretch her out.

"If you've watched porn, then you've had to have watched a good anal scene. They're fucking incredible." He groaned and started to work more of his fingers into her asshole, going deep and hard, stretching her. "One day soon, this asshole is going to be mine, Ava. I'm going to enjoy fucking it and making it so. You want that, don't you? You want to belong to me in every single way imaginable?"

"Yes!"

"Good."

He was so close to orgasm. He removed his fingers from her asshole, grabbed her hips, and pounded inside her, wanting to fill her so completely. Fucking her harder with every passing second. This time, as his orgasm built, he reached between her legs and stroked her clit, getting her off at the same time as he did. He didn't pull out. He slammed in deep, flooding her cunt with more of his cum.

Chapter Eight

"I'm not talking sex with you," Ava said, giggling into the cell phone.

"Why the hell not?"

"I'm in the bank, and you're going to have to wait until I'm not."

"So that means you want to talk dirty to me."

She rolled her eyes. Smokey had been gone one day, and she missed him. What she did love was how he continued to keep calling her. It was almost as if he couldn't seem to help himself, which she loved.

People were going about their daily lives as if there was nothing happening around them. Something was, something huge. She was falling in love. There was no other word for it. She'd tried to stop it each time she realized the signs, but he made her feel so alive.

Smokey had gotten into her heart, and what was more, she didn't care because she loved the feelings he evoked inside her. They were … magical.

Of course, she wouldn't dream of telling him exactly how she felt. She had no doubt he would pull away as fast as lightning. He didn't love her. The club tolerated her. She didn't for a second believe it was a good position to put Smokey in. So, she ignored the need in her heart and just decided to live her life, enjoying the moments they were together.

"Ava?" Smokey asked.

She didn't even realize she hadn't responded to him.

"Yes, I want to, but the bank has to come first right now. Call me in about ten minutes?" she asked.

"Got it. Take care, babe."

"You too." She hadn't figured out a term of endearment for him just yet.

One day, she would, but for now, he was just Smokey. She still didn't know his real name. Not that it mattered.

When it was her turn at the bank, she handed over the check and requested some of the funds from her business account. She tapped her fingers on the counter, waiting.

The lines today were so long.

She waited, and finally, with a brown envelope, the woman returned. Ava thanked the woman and turned back toward the line. She tried to work her bag open, but with how hot it was in the bank and all the gazes on her, she held the envelope within her grasp and quickly rushed outside.

Ava tried to open her bag and wasn't looking where she was going, bumping into a hard wall of a chest.

She dropped her envelope and winced as it fell to the ground. Then she decided she'd bring in a batch of cupcakes to the woman who had the forethought to seal the damn thing. She should have stayed inside the bank.

"Oops, my bad," the hard, masculine voice said.

Ava went to pick up her money, but the man got there first. She looked at him, seeing the business suit on the large, muscular man.

"I should have looked where I was going." She rubbed at her temple. Between the sudden heat and Smokey's phone call, she was all flustered.

"Don't worry about it. I wasn't watching where I was going either." He moved to the side and she turned, frowning.

"I'm really sorry."

"No, it's fine. I don't mind when a pretty lady bumps into me."

This made her laugh. "Okay." She held her hand

out. "Can I have my envelope?"

"Do you want to go out with me?"

This caused her to look up at him. "Er, I'm sorry. I'm seeing someone. No, thank you." She internally winced. No one had ever randomly asked her out on a date.

He waved his hand in the air. "It's fine."

She forced a smile, finding this entire scene uncomfortable. "Can I have my envelope, please?"

"Sure, sure." He held it out to her, and as she reached out to take it, he gave her a tug so she was close and she fell against him. His lips next to her ear. "You're so beautiful. Any guy who has you, make sure he tells you that."

She pulled away from him quickly, finding him so strange. He let go of the envelope, and she put it in her bag.

"Well, thank you for your … compliments. I'm so sorry for running into you."

"Don't worry about it, Ava." He winked at her.

She frowned as he turned on his heel and walked off.

How did he know her name? He must have been a regular man around town or something. She had to get used to people knowing her name without having the first clue who they were.

After crossing the street, she made her way into the diner where Raven sat waiting for her. The other woman was drinking a coffee as she arrived. She nodded to the waitress that she'd have the same.

"I've just had the most bizarre meeting outside the bank," she said.

"Oh, please, the bank is boring. Has Smokey been in touch?"

At the mention of Smokey's name, she forgot all

about the strange encounter and smiled. "Yes. He just called."

"Any word?"

Ava rolled her eyes. "He doesn't talk to me about club stuff. You know that. He only talks about … other stuff."

"The dirty kind of stuff." Raven winked at her.

"You're not making this any easier."

"What? You're the one fucking the boss. This should get me perks being your friend."

Ava tensed up. "Oh, is that the only reason you wanted to have a coffee?"

Raven cursed. "I didn't mean it like that. It was a joke. I happen to like you, which is pretty big news. I don't like a whole lot of people. Ignore what I said. I'm used to the whores who stick around at the club begging for attention. You know how fucked up that can be." Raven sighed. "They hate your guts."

"What did I do?"

"You got Smokey's attention. It makes you enemy number one in their book."

Ava thanked the waitress for the coffee and looked at Raven. "Did he sleep with a lot of the women?"

"Don't go there," Raven said.

"Sorry."

Raven reached out, touching her hand. "I'm the kind of woman who says what went on before you guys met, it doesn't count. It's what happens during and after. Smokey hasn't looked at another woman since you came on the scene. You really need to stop worrying. Smokey's not going anywhere."

"I'm not worried. It's not like that." Was it, though? She wasn't sure.

The other women were nice to her. She'd

accepted long ago that she seemed to be the kind of person no one particularly liked. No one had a bad word to say about her, but she didn't mesh with others. It wasn't without a lack of trying either. People simply didn't like her.

She sipped at her coffee.

"I didn't mean to sound like a bitch before."

Ava waved her hand in the air. "It's fine."

"You really need to stop doing that," Raven said.

"What?"

"Acting like you're not hurt when you clearly are. Don't hide your feelings, and don't make others think they can get away with hurting you. I'm sorry for being a bitch."

"I'm fine. Really."

"I'm starting to think I need to approach you with my bitch radar."

Ava burst out laughing.

"Are we going to get something to eat, or what?"

"Why are you here and not with the guys?" Ava asked.

"They need someone to handle the fort. That's me. I'm the chick who makes sure all the prospects and bitches stay in line." Raven shrugged.

"How did you become a member?"

Raven put down her menu. "Why do you want to know?"

Ava pulled back. "I was just curious."

"Is this about Smokey again?"

She chuckled. "When is it not about Smokey?"

"Babe, listen, the club life, you don't have what it takes." Raven licked her lips. "I'll level with you, okay. Shit gets mean at the club. It gets hard. I've got scars on my body from the hits I've taken. We're not a fairytale. It's hardcore. Don't get me wrong, there are harder MCs out there. Smokey, though, he knows his shit and he keeps us all safe." Raven sat back. "The way he looks at you. He doesn't want you anywhere near the fucking club. He likes that you're … you."

"How did you manage to make that sound like an insult?" She tilted her head to the side and laughed.

"I'm downright fucking talented." Raven winked. "Now, let's eat. I'm starving and these curves will not feed themselves. Believe me."

****

"Why the fuck would I want to align myself with you guys again?" Smokey asked, staring across the table at Sebastian Drago.

He didn't want to have this meeting.

Ryan was currently under the mafia's protection, and that pissed Smokey off. The lying piece of shit had been in the mafia and the Twisted Bastards MC's pocket. Big Dick had discovered the fucker's location. He hadn't gone for extraction because Smokey had told him not to. He wasn't going to risk anyone else's life for Ryan.

Heads were going to roll when he was through.

Sebastian sighed, and his gaze wandered to Ugly Beast.

Smokey slammed his hand on the table. "This is my meeting. Not his. I don't have time for this bullshit."

"We have product. It needs moving, and so far, it has only ended in bloodshed."

"So, I told you last time. My time with the mafia is done. You guys are fucking hypocrites. The way you kept a perv in power, and you guys think I'm an animal. I don't get my nuts off screwing underage girls."

Sebastian tensed up. "There are rules to follow."

"Yeah, well, I follow the main rules which say those who want to fuck little girls need to die."

Smokey glared at Sebastian.

"If you won't consider a connection with the mafia again, why did you come?" Sebastian asked.

"Curiosity. I don't see why *The Boss* sent you and didn't come himself." Smokey smirked at Sebastian, tilting his head to the side. "Unless you are the big man himself."

"I don't want that role. You know who I think is suited to it." Again, Sebastian looked toward Ugly Beast.

Smokey glanced back at his sergeant at arms. Ugly's past wasn't pretty. Born Umberto Garofalo. The bastard child to an underage girl at the hands of the previous mafia boss, Nico Garofalo.

Ugly had been left for dead until Sebastian Drago made something of him. Not many people knew the full history. Smokey was one of the few who did.

With Nico's death, the true heir to the mafia throne was Umberto. Ugly Beast didn't want it. Smokey had talked to him, even tried to reason with the man, but he wouldn't be talked into anything.

The only place in the world he wanted was by his side.

"Now, you being the underboss, which is kind of like the boss in waiting, why didn't you take the job?" Smokey asked.

"Because he didn't want it." The hard voice came from the corner, and Sebastian shook his head.

Smokey smiled as the true boss made his appearance.

"And who are you?" Smokey asked.

"I'm sure you're aware of who I am."

"Carlos Santigo. The brand-new boss of the mafia. You've got one of the worst reputations in your entire outfit, if my memory serves me well. You're not married. No bastards that people know of. Rumor has it that you kill them. I doubt it. Any kid is better than no kid when it comes to your kind."

"My kind?" Carlos asked.

Sebastian tensed up. "Don't, Smokey. Do not disrespect him."

Smokey stood, sending the chair back with a clatter. "He should count himself lucky that the only thing I'm doing is disrespecting him after the insult I've had to deal with. You're all supposed to be men of your word. Your word means absolute shit." He pointed his finger in Sebastian's face. "You're housing a man responsible for hurting one of my men. I want him back."

"I'm under the impression you wish to have power," Carlos said, coming forward.

Smokey eyed the man who was now the new boss. He knew a monster when he saw one. After all, he didn't become the president of the Hell's Bastards MC because he knew how to play with dolls. "You've got nothing I want."

"But you see, I do, Smokey," Carlos said. "I want to come to some arrangement."

"Not going to happen," Smokey said.

"You acquire more land. More turf. The last deal we had with you gained you a great deal."

"And nearly killed my men. I haven't forgotten what went down and what happened with the Twisted fuckers you decided to join forces with." Smokey was so close to grabbing his gun and killing them all. If it wasn't for the mega fallout, he'd have done it already. Ugly Beast stayed perfectly still in his place, watching, observing.

They all had a part to play.

Running a hand down his face, he stared at Carlos, waiting.

"The deal that went wrong had nothing to do with me, or the main outfit. We're sorry if this has led you to believe otherwise."

"I'm not interested in apologies."

"Then maybe you'll be interested in knowing the Twisted Bastards MC have approached me. Creed to be exact."

This made Smokey pause.

Creed was the asshole leading the Twisted Bastards MC.

"He's interested in brokering a deal. He'll be quite happy to distribute our product. He wants guns and the men to take down the Hell's Bastards MC."

He shook his head. "If that's true, you wouldn't be telling me about it."

"Ah, but you see, Sebastian here tells me that Creed is not to be trusted. He'll back out of deals or find ways to renegotiate. I don't like men who don't keep their word."

"And you think you've got a chance with me keeping mine?"

"There's something I like about you, Smokey. You're not here to manipulate. You want what you want and we're all here to play your little puppets," Carlos said. "What I'm offering you is an alliance, of course. One that will benefit us both."

Smokey gritted his teeth. It was on the tip of his tongue to tell him to go get fucked. Instead, he waited. "I'm listening."

"It's simple. You will distribute our product. We will not sell guns to any rival MC. When you need help, our men will back you up if the occasion calls for it, and in return, we will offer you up some more land to help with your club's expansion."

Smokey nodded. "I'll think about it. Come on, boys, we're out of here."

"This is a time-sensitive offer, Smokey," Carlos

said. "I suggest you think quickly."

Smokey spun around and grabbed Carlos around the throat, pulling him across the table. "And I want you to understand while you're throwing your little pussy around, you didn't offer one more thing. I want Ryan, you piece of shit. If I don't get him, then the deal is off." Smokey glanced around the room. His men had pulled their weapons, and it hadn't taken long for the other men to draw theirs. It was a standoff, and he laughed. "I trust my men, Carlos. Can you say the same?"

"They will kill you."

"And you'll be dead right along with me. I'm willing to take the risk. The difference between you and me is I'm not afraid to die for my club. Are you willing to die for yours?" He let Carlos go. "I'll take all the time I need." He glared at Sebastian. "Next time, don't pull fucking tricks."

He turned his back on the mafia and walked out of the warehouse. His hands shook with his thirst for blood, but he shoved it down. Now wasn't the time to go after what he wanted.

He had to take his time. Ryan would be his, and once he was, he was going to find out every little detail that made the little shit turn.

No one stopped him as he climbed on his bike, fired it up, and took off, heading toward the club. Before he could go deal and be with his woman, he had to bring the offer to the brothers.

Getting in bed with the mafia wasn't a safe deal. He knew the risks. He'd dealt with them before and nearly gotten himself killed.

The journey was long, and by the time he landed in the clubhouse, he was so fucking tired, but the church was set up. He handed in his weapons and cell phone, making his way to the head of the table as all the men filed in.

Once they were there, he got Verge and Lewis on the phone. They were the closest chapters and had taken their back a few times.

He gripped the back of his chair as Hunter gave the full details of what they'd discussed.

"Are they going to give us Ryan?" Brick asked.

"That's the only part of the agreement I don't like," he said. "There's not going to be any deal where Ryan lives. Hanson, you're owed his life."

Hanson nodded.

"So we renegotiate," Lewis said.

"Either offer is going to have the cartel breathing down our necks at some point. You mess with the drugs and they're going to become a problem," Verge said.

"One problem at a time. We're going to take a vote. I want honesty. We're all going to be making these runs and doing this deal. I know how fucking messed up it was last time. Do you want to deal with Carlos Santigo with the negotiation we get Ryan?" he asked.

Lewis and Verge voted yea. One by one, his men all voted the same.

When it came to Ugly Beast, the man stayed silent.

"Are you against this?" Smokey asked.

"I don't like Carlos," Ugly Beast said.

"We don't have to like them to do business with them."

Ugly Beast nodded. "If we get Ryan. Otherwise, for me, it's a nay."

Smokey nodded and kept his gaze on Ugly. "Make the call to Sebastian. Without Ryan, no deal." He smacked the gavel on the table.

One by one, the men filed out, and he took off right behind them. He went to his bike, pushing a couple of women out of the way as they tried to get in his path. There was only one person he wanted to see right now.

Chapter Nine

Ava came to as someone kissed up her back. At first, she tensed up, gasped, and was about to pound whoever had broken into her house. Her arms were grabbed and she was pressed to the bed. Her face against the pillows.

"Shh, it's me," he said.

"Smokey?"

"You got plans for any other man to be sneaking in your room late at night?"

"When did you get back?" she asked.

"A couple of hours ago. I've been dealing with the brothers and club shit, but I didn't want to go another night without having your pussy." He pressed his lips against her neck, and she released a moan. With the way he touched her, she was so addicted to him.

Closing her eyes, she sighed as he touched her pussy. His hand slid beneath her shorts to touch her.

"Did you miss me?" he asked.

She chuckled. "You know I did. I always miss you."

He let go of her arm, and his mouth went from her neck and down her back. She pressed against the bed in an attempt to sit up, but he stopped her, keeping her in place.

"I'm not ready for you to move." His hands traced down her back, going to her bed shorts. "This ass should never be covered up." He pulled down her shorts and she stayed perfectly still.

He moved some pillows from the top of the bed and thrust them beneath her pelvis. "Perfect." He grabbed her ass cheeks and spread them open. "I can see your cunt and your asshole."

"Please," she said.

"You want my dick?"

"Yes."

"Then you hold this ass open while I play."

She whimpered as the tip of his cock toyed with her entrance. He held himself still and then slowly began to thrust inside her. "I think it's going to be quite easy for me to get used to seeing you take my cock. I've never seen a prettier sight."

Inch by inch, she took him, holding her ass open.

His hands went to her hips, and she didn't let him go as he grabbed her hips and began to pound inside her. His strokes were rough, hard, almost angry and desperate. She loved it, pushing back against him, wanting more of what he could give her.

Suddenly, he paused and lifted up. Then his fingers stroked across her anus. "This is the one hole I haven't taken, babe. The one hole I want to make mine."

She cried out as he leaned over her, driving his cock deep into her pussy as he reached for the drawer beside her bed.

"I've been keeping this safe in just the right event," he said.

Out of the corner of her eye, she saw the tube of lubricant. She tried to listen to what he was doing but he was so quiet.

He pulled out of her pussy and then something cool and slick teased across her anus. She bit her lip, waiting. The tip of his cock replaced his fingers.

"I'm not going to lie to you, babe, this is going to sting a little."

She tensed up as he started to work inside her ass. She really didn't think he was going to fit, but there was no defying Smokey. He held her hips steady in his grasp as he pushed inside her asshole.

Ava let out a cry and he stilled. One of his hands

circled her throat, pulling her head back and kissing her neck. "I'll go easy. I promise."

With his other hand, he cupped her pussy and stroked her clit. She moaned his name as he worked her body.

The pain of his penetration faded slightly as he worked her clit. She was at a fever pitch within seconds. He didn't allow her to come straight away. He took his time, making her wait as he filled her ass.

Inch by inch, his cock filled her ass until she could take no more. "You've got all of my dick now, Ava. I own every single part of your body. What do you have to say?"

"Please," she said. "Please let me come."

"Good girl."

He stroked her pussy until she came, screaming his name. She no longer cared that there was a big, fat cock in her ass. She wanted him, every single part, and there was no backing down.

Smokey let go of her pussy and started to ride her ass. His strokes started out slowly at first until she became accustomed to the sheer size of him. Then he took her harder until the sounds of their bodies smacking together echoed around the room. She didn't want him to stop, and she loved the slight pain as he took her.

When he came, he wrapped her hair around his fist and bit down on her neck.

The tight heat filled her body, and his cum pulsed in her ass.

The pleasure began to ebb away and all that remained was bliss. She was happy.

Smokey groaned. "Time for a bath."

Before she could stop him, he'd lifted her in his arms. "It's late."

"And as much as I'd love to see my cum dripping

from your ass you're going to be sore if I don't do something about it." He carried her through to her bathroom and placed her on her feet.

She watched, a little embarrassed as he filled the tub with water. "You don't have to do this."

He added some of her soothing salts and tested the water.

She hadn't realized he was still dressed. He wore his shirt and his pants were still around his waist. His cock, now flaccid, hung from the opening of his zipper.

He came toward her, stripping off her shirt. He held her hand as she climbed into the bath. Within seconds, he was naked and climbing in behind her.

She rested against his chest, closing her eyes, feeling the heat and warmth of him surround her. "This is nice," she said.

"It's been a long day."

"Do you want to talk about it?" she asked. He didn't share club stuff with her, but if he needed to talk, she was more than happy to listen.

"Can't, babe. It's club stuff. Did Ryan ever say anything to you?" he asked.

"Who's Ryan?"

"That guy's bar where you were drinking the first night I met you."

"Oh, no. I didn't know him. That night was the first time I'd been there."

"Right."

She frowned and tilted her head back. "I don't like you looking so troubled."

"It'll fade."

She sat up and turned so she could face him. "I know I'm not club, but you can trust me. Whatever we talk about, I won't say anything."

Smokey smiled. "You're so naïve. You don't

have the first clue what my club will do to you. What we can do."

"I'm not stupid. You think I don't see you guys carrying? The way you are? I'm not stupid, Smokey." She tried to stand up, but he caught her waist and settled her against him. "I can be trusted."

"Can you? Do you know I've killed people? That I love hurting people and I consider it a fine art to torture them?"

"I knew you weren't normal."

He snorted. "I'm not a lot of things. You should be running from me, Ava. I know everything there is to know about you, and yet, you're not running. Why is that?"

"I don't need to run. You don't scare me, Smokey. Neither does your club. I know life isn't always easy."

"You've only seen the good in life."

This made her tense up, and she turned toward him. "What makes you think that? My parents? Their wealth? Maybe it's because I got married? Just because I've known happiness doesn't mean I don't know how bad life can be. My parents … they ran several foundations. They didn't raise a daughter to live in the clouds. They raised a woman who was aware of the world around her."

"Then why aren't you running from me? Any sane woman would prefer a man with a nine-to-five job." He stroked her hair back.

She cupped his face. "I had that guy, remember? He hurt me more than anyone else I know. He took great pleasure in doing it." She licked her lips. "I don't want to be hurt ever again. I know that you don't promise me forever, but you don't lie to me, Smokey. I … I love you for that."

He tensed up and pressed a finger against her lips. "No. Don't fucking say shit like that. I can't give you love."

"I'm not asking for you to give me love, but I can't stop the way I feel for you, Smokey. I love you. I'm in love with you. I won't … I don't expect anything from you. I know you don't do love and this is only temporary, but I do love you." She pressed a kiss to his lips.

He gripped the back of her neck and pulled her in close. "You're too good for me." He took possession of her mouth, and she kissed him back, not holding anything in. Letting him know with her kiss and touch that she meant every single word she said.

Smokey moved her so she straddled his waist. Within a matter of seconds, his cock was rock-hard as he pressed against her pussy.

"Again?" she asked.

"You don't like it?"

"I have no complaints."

"Good."

He moved her over him and positioned his cock at her entrance. She cried out his name as he began to fill her.

Smokey wasn't completely erect, but with how he moved inside her, he was so close to it.

"I want you to look at me. No one else, only at me."

She stared into his eyes as he grabbed her hips, and together, they thrust against each other, working the other into a fever pitch of arousal and pleasure. Smokey got her to lean back so he could play with her tits. He stroked her clit, bringing her to another orgasm.

She loved the way he touched her. He had the power to give her pleasure or pain. Each touch and stroke set her on fire, making her desperate for more.

"Come for me, babe. Let me hear you come. I want it all."

She went over the peak. The orgasm was so incredible, she didn't want it to stop, and she rode the wave of pleasure until she had nothing more to give.

Smokey held on to her and thrust up within her, his own release only seconds away. His cock flooded her pussy with more of his cum.

Ava didn't know when he'd stopped pulling out. Did he even realize he wasn't protecting them both? She didn't want to ruin the moment and stayed silent. Nothing good would come of it.

He didn't say he loved her.

She knew he wouldn't.

No one ever did.

****

The deal was reached and an arrangement was agreed to with Ryan being handed over to him. The basement of the clubhouse was already set up to accept rats and traitors.

Smokey sat at his desk, going through paperwork when Hunter came to his office. The doors were shut, and Smokey looked up from the paperwork to wonder what the fuck his VP's problem was.

"These were waiting on your bike," Hunter said.

A brown envelope was placed on his desk.

"And?"

"It's addressed to the club. You need to see what is inside."

Smokey picked up the envelope and turned it over. The club's name was scrawled across the front. "What the fuck is this, Hunter?"

"Open it. Find out."

"You've seen it."

Hunter nodded.

Smokey threw down his pen and opened the envelope. Pictures slid out of it, landing on his desk. The first one made him freeze.

"What is this?" he asked.

"Ugly Beast called it. If you think about it. Ever since she arrived, shit has been going wrong. She was at the bar, and she's willingly available to you. Have you spoken to her about club business?" Hunter asked.

"No."

"Are you sure?"

"I said fucking no."

He had no explanation. Ava was accepting money from Creed, the fucking president of the Twisted Bastards MC.

Rage bubbled up inside him.

"Get the club set up for church," Smokey said.

Hunter nodded and walked right out.

Smokey stared down at the pictures. Women. He should have known he couldn't trust Ava. She said all the right things. Did everything right. She almost had him convinced she was different.

No wonder she kept on asking about the club and wanting him to trust her. He had to wonder what Creed was paying her.

Hunter returned twenty minutes later to tell him everyone was ready. He got to his feet and took the pictures.

Once inside church, he threw them down for all to see.

No one jumped to her defense.

"That fucking bitch," Raven said. "What's the plan?"

Smokey looked at the pictures. "It's simple. I want her here in the basement. We'll take care of that fucking slut, and then we'll deal with Ryan."

Raven smiled. "Let me handle this. I can't believe I was fooled by her."

"Well, we won't be fooled anymore."

Smokey was the first this time to leave church. The tension in the air was palpable. The club had been betrayed. They hadn't made it easy for Ava, but they'd certainly been willing to accept her. Her presence had started to become noticed.

Rather than let the men deal with Ava, he selected three more club women who'd been around the longest. He told them what had happened, and in return, they were going to make her pay.

While Raven and his men got Ava, he went to his office and stared out the window to watch. From his vantage point, he could see the moment Raven arrived.

"I love you. I'm in love with you."

All of it had been lies. He should have known.

Ava would pay dearly for what she did. He wondered if this was why the ex tried to get away as fast as possible.

Running a hand down his face, he tried to gain control of his rage, but it just wouldn't come.

Raven's truck arrived. Kinky and Brick had gone with her.

He watched as Ava, bound and gagged, was hauled out of the back of the truck. She fought against them.

Soon, the sounds of her screams filled the air of the clubhouse. No one stopped them.

Smokey took a couple of minutes.

"Do you want me to handle this?" Hunter asked.

"No. This is my problem."

He grabbed the pictures and placed them in his inner jacket.

After leaving the office, he made his way to the

basement where the women were already pushing Ava around. She was bleeding from above her eye and her nose.

He noticed her shirt was also torn.

When they pushed too hard, she fell in a heap on the floor.

"Why are you doing this? Where's Smokey? I want to see him," Ava said.

"I'm right here, you disgusting slut."

She scrambled to her feet. "I don't know what's going on. This isn't funny. I'm scared."

He laughed.

Raven pulled her hair, and Ava let out a cry. Another of the whores grabbed a chair and they tied her to it.

Tears fell down Ava's cheeks, but she'd stopped fighting.

"Did you think you could fool us for long?" he asked.

"I don't know what you're talking about."

Raven slapped her hard, and she whimpered. Her head flung to the side.

Smokey grabbed a chair, dragging it up toward his woman. Even covered in blood, she was beautiful and so striking. All that blonde hair.

"Cut it off," he said.

Raven smiled. "With pleasure."

Ava screamed as Raven none-too-gently grabbed her hair and began to hack the length off.

When it was done, her hair was thrown to the floor.

"I don't know what's going on," Ava said, sobbing. "Let me out of here."

"You think we're going to let you go so you can run back to Creed? The fucking prick?" Raven said.

Ava's sobs filled the air.

"I've had enough of this." Before Smokey could stop it, one of the club whores had grabbed a scalpel and sliced it through Ava's leg.

Her screams filled the air.

Kinky grabbed the whore and pulled her away.

The club felt Ava's betrayal.

"I don't know who Creed is," Ava said. "I've never even heard that name."

Smokey tutted. "You should know by now that nothing is ever sacred. There is no escape from what you've done." He reached into his jacket and pulled out the incriminating evidence. "Did you have a good laugh? Did you think you'd gotten me to fall in love with you?"

He wrapped his fingers around her neck, cutting off her oxygen. "You were only ever a decent fuck, and you weren't any good at that. You were easy, but I've had better." He let her go, and she gasped for breath.

"Please, stop this. You're making a mistake. I didn't do this. I don't know who that man is." She turned toward Raven. "It was the day I went to the bank. I tried to tell you I had a weird experience. Please."

"She's lying," Raven said. "She didn't tell me anything about the bank trip."

"You shouldn't have done Creed's dirty work, Ava. You're going to wish you never met me." He got to his feet. "Have your fun."

Smokey left the basement.

He didn't need to hurt Ava. His club would get her ready so he could make the final blow. Ava wasn't going come out of this alive.

With her death certificate filed, he needed to go and make some arrangements at her house.

Leaving the clubhouse, he rode his bike to her place. His key still in his jacket pocket, he stepped inside and was hit with the hardest sense of betrayal.

In the back of his mind, he heard her laughter. The sweet sounds she'd made.

The truth was, he'd had every intention of keeping her. She'd gotten under his skin, and he'd even been thinking of a future with her. He should have known better than to make a deal with a woman. They were fucking toxic. No one was different.

Fueling his anger, he made his way up to the bedroom and started to pack a bag. He'd make it look like she was away on a trip or some shit. They'd dispose of her body, and no one would ever find a trace of her or link her to the club.

He'd packed a bag and was heading out of the house when Ugly Beast called.

"What's up?" he asked.

"Where the fuck are you?"

"At Ava's house, why?" The boys had already gone and trashed her bakery. He hadn't given the order, but he didn't care.

She'd lied to their president and was working with their enemy. There was no way out of this.

"I need you back at the clubhouse now," Ugly Beast said, hanging up.

Shaking his head, Smokey closed the door, He strapped the bag of clothes to his bike and took one last look, allowing himself to feel the betrayal. The hope of a future dying inside as he looked at the house.

Creed was going to pay.

That fucker thought he won, but Smokey was going to show him. Maybe he'd take her apart piece by piece and mail it to him.

Arriving back at the clubhouse, Ugly Beast was waiting for him.

"Where are the pictures?" Ugly Beast asked.

"I don't have time for this."

"For fuck's sake. I'm trying to save your ass from making the biggest fucking mistake for your life. Where are they?"

"They're on the floor of the basement."

A feminine scream filled the air.

"Get Raven up here now. I'm in the church room."

"I'm not your fucking minion," Smokey said.

"And right now, you're not behaving like the boss." Ugly Beast shoved him. "Get the fuck in church. I'll get Raven myself."

Smokey was going to beat the living shit out of Ugly Beast. Maybe even leave him for dead.

He went and took his seat at the head of the table when Ugly Beast returned.

"What the fuck is this, Ugly? I've got shit to do," Raven said.

Smokey noticed her knuckles were red with blood.

He didn't care. Ava deserved it.

"Watch," Ugly Beast said.

He hadn't realized the TV had been brought into the room. Bored, Smokey watched, noticing Fort Clover's bank and Main Street coming into view. He frowned as the bank door opened and Ava stepped out. She wasn't watching where she was going, and Smokey tensed up even more when he caught sight of Creed. The fucker had been waiting for her and was dressed in a business suit.

Ugly Beast pressed the remote, and this was the camera inside the bank. It showed Ava waiting in line and then taking a brown envelope from the woman behind the desk.

"Ava's not Creed's accomplice," Ugly Beast. "I

don't know who took those pictures, but it wasn't her."

"You've got to be shitting me," Raven said. "We can see it."

"No!" Ugly Beast said. "Ava's not like that. My wife made me realize it, which is why I decided to go to the source. Ava's innocent, Smokey. She's not an accomplice. Creed's messing with your head, and looking at the way he worked her, he did this on purpose so you'd hurt her."

"Fuck, I left those bitches alone with her." Raven turned to leave, but Smokey was on his feet, charging out of the room and rushing toward the basement.

He was too late. The undeniable sound of bones breaking filled his ears.

He got to the basement. They'd pulled Ava from the chair. Two of the women held her down while the other brought the hammer down on her hand. Her hand was broken. The hammer was raised again.

"Stop!" His voice echoed around the room. The ramifications of what he'd done rushed through him.

"Get away from her," he said.

The moment they were away, Ava curled up into a ball.

Smokey knew the club was at his back. Running a hand down his face, he couldn't believe what he'd done. He went to her side, and as he tried to pull her into his arms, she screamed, trying to get away from him.

She was soaked with blood. "Don't you touch me."

"Ava, I'm so sorry."

"It's a trick. Leave me alone."

He had no idea what to say.

"I want to go home. I won't ever come near you again. I promise. I just want to go home. It's safe there."

His heart broke.

The woman with the sweet smile was gone. He'd broken the only good thing in his world.

Chapter Ten

Ava couldn't recall exactly how she got out of hell, only that she somehow did. She couldn't stop crying even as Hanson drove her to the hospital. He was the only one who hadn't been close to her.

She had asked for Abriana, but she was still taking driving lessons.

Hanson looked nervous, and she ignored it, preferring to stare out the window. He'd been with her when she'd walked into the emergency room reception. Doctors and nurses had tried to separate them to get her to talk. She lied, blatantly. Falling down the stairs, and a bowling ball had fallen on her hand.

"How are you?" Hanson asked.

She turned her head to look at him. One eye was completely swollen shut. She had a hand crushed, a couple of bruised lips, a split lip, along with a stab wound in her thigh. Not to mention several cuts to her arms and back. When Raven had left, the club whores had really gone to town on her.

Ava had a feeling Raven had been holding back, but the woman could punch.

"Stupid question."

"Just take me home."

"Smokey didn't mean it."

"Don't." The last thing she wanted to hear was his name right now. He hadn't lifted a single finger, but what he'd said had hurt in ways she didn't think was possible. She knew he was a monster. Had accepted him for it, but she didn't realize the level he'd go to. He hadn't once considered her innocence. All he'd seen was her guilt, but she hadn't had anything to do with any Creed.

"I know you're hurting right now."

"Hanson," she said, pressing her lips together to try to contain her sobs. "We don't know each other that well, but I'd really appreciate it if you were quiet. I was dragged from my bakery, hit, beaten, tied up, stabbed, and I just ... no. Okay? Just no."

Tears leaked down her face, and she swiped at her cheek. The one that was still good. The other had a giant bandage over it to help heal her other eye.

She took a deep breath, counting in her head. She wouldn't break. Not in front of him.

It felt like a lifetime before he pulled up outside of her house, but not a whole lot of time had passed. It was dark now. Raven, Kinky, and Brick had gotten her during a lull. The moment Hanson parked, she climbed out of his car. She heard him park and leave the vehicle.

"You don't have to do anything more," she said. "I'm perfectly fine. Thank you."

"Please, Smokey asked me to take care of you."

"I don't want you to take care of me. I don't want any of you or your club near me again. Get out, or I will call the police."

She reached into her jeans pocket and retrieved her key. Sliding it into the lock, she closed the door with a slam and flicked the lock right back into place.

Spinning around, she collapsed in a heap and allowed the tears to fall.

All it had taken was a single day. Not even that long. She'd woken up that morning so happy with the world and with her life. After ten years of misery, she'd found happiness. Now it had been stripped away.

She didn't know what was worse, finding Derek cheating, or this.

Ava rubbed at her chest. No, this had to be the worst. She'd never felt so empty, so lost, so alone.

For the first time since her parents died, she

wished they were here. She didn't know what to do.

The life she thought she'd been building had been swept out from beneath her.

"Ava," Smokey said.

She jerked up. "What are you doing here?"

"I have a key."

"Leave the key and get out." Her hand shook as she tried to open the door to make him leave.

He pressed his body against her back, and she screamed, throwing herself away from him.

She saw the pain in his eyes but didn't care. "Get out."

"We need to talk."

"No. We're done talking. I've got nothing to say to you."

Smokey kept on staring at her. She couldn't handle it, so she looked at the floor. At anything but him.

He was a monster. He'd destroyed her.

"Get out." She repeated it so he'd listen to her. This wasn't a joke to her, or a game. He'd hurt her in the worst possible way.

"I brought your clothes back."

She frowned. "My clothes?"

"I packed up some of your stuff."

Her heart broke. "You were going to kill me."

Smokey's jaw clenched.

"I'm sorry to have disappointed you that you can't get rid of me that easily."

"It wasn't an easy choice."

"Sure it was." She clicked her fingers. "One fire of a bullet. You could have stabbed me. There are any number of things you could have done to me." She pressed her lips together even as more tears flooded her eyes. "Leave."

"I thought—"

"I know what you thought. What you and your whole club thought. There's no way you could have ever imagined a woman, someone like me, showing you loyalty." She closed her eyes. "I can't do this now. I don't want to. You've got to leave."

"Not until I know you're okay."

Ava started to laugh. "Okay? You want to know if I'm okay?" She bent over as if it was the most hysterical thing she'd ever heard. "Look at me, Smokey. I'm not okay. Nothing about this is okay." She kept on repeating the same word. She took a deep breath. "We're done. We're through."

"Ava?"

He went to touch her, and she backed away. "Don't you dare touch me. After what you did and said, you have no right."

Smokey stopped, hand clenched into a fist.

She stared at him, not sure what exactly he wanted.

"How are you?"

Ava shook her head. "Please, just leave."

"I need to know that you're all right."

She opened her mouth, closed it, and then snorted. "I can't do this with you. I don't want to do this with you. Please, I need you to leave."

"Ava."

"Get the fuck out!" She screamed at him. Why wasn't he listening to her? After everything he'd done, she wanted him gone as far away from her as humanly possible. The clubhouse even seemed too close.

Her heart was broken.

"I know you love me," he said.

"Yeah, and the story of my life is that you will never love me. Club comes first. Even when an innocent woman is begging for you to stop." She pressed her lips together and shook her head. "Get out." She was growing tired of repeating herself around him.

He stayed perfectly still. She couldn't even see out of one eye. Her hand hurt and the doctor had given her some pain medication to help her sleep. She'd been advised to take it easy and to rest.

All she wanted to do was make herself a hot cup of chocolate and go curl up beneath a warm blanket. Anything beat being near him.

"Ava, please."

"You're not even going to apologize to me. No *I'm sorry*."

"I did say I was sorry."

"It's not good enough. If you really regret what happened, then leave. I don't want to see you or any member of your club again. I'm begging you to go."

He still didn't move as it looked like he wanted to say something, and Ava hated herself as she collapsed to her knees. "Is this what it's going to take? My body is broken. I told you that you could trust me, and still, you didn't believe me. I've never done anything to warrant your treatment, Smokey. Now, get out. I don't want you near me. I don't want to even talk to you. Do me this respect and get the fuck out." She pressed her hands together, almost begging him, and she saw his teeth were gritted.

She didn't care.

He had to leave. There was no way she wanted him near her.

He stepped toward the door.

"Leave the key behind you."

She'd loved it when he'd snuck into her house. The way he'd taken her, made love to her. It was all a lie. A stupid fucking lie.

"No."

"Fine. Take it." She'd have the locks changed tomorrow. She was done arguing with him.

"I'm going to leave Hanson outside your house. He'll keep watch."

"Scared I'll run to the cops?" She refused to look at him.

"It's for your own safety. In case Creed decides to do something else when he sees he hasn't succeeded."

She snorted. "He did, Smokey." She turned toward him. "He completely tore apart what I love. It's one thing to know of what you do. It's quite another to be the victim of it, especially when I didn't do anything wrong." With her good hand, she rubbed at her temple.

Smokey looked like he wanted to say more.

She waited, not really sure what to expect.

He was a man who'd certainly surprised her. He'd broken her heart. Her relationship with Derek had never come close to the kind of passion and feeling Smokey evoked.

It was all gone.

After several minutes passed, Smokey finally let himself out of the door. She rushed toward it to lock it, and then with as much grace as she could muster, she made her way into the kitchen.

With one good hand, it took a lot more work, but she made herself a nice mug of hot chocolate and then proceeded upstairs where she took a short bath.

Even the bathroom held so many memories, and the tub itself. She could see herself laughing with Smokey, moaning as he touched her in the most intimate of ways.

"It's over, Ava. You're not going to allow him to get away with this. You've always been open with him. This time, you're done. You're not going to be a doormat."

She sipped at her hot chocolate as her heart continued to break over what might have been.

Life wasn't fair.

The moment Raven had entered her shop, she'd been happy, figuring the woman had wanted a girl's chat. Instead, she got a punch to the face and then was tied up and dragged out the back toward a waiting truck.

Never had she been so terrified. Not even when Derek had lost his temper with her.

The club whores had been joyous in hurting her. The pleasure they took was almost scary.

"Don't think about it." She put her hot chocolate down, and without wetting the cast, she washed her body.

She tried to wash part of her face, but that was useless.

When the hammer had been brought down on her hand, she thought they'd smashed all the bones, but it was only a small break. One that would be fixed with some rest.

The doctor had constantly been looking at Hanson as if he was the culprit.

All her injuries had been caused by women. Strong women.

Climbing out of the tub, she let the water run away, ignoring the fact it was tinged red from the dried blood on parts of her body.

She wrapped herself in a towel and moved toward the bed. Lying her head down, she pulled the blanket over her. All she wanted to do was block out the world and pretend no one existed.

The truth was, a part of her still wanted Smokey to come and wrap his arms around her, to make her feel safe. It was never going to happen. She'd never allow herself to succumb to him again.

Even though it broke her heart, she and Smokey were well and truly over.

****

The following day, Smokey stood in the church room. The club brothers and Raven were all present. No one had spoken since Hanson had hung up. There was no sign of Ava leaving her house.

He ran a hand down his face, wanting to hurt someone. More importantly, Creed.

"Tomorrow, we collect Ryan," he said.

Dwelling on what he'd done wasn't the answer. Not with the club. He had to stay in perfect control.

"We don't go alone," Hunter said. "I don't trust this Carlos at all. It's a trap."

"I don't think it is," Ugly Beast said. "Sebastian came to us."

"He's not the one in control of the entire outfit. Carlos is," Smokey said.

"Are you guys fucking kidding me right now. That's it?" Raven asked.

Smokey turned toward Raven. He didn't dare look at her knuckles. He'd caught sight of them last night when she'd placed a pack of frozen peas across them. Neither of them had spoken any words, but the guilt was so easy to read.

"There is nothing to discuss."

"There's not? Are you ... fucking wow. We need to go after Creed," Raven said. "Look what he did."

Smokey shook his head. "Our time with Creed will come, but not today." He turned toward Hunter. "I suggest we pack hard. I don't want to be caught off guard. Ryan's coming home, and he can be Hanson's birthday present."

"No!" Raven slammed her hand down on the table, drawing everyone's attention. She often sat in the back and only contributed when she really needed to.

"You can leave."

Raven held her hands up. "This is what Creed did. You think I don't feel the guilt over what I've done?"

Smokey's hands clenched into fists as Raven continued.

"We've got to hit back and hit hard. First, he went after territory, now he's done this with Ava."

"What did he do?" Smokey asked. "Fuck all. That's what he did." He answered her before she even had a chance to. "Creed didn't do this. He set the fuel, but we're the ones who stoked the fire. We're the ones who took an innocent woman."

He stopped and pressed his lips together. The way Ava cowered away from him last night would be forever embedded in his mind. "I did that yesterday. Not Creed. I should have looked at those pictures, tore them up, and burned them. He won. I didn't." His own insecurities about women had stopped him from doing it.

He'd believed the worst of a woman who'd only shown him to trust her. To love her even.

In one simple action, he'd lost a great deal. Ava was ... precious. She would never have betrayed him. He'd waited all night for the police to come knocking at his door. Instead, he was left alone.

Ava hadn't even called the police. Hanson had told him that she'd been questioned at the hospital repeatedly, looking at him as if he was the one to hurt her.

"We've got to do something," Raven said.

"We do. We ... we make sure that Ava is well taken care of. For the foreseeable future, I advise that you keep your distance. I tried to see her last night." The memory of her flinching away from his touch was right there in his mind. Mocking him. He fucking hated it.

She didn't deserve any pain he'd caused her.

"Are you okay?" Raven asked.

Smokey pulled out of his thoughts and looked around him. He quickly got back to the arrangement on Ryan. The pickup should be easy so long as there were no tricks. He didn't anticipate any.

When no one offered up any questions or conclusions, he smacked the gavel down, drawing the meeting to an end. He leaned back and rubbed at his head.

Raven cleared her throat, and he sat up, surprised to see both her and Ugly Beast still in the church. He wasn't in a rush to leave the room. He needed the peace and quiet. Last night, he hadn't slept once.

In a few hours, he intended to take over from Hanson.

"This isn't your fault," Raven said. "This my fault."

He sighed. "Raven, go away."

"I know you're angry."

"Then why are you still here? You're a club brother as far as I'm concerned, and that means I can beat the shit out of your ass." He stood up and the chair flung across the room with the speed at which he moved.

"I'm sorry," she said.

"I don't need your apologies. Go and do whatever job you need to fucking do. I'm done listening to your shit."

He was through with her. The last thing he wanted was to listen to more excuses.

Raven's hands tightened into fists.

"Do you want to throw down?" Smokey asked.

When Raven had been initiated, she'd taken on five of the club brothers, showing she could have their backs just as much as they could have hers. He'd also made her lift one of the brothers and carry him across the parking lot.

She'd done it all. She was a strong woman, but he knew deep down inside, she was vulnerable. The world hadn't wanted her. They were the only family she had. She needed this club. Abriana was the closest person Raven had as a friend. That had increased to two with Ava.

He'd fucked it up.

"I hope you can make things work with her," Raven said. She turned on her heel and left.

All that left was Ugly Beast.

"What?"

"I wanted to make sure you're all right."

"I don't need any hand-holding. I'm not a fucking pussy." He was done being treated with kid gloves. What was done was done. Nothing he could do to change that.

"How did you know again?" Smokey asked. "When you saw the pictures, you were looking for blood. You went home to your wife."

I ... I asked her what she thought of Ava. I looked at the pictures, and it seemed too perfect. I also can't deny that Ava's won me over in the past few weeks. Her cooking is the best and even though Abriana's improving, she's never going to be able to cook well." Ugly Beast shrugged. "Apart from you, Raven and Abriana are the only two people she's been around and well, I trust my wife's judgment."

"I made a rash decision."

"You thought Ava was like every other woman. I hurt Abriana before I admitted I was in love with her and I couldn't live without her."

Smokey chuckled. "You think I'm in love with Ava."

"It shouldn't hurt."

"What?"

"If you don't have any feelings for Ava whatsoever, none of this should hurt. You shouldn't feel a damn thing. My question to you, Smokey, is do you?"

He stared at Ugly Beast.

Even though they'd had their differences, he still considered him a friend, even outside of the club.

"You can't even admit your feelings to me."

"I don't know what I feel for Ava right now."

"She's innocent. Your decision, your lack of trust did this. How does that make you feel?"

"Like I want to hit something and to keep on hitting it until there's nothing left. I want to destroy Creed."

"And you don't think that comes from some feeling for her?" Ugly Beast asked.

"When did you become some kind of expert?"

"Since I fell in love with my wife and have the most perfect daughter in the world. I don't know why you picked me to marry Abriana. You've got your reasonings, and now, it doesn't matter to me. She's the love of my life. You gave that to me. One day, I hope you're able to feel something for a woman besides anger."

Ugly Beast made his way outside of the room, leaving him alone with his thoughts.

What did he feel for Ava?

Guilt. That was a big one.

Loss. He'd fucked up.

Love. He stopped.

She'd told him she loved him. She hadn't expected anything from him. No reciprocation of that love. She'd just told him how she felt.

That love had come out of nowhere.

You love her.

Smokey refused to listen.

Ava's smiling face invaded his mind. The way she moaned. His name falling from her lips. Her touch.

All of it ran through his mind, threatening to consume him. He ached for her.

Then he thought of the way she'd scurried away from him. The pain in her eyes.

Last night, before he'd made his presence known, he'd heard her sob.

He'd done that. No one else. He was responsible for hurting her, and it killed him.

He wanted to protect her. To show her that she could trust him.

Instead, there was nothing he could do. When she'd needed him most, he'd trusted the lies of the camera. Creed had done this on purpose, and rather than trust her, he'd figured she was lying to him.

He was the monster in her world, no one else.

After picking up the gavel, he launched it across the room. One by one, he threw the chairs out of his way. One of them crashed into the window, smashing it.

He didn't care. Rage coursed through him. He was used to the feeling, but not this strong. This was something more. It didn't scare him.

Feeding that anger, he trashed the room, taking anything down that stood in his way. He completely tore it apart, not caring what survived or not.

No one came to stop him. They left him alone as he tossed the table into the air. When there was nothing left, he stood, staring around at the mess he'd created.

Books were thrown everywhere. Chairs were broken. The table was as well.

Again, he didn't care. No matter what he did, or how he destroyed something, he was not going to get back his woman. She was lost to him forever.

Collapsing to the ground, he pressed his face against the palms of his hands. Fear and sadness worked together in his hands. He'd lost the one good thing in his life.

Ava. The only woman he'd ever loved.

He fucking loved her and now it was too late to tell her how much. He'd destroyed her. There was no coming back from that. It didn't matter how many rooms he trashed. Ava was lost to him.

His cell phone rang. He pulled it out of his pocket and saw it was Hanson.

Smokey didn't even realize he'd been crying until a single teardrop landed on his cell phone.

He wiped at his eyes and took the call. "What?" he asked.

"She called a cab and I followed her."

"Where is she?"

His heart raced at the thought of her leaving town.

"She's in the bakery and … they didn't leave anything alone, Smokey. The place is torn up. The windows smashed in. All of it is destroyed. What do you want me to do?" Hanson asked.

"I'll be there in a minute." He hung up.

The bakery. He'd forgotten about that. Kinky and Brick had gone back to take care of it.

The town would know she was on the club's shit list. When he didn't think it could get any worse, it did.

Ava didn't deserve this. She never did.

Feeling like a fucking monster, he left the church and ignored the people who watched him leave.

He had to get to Ava's. She was going to be so upset. All her life, she'd wanted to own that bakery. She had told him all about that dream. Derek had stopped her from seeing it, and now he'd stopped her from even being able to live it.

He was a fucking monster. He hated himself.

Climbing on his bike, he took off into town.

How the fuck was he going to fix this?

Chapter Eleven

Gone.

All of it was gone.

The windows were smashed.

The door hung off the hinges. The counter where she stored her baked goods. It was all well and truly gone.

She took a deep breath, trying not to feel anything as she looked around at the mess.

The food was also on the floor. She'd been midway through her shift when they'd taken her.

Biting her lip, she didn't know where to start. This was her dream, and look at it now.

Anyone who walked on by, and there were a lot of people, would know. She was out of favor with the Hell's Bastards MC.

No one would come here. No one would care.

She closed her eyes and took a deep breath.

"Honey, you will realize in life, that you can do anything. You're an amazing person. Strong. Nothing will ever break you."

Her mother's words whispered in her mind as if she stood right next to her. She put her hand on her hip and stared around her.

It was easy to do. She pulled out her cell phone and started to call for cleaners to help clean the mess up and builders to take care of the windows and doors.

No one.

Each cleaning service was currently fully booked, and no builder would come to her shop. They were happy to help until she said her shop name.

Blacklisted.

Had Smokey done this? Was it the state of the shop?

The gossip mill had run all kinds of rumors. No one would touch her shop.

Tears filled her eyes, but she refused to be broken. There was always something to be done. She walked into the back and picked up a sweeping brush.

Ava started in the back, ignoring the pain in her hand. When it got to be a little too much, she'd attempt to use it one-handed.

"We're closed," she said, calling out when she heard the sound of footsteps walking on broken glass.

Smokey rounded the corner, and she held the brush in her hand even tighter, not wanting to let it go.

"Why are you sweeping the floors?" he asked.

"I've got to clean this mess."

"Phone someone."

"Smokey, this is none of your business. I don't want you here. At all. Please, leave."

"Don't be stubborn."

"Get out." She didn't want to see him. It hurt too much. In the past few hours when it came to her encounters with Smokey, she'd started to feel like a broken record. Still, he wasn't budging.

"I'll leave if you tell me why you haven't gotten cleaners and builders in."

Ava glared at him. "Why do you even care? The message is loud and clear for everyone to get, Smokey. Ava's is a bad place. She's not on speaking terms with the Hell's Bastards MC." She pointed around the back room. "What did you think was going to happen, trashing my place?"

He opened his mouth, but she didn't want to hear whatever the hell he was going to say.

"But that's fine. You didn't think of what this would mean because you had no intention of letting me live. How thoughtful of you." She rolled her eyes and started to sweep. She held the brush in the wrong way, and pain radiated up her hand and into her arm, making her cry out.

Smokey went to take a step toward her, and she backed away.

"You're hurt."

"I'm fine." She wasn't going to ask for help from the man who'd ensured her life would be a living hell.

Silence fell between them.

Still, Smokey didn't leave.

She took several deep breaths until she no longer felt sick. The pain was hard to work with. At least she had some time to heal her hand before she opened up the shop again. If no one would even come and work for her, and she was willing to pay them well for it, she doubted her shop would last. No one would come for baked goods. Not anymore.

Her life was over.

"No one will come and work for you?" he asked.

She smiled. "Nope. They're suddenly busy. Well, they're not busy. Not until I give them the location, and all of a sudden, their calendar is full. They don't want to double-book. So, there you go, Smokey. I got my ass beat and my business is pretty much in the toilet. No one will touch me."

She would have clapped her hands, but that would only cause her more pain.

Right now, she wanted to sob.

How she was keeping it together, she didn't know. Or she was just holding on by a thread. She wasn't sure which.

"I'm sorry."

"I don't accept it," Ava said. She took a deep breath. "This is hard for me right now. I don't want to do this with you. My life is in the toilet. Please, just leave me alone. Let me drown in my misery alone."

"You don't have to be alone."

"I'm not going to be with you, Smokey. Never. I mean what I said. It's over between us, and there's no way to fix it."

"I don't believe that."

She shrugged. "Believe what you want. I'm done. We're done. I'm glad it happened now instead of a few years down the line. I've already wasted ten years of my life with a man who never loved me."

"Ava…"

"Hey, don't sweat it, Smokey. Your breakup was certainly one I won't forget. I'm getting used to it. Believe me. I need some air." She turned on her heel and walked out the back to where she normally took deliveries. The other shops were enjoying the fully functioning workloads with all their employees while she leaned against the wall, taking deep breaths.

The bakery wasn't going to make any money. She'd lost it. She knew that now. She'd have to sell the place and would probably lose any kind of profit there as well. The only way to get her shop fixed would be to call through to the city. Pay for someone to travel to her place and to get the job done. It was going to be a headache, but something had to happen.

The shop couldn't stay that way for long.

She stayed outside long enough, hoping Smokey got the message. That he had to leave.

After opening the door, she came to a stop in the stockroom. Brick was there, picking up the flour that had been tossed across the side. One of the club whores who'd taken pleasure in holding her down was there, holding a trash bin.

Ava tensed up. "What the hell are you doing?" she asked.

Brick stood. He held a pack of chocolate chips this time. All of this was useless. She couldn't use any of it to bake with and to sell it to the public.

More noise greeted her.

She wanted to go and see what was going on, but the thought of passing Brick and the other woman filled her with fear.

No one moved.

Brick cleared his throat and stepped out, grabbing the woman's hand as he did.

She stayed perfectly still, and Brick took another step back, keeping his distance.

Her heart raced as she took a step forward, then another, until she was out of the kitchen, but that didn't make her feel safe.

More of the Hell's Bastards MC were in her small shop, cleaning. Their leather cuts holding their emblem clear for anyone to see, and it filled her with fear as they all worked.

They were too close.

"Smokey!" Brick yelled for their president.

She put a hand to her chest in an attempt to calm herself.

It didn't help.

Nothing seemed to be helping. They were in her shop, and when she caught sight of Raven, she covered her ears, bowing her head.

It's going to be okay.

It's fine.

She counted to ten again. The first ten numbers were starting to piss her off.

When hands touched her shoulder, she screamed and pulled away. Smokey had tried to touch her.

She'd tried not to cry, but tears were already falling down her cheeks. "Get out," she said.

"We're here to help."

"I don't want your help. Get out. Please." She started to pant.

"This isn't good for you."

Even as she struggled to breathe, she stared at him. "And neither are you. So get the fuck out before I call the cops."

"We're trying to help," Raven said.

The panic rose, her chest rising and falling with each quickly indrawn breath. This wasn't good.

In and out.

She watched him.

Waiting. Desperate.

Smokey clicked his fingers and one by one, the club left the bakery.

"Ava, I'm so—"

Smokey snapped his fingers again, and Raven shut up, and much to her surprise, left.

"We will pay for any damages," Smokey said.

"I don't want your money."

"Damn it, Ava, let me do something."

She looked at him. "You want to do something?"

"Yes."

"Then respect my wish for you to leave me alone. All of you. I don't want you or your club anywhere near me. Tell Hanson to stop following me. Please, just leave me alone. Give me that."

Smokey stared off to the side. "Anything but that."

"This isn't going to work. You and I, it's done. It's finished."

"No."

"Smokey, I don't want to be with a man who would rather trust the lies of a picture than me. This isn't going to work. I don't want to be with you anymore."

He closed the distance and cupped her face.

The tears fell thick and fast. She tensed up and he growled. "I'm going to find a way to make this right, Ava. I'm not going to lose you. I fucked up. I know this. I know you can't just stop loving me because you say so."

She shook from his touch.

Smokey pressed a kiss to her head and then he pulled away.

She watched him leave, thankful that he did.

Collapsing to the floor, she curled her legs close to herself. Everything was hopeless. All of it.

This was her dream, and it was gone as quickly as she thought it could be possible. She was the biggest fool.

Resting her forehead against her knee, she didn't know how much time had passed. The energy to get up and clean was gone. All she wanted to do was go curl up and forget this had ever happened. This was the nightmare she didn't want to come back to.

She stared across the floor at all the mess. Tomorrow, she'd clean it up. As she began to work out a plan, her cell phone rang.

Pulling it out of her pocket, she recognized the cleaning services number.

She frowned and clicked *accept*.

"Hello," she said.

"Is this Ms. Ava Sinclaire?"

"Yes."

"I'm so sorry about my misinformation. We have plenty of openings. We have a cleaning crew on their way to your shop right now."

"Wait, what?"

"And please, don't worry about the bill. It has been settled, and my sincerest apologies."

The line hung up before Ava could ask for more details.

Just as she was about to call them back, her cell phone rang. This time, from one of the builders.

She took the call, and the same thing happened. They were on their way to get measurements for new windows and to board them up until they were able to fix them. Again, the bill had been taken care of.

As she stared at her cell phone, she knew it didn't take a genius to work out what had happened.

Smokey had taken care of it.

She didn't move.

When the cleaning crew arrived, no one approached her. No words were spoken. They just got to work as if it was an everyday occurrence to see a trashed shop and the owner sitting in the corner.

People worked around her as if she wasn't there. She watched them work.

The pain in her body was the only indication she was alive because every other part of her felt so numb.

****

Three days later

Smokey stared down at the check written to him.

It was in Ava's writing.

The money was the exact amount for the cleaning crew and the builders.

He'd ridden past the shop earlier to find it had been perfectly cleaned and the windows were back in place. The shop looked brand-new. Only, it was closed.

There was no sign of Ava either.

Several of the brothers had gone past on each day to see. The windows had been fixed within twenty-four hours as he'd paid the extra to have the process speeded up.

"Are you okay?" Hunter asked, coming to stand

beside him.

He didn't hide the check.

The club felt Ava's loss. They all did. No one had any idea of how to make it up to her.

"She wouldn't even let you pay for the damage."

"I don't blame her," Smokey said.

"What are you going to do?" Hunter asked.

Smokey stared down at the rectangular piece of paper. He'd never been hurt by something so trivial. He had a lot of money and was aware Ava wasn't hurting for money either. Her parents had been sure to take care of her.

Tearing up the check, he refused to take her money. She was going to realize there was no running away from him.

"Has Hanson finished with Ryan yet?"

Collecting Ryan from Carlos had gone without a hitch. He was starting to believe the man was true to his word.

People were surprising him left and right.

"Smokey?"

"Well?"

"He's still enjoying torturing him."

"I don't want him to make the final blow until after I've spoken to him." Smokey tossed the torn check into the trash bin.

"What do you want to do about her?" Hunter asked.

"Nothing yet. She's hurting. I'll take care of the bills when they arrive. I want a set of eyes on her at all times. Creed will be watching for the fallout unless he's already aware of it."

"You want me to set up a meeting with him?"

"No. I'm not interested in talking with that asshole. The only thing I want to do is kill him." He thirsted for Creed's blood and wanted to hear the son of a bitch's screams. All in good time.

He and Creed had been able to exist so long as they stayed out of each other's business. Now that Creed had invaded that, all bets were off.

"I want to call in every single favor we have. By the end of this week, I want to know everything the Twisted Bastards are into. Got it?"

"Got it. The boys will love going to war with them."

Smokey turned on his heel and made his way into the clubhouse. Ignoring the bar, even though he really wanted a drink, he went straight to his office. Sitting down in his chair, he stared up at the ceiling.

Anger pulsed through every single fiber of his being. The need to kill rushed through him. Acting out now would only cause more problems, and he'd fucked up enough for one day.

There was a knock at the door, and he called out for whomever it was to come on in.

"Smokey."

The husky feminine voice made him open his eyes to see the blonde who'd brought the hammer to Ava's hand. Darla, he believed her name was.

He'd wanted to kill the three women who'd hurt Ava, but it was wrong of him to even want to do that. They had been acting on his instruction. His and Raven's. They shouldn't have left them alone.

This was his mistake. The biggest fucking mistake he'd ever made.

"I want to come in and apologize."

"You should be going and servicing one of the men. I don't want you in my office."

"I did what I thought you'd want. She's a rat. A traitor."

"No, she wasn't."

Darla shook. Her clothes barely covered her body. The sight alone sickened him. Before he'd met Ava, he'd fucked this woman a few times. She'd never been a favorite. It was what a lot of club pussy hoped to be, a favorite.

"You need to get the fuck out before I throw you out of the club for good." He was tempted to do that already. Raven had already approached him and offered up her patch. Her guilt equaled his.

"I … let me make this good for you. You'll forget about her before long, and I know I can make you love this."

Smokey started to laugh. The idea of ever being fine with anything again fucking sickened him. "Fine. You think I'm fine with the fact the woman I love can't stand to have me touch her?"

He got up and rounded the table. Darla didn't move, so he made sure she moved. He grasped her neck and started to march her outside of his office, speaking as he did. "Let's get one thing clear, the only reason you're still around is because you were acting on orders. If I could, I would have you buried six feet under, alive. I'd make sure you knew pain long before I granted you an easy death. You want to stay alive, I suggest you stay as far away from me as possible, because I will end you. I've killed bitches before, and I've got no problem hurting you."

And yet you didn't raise a hand to Ava. You let others do your dirty work. Why was that?

He slapped his head, trying to shut off the voice taunting him. He knew the reason why. There was no silencing the truth. He'd been able to hurt Ava with words, but that was all it was, words. None of it had any meaning. Physically hurting her was a whole other thing entirely.

After entering his office, he slammed the door closed and hoped no one else interrupted his thoughts.

Carlos Santigo had already gotten in touch about a bunch of product landing at one of the ports. They wanted them to be there for when the transition went through. Their men would be present to do the hand-off, but they would be doing the drop-off.

Right now, Smokey wasn't interested in leaving town or being far away from Ava. Not with him waiting for Creed to make the next move. He didn't like being kept out of the loop. With his men ready to kill, he wanted to be prepared.

Creed would make his move, and when he did, he'd be ready for him.

Hunter arrived minutes later. "Hanson said he's all yours."

Getting to his feet, he made his way straight to the basement. Once again, the brothers gave him a wide berth, not wanting to get under his feet.

As he advanced on the man tied to a chair, Ryan groaned then laughed. One of his eyes was swollen shut. Knives were protruding from his legs and hands. Hanson had really gone to town.

"You look like shit." He grabbed a chair and dragged it across the basement floor.

"I'm still prettier than you."

Smokey laughed. "Yeah, well, the chicks will still be hanging off my dick. So, tell me, Ryan, why did you do it?"

Ryan groaned. "I don't have to tell you shit."

Smokey reached out, taking the handle of one of the knives and twisting it.

Screams filled the air.

"You don't have to tell me shit, but you see, I'm

better at this than Hanson. First of all, you didn't get me stabbed and landed in the hospital, and well, I got a better deal out of it. I'm fine."

"What about that chick you're banging?" Ryan asked. "How's she handling it?"

Smokey froze. "What the fuck?" he asked.

"I was there when Creed made the decision to go after your woman." Ryan laughed. "I didn't know shit was going to go down like that when I made my deal. I didn't want to betray you, Smokey. I needed the money."

"I pay you well."

"Not enough. The bar doesn't make enough, and I like shit." Ryan started to sob. "Creed said he'd protect me, but the moment he made the decision to go after that fat fucking slut, he cut me loose. Then Santigo picked me up, and the rest is history." Ryan let out a cough.

Smokey stared at him, sickened. "All of this is about money?"

"Money is everything."

"Money's not everything."

"Says the man who has it all. Live in my shoes for a couple of hours, and you'd see why." Ryan shrugged. "You didn't pay me enough."

"The bar is mine now. We'll see how much we can get that bar to make."

"You're going to kill me, aren't you?" Ryan asked, already pissing himself as he said it.

Smokey stood up. He pulled the blade from Ryan's thigh and without warning, stuck it in the man's neck.

He watched as the last rays of life left Ryan's eyes. The man's head slumped forward.

Hunter was on the stairs.

"Clean this shit up."

He went out of the clubhouse and toward his

bike. Straddling the bike, he turned over his ignition and then gunned out of the main grounds, taking to the open road. Killing Ryan didn't fill him with regret. It didn't do anything for him. There was no victory here. He felt nothing.

Money.

Greed.

It was all the same kind of shit.

He was done with people.

Ava. He wanted his woman. He'd failed her.

There had to be a way of getting her back. He didn't know what he could do. There was no fucking hope right now. She wouldn't accept money from him, nor his help, or his time. He was failing at everything.

Smokey didn't know where he was going until he saw the sign confirming he was in Creek Springs. Twisted Bastards territory.

He didn't give a fuck about the danger surrounding him. Driving straight to the main bar, titled *No Name Bar*. Original. He parked up his bike.

Without a glance at anyone, he walked directly to the main bar and slammed his hand down on the counter. A blonde with a huge pair of fake tits walked toward him.

"What can I get you, baby?" she asked.

"A whiskey. Make it the good stuff."

Whispers followed his entrance.

Within seconds, Creed would be well aware of who entered his territory, and that was exactly what he was hoping for.

The blonde put the drink down. "I haven't seen you around before."

Smokey noted the ink around her wrist marking her as one of the Twisted Bastards MC sluts. He knew how the club marked their women. All of them had to have a mark. One around the wrist claimed them as club property. The women had to have something across their back, or somewhere more personal. The sluts had barbed wire around their wrists, while the owned women had intricate roses mixed with thorns. This woman had the barbed wire. Any Twisted Bastard could fuck with her.

"You know I'm not from around here, darling."

"I know who you are, and you're not welcome here." The blonde wrapped her fingers around her wrist.

"I wonder if he would come running if I put a bullet in your face." He pulled out his gun and saw the flash of fear in her eyes.

"I've done nothing wrong."

"Everyone has done something, babe. There's no question about it. You're not an innocent. Now tell me where your owner is," Smokey said.

She licked her lips and shook her head. "I'm going to have to ask you to leave."

Smokey tilted his head. "Does he fuck you? Are you his little bitch?" He thought about Ava, and when the woman started to walk away, he grabbed her arm, pulled her across the counter, and held her neck tight. The woman screamed.

"Tell me."

"I'm right here, Smokey. I suggest you let the woman go."

He smiled and turned to face Creed. "Long time no see, asshole."

Chapter Twelve

Ava took another spoonful of intense chocolate ice cream. The flavor exploded on her already cold tongue, but it didn't do anything to appease the hunger deep in her soul. Her hand still hurt, but she hadn't touched much in the way of painkillers. She didn't want to get addicted to drugs and the pain helped her to remember. Not that she needed reminding. In the past few days, every time she slept, she was back in that nightmare. Every single night, she woke up covered in sweat, fear lodged in her throat, pain breaking out through her whole body. She couldn't make it stop.

No matter how much ice cream she ate, or chocolate, nothing seemed to be helping her mood.

She hurt everywhere, not just physically but emotionally.

There was no one to offer her comfort. No one to talk to. She was all alone.

After her parents died, she'd felt lost and alone. This was the same feeling. Alone. The bakery remained closed. Her hand was useless in her attempts to bake. The machines were only good for so much.

The sound of the doorbell ringing made her pause with the spoon close to her mouth. She opted to ignore the sound, only it came again.

On the third ring, she pushed the spoon into the tub of ice cream and got to her feet. She checked through the peephole to discover Abriana standing there.

What was she doing here?

"Ava, I know you're in there. Please, open the door."

She kept the bolt across the door but opened the other locks. With Smokey refusing to hand in her key, she'd called an out-of-town locksmith to come and change all the locks and to add in a few others for safety measure. She didn't feel safe. If someone wanted to get into her house, they'd find a way to do it.

"What's the matter?" Ava asked, looking at Abriana through the small space she'd made.

"I wanted to come and see you," Abriana said.

"You've seen me." She didn't want to get too close to Abriana. She was married to one of the club, and Ugly Beast hadn't exactly been her biggest fan.

"Ava, please, don't … don't do this. It's only me here. Ugly Beast will go as soon as you let me in."

She couldn't see much of the road or anything of the street behind Abriana, so she had no choice but to release the lock.

Opening the door wide, she saw Ugly Beast sat in the car. No one else was around.

"What do you want?" she asked.

Abriana winced. "I know we haven't been close. We haven't had the time to get to know one another. Raven told me what happened."

At the sound of her name, Ava flinched.

"Shoot, I know it must hurt you for me to say her name."

"I'm fine." She had to get over it.

"You're not fine. I wanted to come and hang out. Maybe we could talk."

"I don't want you to take this the wrong way, but I want nothing to do with the club."

"I know. Er, I'm … I'm club, but I'm not. I'm Ugly's wife and I have his child. He's the love of my life, but I'm not club."

Ava rubbed at her temple. Her eye was still covered. The swelling had reduced significantly but hadn't completely disappeared.

"I'm not in the best place to receive guests. It's

nothing personal. I just want to be left alone." She wore a pair of old sweatpants and a large shirt that had a couple of holes in the front. The clothes were ugly but comfortable. All she wanted right now was a bit of comfort.

"Please, let me be your friend."

"Abriana, you're club. You might not wear the patch or be there for meetings or whatnot, but you're club. I don't think it's a good idea."

Abriana took her hand. "You need a friend. I know you want to push everything that reminds you of him and the club away, but I'm me."

Before she knew what was happening, Abriana had stepped into her home and closed the door.

"Now, Ugly Beast will drive off and he won't be worried. I had your back. Ugly Beast told me what was happening, I told him there was no chance."

Ava was hit with a wave of exhaustion. If Abriana wanted to stick around, then fine, but she didn't have to sit and listen. She went back to the sitting room, picked up her melting tub of ice cream, sat down, and tried to ignore the woman who entered the living room.

Even though her life was in tatters, her house was still very clean. She couldn't stand living in filth. She liked neatness and order. Those were the two most important things.

Love and friendship were too hard. She'd tried to experience both and they'd failed her.

Abriana took the seat opposite her.

"How is Bella?" she asked. So much for ignoring the other woman. She didn't want to be too rude.

Abriana smiled. "Growing so fast. I don't think it's fair that they get to be babies for such a short time. You don't have any children, do you?"

"I'm thirty years old. Even if I had a kid at

eighteen, it would still be living with me."

"Right, of course."

"How old did you think I was?"

"No, I was making conversation. You were married before."

"Yep, to an asshole that with everything that happened, Smokey makes look like a saint. Who would have thought it?" Ava laughed, even though amusement was the furthest thing from her mind.

She wasn't happy. Sadness overwhelmed her.

"I'm so sorry for what they did. I know Rav— I mean, she is really upset about what happened."

"I get that the two of you are best friends, but I don't want to hear about her." She had some more ice cream, but she suddenly started to feel sick.

"I know. This is so awful."

Ava got to her feet. She didn't need to hear how awful it all was. She'd lived it. Every hit and bad word that came her way.

Even what Smokey had said to her. "You were only ever a decent fuck and you weren't any good at that. You were easy, but I've had better."

Ava reached up and touched her hair. Raven had cut it all off.

She had yet to go to the hairdresser's to try to repair the damage. She'd loved her hair. The natural blonde locks had been a joy to brush at night. What remained of her hair, she currently had pinned to the base of her head. She stopped in the kitchen and stared around at the clean counters. Everything was in order.

"Ava?"

"They cut my hair off," she said. "Did you know that?"

She reached for the clips and let what little hair she had fall out. There was no straightness to it. The hair had been hacked off.

Abriana went to her, and she stared at the other woman, tensing as she wrapped her arms around her, holding her.

Ava stayed perfectly still.

She wasn't used to such physical contact. The sweetness that was Abriana brought tears to her eyes.

"I'm here for you, Ava," Abriana said.

"I think I want to go and get my hair done."

Between the hospital visit and the bakery, she'd put so much of her life on hold.

"Do you want me to call Ugly Beast to come and take us?"

Ava shook her head. "No. I want to call a cab." She wasn't going to drive just yet. Anytime she put any pressure on her hand, the pain was too much.

Abriana nodded. "I will have to tell Ugly Beast what we're doing."

"You do that. You don't have to come with me. I can go to the salon myself."

"No." Abriana took her hand. "We'll do this together. I want to be there for you."

"Okay."

She called for a cab as she made her way upstairs to change her shirt. She kept the sweatpants on but she couldn't go to a salon with holes in her shirt. She had some standards. At least, she hoped so.

With a fresh shirt in place, she made her way downstairs, stopping when she heard Abriana.

"They cut her hair! No, Ugly, this isn't funny. I had no idea. Have you seen what they did to her? Raven was lying to me. I don't want her near me for a long time. I'm so mad at her. I don't care what you have to say to defend yourselves. It's wrong. Ava had never given any of you any cause to doubt her."

She shook her head and watched as she hung up.

"You don't have to do that for me," Ava said, startling her.

Abriana whirled around. "You weren't supposed to hear that."

"Kind of hard not to when you're yelling."

The sound of a car tooting its horn caught Ava's attention. "That was fast."

"Smokey's made it so."

Ava paused. "What?"

"He's, er, he's made sure everyone in town knows that you're a priority. He wants everyone to be on their best behavior. What you want, they have to get."

"I didn't ask for that."

"I think it's one of the many ways he wants to attempt to make amends." Abriana shrugged. "I'm sorry. I don't know much. I tend to stay out of the whole club thing."

Ava nodded. "You can be friends with her. It doesn't bother me. I'm not going to be part of it. I'm not even thinking of sticking around for much longer." She opened the door as Abriana caught her arm.

"What do you mean?"

She looked at the hand on her arm and waited for Abriana to let her go, which she did within a matter of seconds. "I'm so sorry. I didn't mean—"

"I get it. I'm thinking of selling this place and the bakery. I haven't replaced the furniture inside, and I have no fresh products waiting to be used. It's an empty carcass."

"But you love this town."

"I thought I did, but feelings can be easily changed."

"This is about Smokey again."

Ava smiled at Abriana and pulled away slightly.

"Please, don't worry about it. I've got an appointment with a realtor in a week. It's where I intend to talk to them. I'm looking for another place to live."

"You'll wait to make that decision."

"There's nothing keeping me here, Abriana. If I decide to make the move, I will. I've just got to find someplace where I can set down real roots." She was checking towns extensively. She'd already made the decision not to live in the city. What she wanted to make sure of was that there were no towns with an MC club.

Fort Clover was the last town she ever wanted to be in. As she climbed into the back of the cab, Abriana joined her, and Ugly Beast tailed them as they made their way into town.

"Will you tell Smokey?" Abriana asked.

"No. I have no reason to tell Smokey anything. He's not my boss, and I'm not indebted to him. I'm a free woman." She rubbed at her chest, praying for the pain in her chest to go away.

Thinking of Smokey always made her hurt. She loved him. No doubt about it.

A part of her always would, but she wouldn't fall for him, not again.

****

It had been a long time since Smokey had experienced a beatdown. His fists were bloody, his nose broken, again. One of his eyes was sealed shut, and his lip was cut. A tooth was missing, and he'd bitten a section of his tongue as well. Aching ribs and a hell of a lot of bruises, but he'd taken on Creed.

Of course, his boys had been alerted that he was in Twisted Bastards territory and the fight hadn't lasted as long as he'd wanted.

He hadn't gotten to kill Creed.

Instead, his aching ass was dragged right back

home, to where he sat now, in the clubhouse, getting stitched up by the doc.

"What the fuck were you thinking?" Hunter asked.

"That's your first mistake," he said, laughing.

"Does it look like I'm laughing?"

"Does it look like I give a fuck?" Smokey asked. "I did what I had to do."

"You go into their turf, you can guarantee retaliation."

"We'll be ready for them."

Hunter growled and looked ready to punch him. Smokey was more than ready for another throwdown. Any of these bastards wanted to take a turn, he'd be right on them. As soon as the doc had stitched him up, he'd pop them right on open.

"Someone try to reason with him. I'm done trying. He's not fucking listening to reason." Hunter shook his head.

"I think it took balls," Kinky said, who was nursing a bruised jaw.

"Thanks."

"This because of what he made you do to your woman?" Doc asked.

"Be careful," Smokey said. Ava wasn't his woman and knowing that hurt.

He was struggling with not being able to hold her. He'd give anything to wake up with her in his arms. As it was, he just had to relive the memories of all the times he'd taken for granted.

He'd give anything to have Ava back in his arms. Anything.

Doc nodded and went back to finish stitching him up. The doc was leaving as Abriana and Ugly Beast came into the clubhouse.

Ugly Beast held his daughter against his chest, and it looked like little Bella had puked down the leather of his cut.

"Gross," Smokey said.

Abriana stormed right up to him and glared. "You butchered her hair!"

Smokey looked past Abriana's shoulder to Ugly Beast, who shrugged. "You asked for Abriana to go and see her. You were right. Out of all of us, she got into the door."

"And we went to the salon. She hadn't dealt with her hair, and it looked like a mess. My God, how could you do that to her?" Abriana looked toward the bar. "And you, I don't like you at all right now." Her words were directed at Raven.

"Join the club," Raven said. "You can hate me all you want to, Abriana. It's not going to change the fact that I already hate myself."

"How is she?" Smokey asked.

Abriana laughed. "Well, she has less hair now. The stylist did some kind of short cut. It's layered and comes around to beneath her neck." She shook her head. "But she's not in a good place. Her home is neat and tidy. It's spotless. I don't think she's doing a lot all day. Her hand is bandaged up and she's eating ice cream."

"Tell him, Abriana," Ugly Beast said.

Her shoulders slumped.

Alarm bells went off inside his head. "Tell me what?"

Abriana took a deep breath. "Ava's meeting a, er, realtor."

He tensed up. "What?"

"She's considering selling. The bakery is empty. No equipment or ingredients. It's completely empty."

He looked toward Ugly Beast.

"I don't think she's going to stick around all that long," Abriana said. "She's alone, and I do think she's lonely."

Smokey got to his feet and grabbed his keys.

Hunter was on him. "Where the fuck do you think you're going?"

"I've got to go see Ava."

"Not in your condition."

"I'm not pregnant, and I'm not about to drop a brat. I'm going to go and see her."

"No."

Hunter stepped in front of him, holding up his hands.

"I mean it, Hunter. Step aside. You do not want to get in the way right now." He waited and tensed his body, ready to strike.

"You're not in a position to go. After what we did to her, do you really think she needs to see you like this?" Hunter asked.

"Today, you don't get to be the voice of reason," he said. He was done listening to anyone else. "Look, I made a judgment call. I fucked up. I'm owning my shit and I'm dealing with it. Ava can't ... I don't want her to leave. She can't leave."

"Let her go," Hunter said.

"No." He growled the word loud and clear.

"And why the hell not?" Hunter asked.

"Because he's in love with her," Abriana said. "It's why he can't stand what he did, nor believe why he did it. He's hurting because of what he did. He wants to make amends, but he can't figure out how. You're not going to win her over by being mean."

Smokey snorted. "Why can't you go back to being the scared little girl Ugly Beast took?"

"I grew up and found you guys. You've all taught

me to stand up for myself. You're my friend, Smokey. I may not like you very much right now, but I do care about you."

"You love her?" Hunter asked.

Smokey's jaw clenched. He didn't believe in love. That kind of emotion was for pussies, and he wasn't one.

Staring into his VP's eyes, he knew he owed him a level of honesty. He'd given the order to hurt Ava, even kill her. They were all following orders, and he'd been wrong. If it wasn't for Ugly Beast, she'd have been dead already.

"I love her," Smokey said. "I love her more than anything else in the world. I miss her so fucking much, and it hurts to know I did that to her. I didn't trust her enough to hear her side. I didn't second-guess those ... pictures. I've got to live with that. Now are you going to stand in my way, or are you going to back the fuck off?" He was willing to fight his VP if he had to.

"You sure you're up for the ride?" Hunter asked.

"I'm good." His body hurt in so many different ways, but he had to do this.

After Hunter stepped out of his way, Smokey went straight to his bike, straddling the machine. He ignored every single stab of pain in all the different areas. Several of the guys came out, watching him leave.

He ignored them and rode in the direction of town. Rather than go straight to Ava's house, he took a detour to the town. People were still milling about even though it was dark. A couple of the streetlights were out as he parked across the street from his woman's bakery.

There was no light in the windows. She normally had something on display that he knew from personal experience she either ate the following day or tossed out. There was nothing. No sign of any life.

Seeing her shop like this hurt.

He'd caused this. His actions had seen to it that his woman would give up.

Revving his engine, he took off, this time heading toward Ava's house. The journey wasn't enjoyable, but he wasn't going to give up.

Arriving at her house, he noticed only a single light was aglow in her bedroom. Smokey took out the key he carried on him at all times and went to the front door. The key didn't fit.

She'd changed the locks.

Cursing, he stepped back and looked up at her window. He stared at the door. Bringing his knuckles up, he knocked. The blood that had been on his hands was dried, so he didn't leave any blood spatter.

He waited.

And waited.

Smokey knocked again.

Nothing.

He moved to be able to see her window. The light was still on. He couldn't hear any music and so he did no more than reach for a couple of small pieces of gravel and throw them at the window.

Seconds passed and the curtain twitched. Ava opened the curtain.

"Come on, Ava."

She closed the curtains, blocking his view of her, but he saw her shadow, still holding them closed.

"Ava, babe, come on." He picked up another couple of pieces of gravel and threw them up at the window.

Another pause.

Going to the door, he began to bang. He wasn't going to give up or give in. He settled on screaming her name.

After several minutes, the light near the door flicked on. Seconds later, Ava opened it. "What the hell are you doing?"

"Don't sell. Don't leave." They were the only words he could form. It was stupid how desperate he was for her to stay.

"This is ridiculous, Smokey. You have no right to come yelling at me and throwing stones."

"They weren't too big."

"I don't care if they were big or not. This isn't funny." Her eye was still covered. She frowned and reached out to the wall. The lights outside suddenly glowed and she gasped. "What happened to you?"

"Nothing important."

"Let me guess, club stuff."

Smokey shook his head. "Not club stuff. I decided to go and pick a fight with the bastard who sent me those pictures."

"And you look like this."

"He's not doing much better. He had more people on his side. I went solo. Didn't take the club with me. Next time, I will."

"Don't—" She stopped, closed her eyes, and took a breath. "Don't do this on my account."

"I have to. He fucked everything up."

"No. All he did was provide you with the gun. You chose to load it and fire." She held her hand out. "I don't want to talk to you about this. Why are you here?"

"Please don't leave."

Ava snorted. "Abriana. So much for friendships, huh?"

"Look, she would cut my dick off if she could. She's pissed, and I get it. We don't deserve your forgiveness, Ava. I know I don't."

"Smokey, stop doing this. I've already made my

decision. When I find the right place, I'm going to leave. It's the right thing to do. I don't want to be here anymore."

"I'll keep my distance until you can bear to see me again."

"You lived here first."

"And you fell in love with the place. Ava, I don't want you to go."

He saw her eyes glisten with tears.

"It's not your decision, and it will never be yours to make. I'm already looking for potential buyers for the bakery, and then I'm going to put this place on the market."

"If you loved me at all, you'd consider the next moves you make, please."

Ava stared at him. "That's cruel even for you. I consider everything. Don't you think I've thought of everything first? It's what I do. You're right. I loved this place. I'd hoped to make a lot of memories. Good ones, and you had started to help me build them. There are places I pass and I can't help but smile."

He took a step toward her. "Then don't go. Please, don't fucking go."

"You're not the boss of me, Smokey. Two weeks ago, I'd have given anything to hear you say those words. Those memories that were once sweet to me, they're not dead. I can't have them anymore. You killed them for me. There's nothing for me here."

"There's me."

"I don't have you."

"You've got all of me, babe." He took her good hand and placed it against his heart. "I know you hate me a lot right now, and I get it. I'm an asshole, but you loved me. You still love me. It's why it hurts so fucking much."

She tugged on her hand, and tears fell down her cheeks. He saw the pain in her eyes. How her face scrunched up, the tension in her body. Gone was the women who loved his touch. He wanted her back so fucking much.

"Love you or not, Smokey. If I decide to go, then that is exactly what I'm going to do, and nothing you or anyone else says can stop me. Please tell Abriana I don't want her at my home again."

"Don't shut her out. She was pissed off. She wasn't bragging or trying to update me. It wasn't like that."

"Then what was it like?" Ava asked. "You're telling me I've got to be friends with Abriana, yet the first thing she came and did was tell you. You want forgiveness. You and Raven, and the truth is, I've got nothing to give. You broke my heart."

The last ended on a sob, and she took a deep breath as her body shook. "I would have done anything for you, Smokey. I still think part of me would, and that scares me. You had me beaten. I can't even use my hand properly, and we both know you were going to bury me once you were done. Now you're asking me to stay."

"I know I'm being unreasonable."

"Yes, you are, and unfair. We're not together anymore, Smokey. You don't get to dictate where I go. Now please leave." She slammed the door in his face.

"I love you too," he said, putting his hand against the glass.

Chapter Thirteen

According to the realtor, there wasn't a lot of interest in buying a shop so small. Where Ava had found it charming, others found it really small. Her bakery was enough for a one-woman operation, and so one month after the attack, she still hadn't found anyone to buy her bakery.

Then there was the trouble with her home. She'd loved the place and had gotten it at a bargain price because it had been on the market for so long.

They were living in difficult times and with those times, no one wanted to buy a place out of the town or a city.

She sat in her yard, drinking some fresh lemonade she'd just squeezed. The lemons had been on sale at the grocery store. They'd looked amazing, and she couldn't resist a bargain.

Now with an abundance of lemons, her creative desires were in full flow. She wanted to bake. Her hand was improving. She'd gone for another X-ray and the doctor was happy with the improvements. He didn't think for a second she'd need surgery and she'd be able to work with it within another month.

Not being able to do anything but sit and eat was starting to get to her. She didn't want to stay indoors all the time.

The nice warm weather offered a slight reprieve, but again, it wasn't enough to stop the itch to do something.

Eating ice cream had lost its appeal. So had eating herself out of house and home. It was why she'd ended up at the grocery store, and now back in her yard, drinking lemonade.

What she hadn't realized was that there was a fair

in town. She'd been so out of the loop with everything.

As she sat drinking, loneliness began to creep in.

Would it hurt for her to go and enjoy the fair for a couple of hours? To be around actual people?

She finished off her glass of lemonade and decided it was time to get off her ass, to go enjoy some other company.

Ava placed the jug in the fridge, changed from her shorts to a blue summer dress with white roses on the front. She called a cab because she didn't like driving with her hand. She was taking every single precaution when it came to helping the healing process.

At the door, she gave herself one final look in the mirror. Most of the bruises had faded. The worst ones around her eye still had some slight mottling to them. Her lip had healed up as well. Her hair, she hated it. The hairdresser had done what she could to fix the hacked locks, but she missed her long hair. She'd gone out of her way to grow it.

Just another thing they'd taken away from her.

Squaring her shoulders, she heard the cab's horn, letting her know it was here. She locked her home and made her way to the cab. Climbing in the back, she told him where she wanted him to go. He took her there without making any conversation.

Being in town, she did notice more people were trying to make nice with her.

The truth was, she wasn't interested. After what Abriana said about his warning to them, she didn't care to make friends that way. She'd rather people just want to be friends because they happened to like her.

Once the cab driver arrived, she paid him and gave him a generous tip. She climbed out, and at first, panic seized her as she looked at the large crowd. Not only was this a big event for the town, but several tourists had arrived.

When she purchased the bakery, she'd been told about this time of year. How wise it would be for her to participate. She'd been looking forward to it. Even planning for it when she first opened up.

All that time had been wasted.

Rather than dwell on the dull ache in her hand, and where there were once bruises on her body that seemed to want to come to life, she stepped into the throng of people.

Everything is going to be fine.

She had always hated crowds. Another reason for Derek to dislike her. He loved to go out and party. She loved to stay in.

Watching people was a favorite pastime of hers, though. Ava didn't immediately get stuck in with enjoyment. She took her time. Observing everyone. The laughter was somewhat infectious.

After what felt like a lifetime, she started to relax.

She had clocked the Hell's Bastards MC, and Smokey, in particular. She ignored them all.

Stepping toward a game that required her to throw a ball in the net, she took three turns, failing each time, laughing as she didn't come close to the shot. The high school teen manning the booth convinced her to have another three turns. She failed the first two and as he went to hand her the ball for her third and final turn, muscular, inked arms surrounded her, taking the ball.

"Let me," Smokey said.

She tensed up. The last thing she wanted to do was cause a scene, and he knew that.

Gritting her teeth, she stayed perfectly still, feeling the heat of him surround her. He took aim and landed the ball directly in the net.

"Pick your prize," the teen said.

She wasn't picking anything. Smokey nodded at a monkey teddy. It was cute. Ava refused to take it when the teen tried to hand it to her. Smokey took it and she ducked under his arm and moved on.

Smokey didn't follow her. He held the teddy in his arms.

She refused to participate in the gun shooting water game. Her hand was still her first priority to fix.

Using one hand, she came to a stop at catching some rubber ducks with little hoops on them. The poll was heavy, but she had a few minutes to be able to grab one.

She failed. Her hand wasn't her strongest. At the last thirty seconds, Smokey took the pole and grabbed one of the ducks with ease.

He was applauded and handed a teddy. Again, he picked one out.

Smokey turned toward her, and she stepped around him. She refused to play this game with him.

She attempted to play two more games, and she failed both of them. Smokey took over and won. He now carried around four teddies. All of them were so cute. She ignored them and went straight to the crazy house. She paid her money and stepped inside.

Ava couldn't recall a fair she'd ever been to. She'd tried to get Derek to go, but he hadn't wanted to. Said fairs were for kids.

She enjoyed them. They were fun.

Rounding a corner, she came to a stop as Smokey was there, minus the teddies.

"Stop following me," she said.

"I'm only doing it for your own safety."

"I don't need you to protect me. You're the problem, remember?" She held up her hand for him to see and he winced.

"I am sorry about that."

"I don't care." She moved past him, and the house had lost its appeal. They had gotten to the crazy mirrors. Their reflections were everywhere. She couldn't deny having Smokey at her back gave her a thrill. It only served to enrage her even more.

She shouldn't care about him. He was a monster.

Ignoring the pull he had over her, she took a step forward, but Smokey captured her waist, drawing her back.

"I know you hate me, but I can't stop thinking about you, Ava. I'm going to help you regardless of whether you want it."

"Are you interfering with my realtor?" she asked, turning around to glare at him.

"No."

"So you're not stopping the interest in my bakery?"

"No."

"I don't believe you."

"Ava, you know I don't want you to leave, but the truth is that shop had been vacant for fucking years before you came along. I didn't know what you saw in the place, but believe me when I say this. You were the only one."

"I don't want to hear this. I'm tired of hearing this." She tried to step away, but he still held her.

Even with the slight, dull pain in her hand and her short hair, and all the memories of what Raven and those women did to her, she ached for him. Her pussy grew slick and her nipples tightened.

The want in her body wouldn't fade, and she hated it so much.

Staring at him now, she wanted to hurt him. To punch him, to do anything that would make him feel even an ounce of what she felt.

Nothing.

"I've got to go," she said.

"I know you feel it too."

"Yeah, and I still remember what you called me. The horrible words you said to me. I'm not going to fall for this, Smokey. Go ahead, win all the games. Take me around on rides. I don't care, and I don't want them."

This time when she pulled away, he let her go. The house lost its appeal, as did the fair. Being around Smokey was too much. She had to be somewhere else.

He followed her all around the house, and finally, when she got out, she didn't linger. A couple of his men stood there waiting for him. Hunter and Brick were there, as well as Kinky and Raven.

They looked at her with pity.

She turned on her heel and walked away. Coming to the fair had been a big mistake. She pulled out her cell phone and waited for the cab to come get her. The same man who'd dropped her off collected her.

He drove back to her house. No words, once again. She didn't want to make conversation. Ava paid him the moment they arrived at her house. After climbing out, she headed toward the front door and came to a stop.

The four teddies were waiting with a card that read: *We need a home.*

They were the same teddies Smokey had won for her. She didn't know how he got to her house before her.

She bent down and picked them up. In the back of her mind, she was tempted to throw them out in the trash. She couldn't do it. When Smokey had won, each time, he'd picked the exact teddy she would have wanted.

That wasn't really important, though. Sheer coincidence. She wasn't going to believe he knew her so well as to pick out the right teddy bears.

Even still, she couldn't help liking that he had picked them out.

****

Smokey was getting antsy. The first run had gone smoothly. They'd picked up the dope at the port and it was waiting in one of the warehouses to be collected. The ride across the county had gone off without a hitch. No interference.

He'd expected Creed and his Twisted Bastards to have interfered. To have done something to make sure it went badly. Nothing. With Creed silent, Smokey knew the bastard was up to something. He just needed to figure out what.

The club was excited for their return.

Club pussy ran into their open arms. A couple of women approached him, but he ignored them, heading straight inside. He went to the bathroom first. After stripping out of his clothes, he took a long shower. Turning it to cold to wash away the fatigue.

Once he was clean, he took off and headed back to church. The money they'd earned was distributed to each member with an amount being put aside for the club. This was how they always did business.

Overall, the club had the highest percentage. In time, it would be invested back into the bank, but at such a rate no one would know where the money came from. Their businesses helped to hide that money as well.

He waited to see if anyone wanted to contribute. Everyone was happy. He slammed the gavel down, and this time, he was the first one out of the room. Women were waiting to party, but there was only one place he wanted to be. Going straight back to his bike, he straddled the machine and took off, heading toward town. The first place he went was the bakery.

No sign of life.

His shoulders slumped. There wasn't a single buyer.

He'd checked. He hadn't interfered with this one, but he wanted to. If he purchased the shop, Ava would leave.

She had the means of starting over. His thorough background check of her had told him of her wealth. She didn't need him or the club. No man. Her money was what lured Derek to her.

This pissed him off because there was nothing he could do.

"She's still not opening."

He turned to see Larissa, a sweet librarian, standing a couple of feet from him. She was the priest's daughter.

"Has she been in town?"

Larissa shook her head. "No. I've seen her at the grocery store. That's about it."

Smokey nodded his head. "Tell your dad I said hi."

She smiled. "He told me to tell you that if you ever feel the need to talk, he's always open."

Smokey nodded. He liked Larissa's father. Jonah Adams. They had learned to accept each other within this small town.

"Do you need a ride home?"

Larissa shook her head. "I like to walk. Good night, Smokey."

He offered good night and then kept an eye on her until she made it home. There were some people who needed protection. Larissa was a sweet woman. She was only eighteen years old, but damn it, the world was too cruel for her. She trusted everyone and people took advantage of that. He knew her father had to even be cautious with new people coming along.

With Larissa back home, he went to the only other place he wanted to go. Ava's.

Parking his bike, he stared up at her house.

The curtain twitched and he smiled, offering up a wave for her to see. She closed the curtain, and seconds later, she came out, wrapping a robe around her.

"Smokey, what are you doing here?"

It was the first time in a week since he'd seen her, and his heart pounded at the sight of her. He did notice the paleness of her complexion. She looked like she'd been sick.

After climbing off his bike, he made his way toward her. Ava stopped, and realizing he was scaring her, he paused and cursed. "Shit, I'm sorry."

"You don't have to come here anymore."

"Have you been sick?" he asked.

Ava frowned. "A little. Not a lot. I'm going to go and see a doctor. Not that it's any of your concern. You look … you're tired, Smokey. Abriana said you were on a run or whatever it's called. Go home. Get some rest."

"I miss you," he said. "I don't like that you're sick."

"I'm not sick. It's, it's kind of hard to explain. I feel fine most days. It's just the mornings. I'm thinking I'm developing some allergies to some foods." She shook her head. "But that's not the point. You can't keep doing this. You think I don't notice that you're always hanging out here? It's not right."

"Why is it not right?" he asked.

"Because we're not together anymore." Her hand was still bandaged up.

"When will that be completely healed?" he asked.

"You're not listening to me."

"I'm listening. I'm just not liking what you say."

He shrugged.

"You need to move on. I know there are plenty of women at the club who would be more than happy to have you around."

"None of them are you."

"This is hopeless, Smokey." She had tears in her eyes. "Damn it. I hate crying all the time."

"I fucked up, Ava, and I miss you so much."

She shook her head. "I wish it was that simple."

"Forgive me, please."

She stared down at the floor. "'You were only ever a decent fuck and you weren't any good at that. You were easy, but I've had better.'" She looked up and tilted her head to the side. "That's what you said to me. Do you remember it?"

"I was fucked in the head, Ava. I swear it was all lies."

"But you said it, Smokey. Lies or not, you thought it." She pressed her lips together. "I told you that I loved you. I even accepted there was no way you could love me back. I knew that. I still know that and it hurts. Everything you said hurt so much."

Smokey witnessed the pain in her eyes and wished there was something he could do to make it right. What he'd done and said was all crap. All of it.

"Ava, I'm so sorry."

"They're words, Smokey. The people in town being nice to me. How welcoming they all suddenly are. Do you have any idea how much I've longed for that?"

He'd done something right.

"But it's not real. You've asked or threatened them, and it's not fair. None of this is fair." She swiped at the tears in her eyes. "I'm sorry, but I can't just forgive and forget. I was loyal to you, and you'd rather believe a bunch of pictures than question me. I didn't even get a fair trial in your eyes."

"I fucked up, Ava. I know this."

"And what about next time? Say I accept that you're sorry. We move on. We go back to fucking each other again. I can be around the club. What happens the next time someone uses me to make you lose your shit? What do I do then? Go through this or should I wait until Ugly Beast or another of the club thinks I'm innocent?" she asked. "I can't live like that."

"It won't ever happen again."

"That's the point, Smokey. Again. It shouldn't have happened the first time. Please, go home and leave me the hell alone." She turned on her heel and walked inside the house, closing the door.

He heard the locks as she put them all into place.

Smokey didn't go home.

He stayed right where he was, staring up at her house. The light in her bedroom window went out after a couple of hours.

Smokey tensed up when he heard the sounds of another bike making its way toward him. He reached into his jacket for his gun, but recognized the rider and the bike as it drew closer.

Ugly Beast parked his bike and came toward him, offering him a flask. "I can't guarantee it's good, but Abriana put a lot of love into it."

"There's no way we can complain when it comes to feeling. Your wife has a whole lot of it."

They both laughed as he opened the flask.

"Soup?"

"I think so. It didn't taste too bad, but that was when I ate it a few hours ago."

Smokey poured some soup into the cup provided. It didn't smell awful but when it came to Abriana's food, scents and looks could be deceiving. It didn't make his mouth water. He took a taste, and there was a weird twang in the background that he was almost afraid to ask about.

"I think it's easier if you just drink it without trying to compare it to anything else you've ever tasted."

He laughed and took another sip.

"Abriana's rooting for you," Ugly Beast said.

"Why?"

"She wants you to win her back. She thinks you have a real shot."

Smokey snorted. "I can't even get too close." The last real time he'd touched her was at the fair, and that hadn't been a lot of touching. He missed her. Not just for the sex, he missed *her*, the woman.

"Do you have any kind of plan?" Ugly Beast asked.

"Did you?"

"Nope. I just wanted to love her, and she gave me that chance. There's nothing else any of us can do after that. Abriana's not like Ava, though. I did hurt her quite badly."

Ugly Beast had said some awful things to Abriana while he'd had the women hurt her.

"Saying stuff and getting others to do your dirty work is a different thing altogether," he said. "Ava's never going to forgive me."

"Never is a long time."

"Would you forgive someone who signed off on you being beaten? I seem to recall the people who fucked up your face are all dead."

"Are you trying to tell me, Smokey, you'd die for Ava?" Ugly Beast asked.

"Yes. I would."

Silence rang out. The only person he'd been willing to die for was the club, and that included all of his brothers. His devotion had been to the patch. No one else.

"Then you can't give up."

Smokey turned toward Ugly Beast. "You don't think I'm a pussy?"

"No. You sound pussy-whipped, but you forget, I know what it truly means to be loved by an amazing woman. There's nothing like it."

Smokey took another sip of the soup and wrinkled his nose. "This is fucking disgusting."

"Yep, but to Abriana, it's better than the last one. I struggled through the other soup, and believe me, I never knew there was much I couldn't stand. I think the next time we torture someone, I'll save all of Abriana's leftovers."

"We'll feed them to death?"

"Nope. They'll talk before we get to that part."

Smokey snorted. He finished all the soup because he was hungry.

"Staring at her window all night isn't going to win her back," Ugly Beast said.

"No, but it gives me comfort to know she can sleep all night. No one else is going to hurt her."

Silence fell between them.

Smokey handed him the empty flask. "Thanks."

"Why did you do it?" Ugly Beast asked.

"Do what?"

"You saw the pictures. I know you, Smokey. You don't react like that. You never have. You always consider every single possibility, and yet, you didn't that time. Why?"

Smokey ran his fingers through his hair. "I was falling for her. I knew it. Feelings like that cloud people's judgment. She was different from the start. I knew that. I saw it every single day. She told me she loved me, and I felt like a fucking king. They were all feelings I didn't recognize. The fact … it was easier to believe the worst in her." He turned to look at him. "I've only ever known the worst."

"True, but it's still a lame-ass excuse." Ugly Beast saluted him and got on his bike.

Smokey watched him go, and he settled in to watch his woman. He'd sleep for a few hours during the day if he had to.

Chapter Fourteen

The cast was finally off. Her hand was healed, but she'd been advised to still take it easy. Ava agreed with the doctor, however, when she'd asked him to give her a physical and told him her symptoms, he'd gotten this strange look across his face. She was vomiting in the mornings, and some foods were making her feel sick. She was experiencing tiredness all the time.

He'd taken her blood and promised to have the results back as soon as possible. It was why the following day, she sat in his office.

"How are you feeling today?" the doctor asked.

"I'm okay. A little nauseous, but I'm getting used to it. Did my blood tests reveal anything?"

The doctor ran a hand down his face. "Ava, the tests show that you're pregnant."

Ava froze. "What?"

"Yes. I was supposed to ask you several questions yesterday, but we've been rushed off our feet with this sickness bug. I did think it was the same, and I didn't suspect anything else. Your symptoms were minor, but … anyway. You're pregnant."

"You're sure?"

"Blood results don't lie. Do you think there is a reason you shouldn't be pregnant? Have you had unprotected sex recently?"

She wanted to lie. She wanted to tell the doctor there was no way she could be pregnant. She hadn't had sex for a couple of months, but before her … accident, she had unprotected sex multiple times with Smokey. He hadn't wanted to use a condom and neither had she.

This was her fuck-up.

She pressed her lips together, wanting to fight the inevitable, but it was a complete waste of time. There was nothing to fight.

"I can do a quick ultrasound if you'd like?" the doctor asked.

"Yes, please, yes."

Maybe then the blood work was wrong, or perhaps they mixed it up with another woman who wanted to get pregnant but couldn't.

She climbed up on the table and rolled up her shirt.

The doctor had left to get an ultrasound machine.

Do I want to be pregnant?

Happiness rushed through her body at the very thought of carrying life, but with it, the harsh reality that the same life was attached to Smokey. He'd helped her to create it, and because of that, she'd have to tell him.

"I'm not pregnant," she said.

The doctor came into the room and set everything up. There was also a nurse present.

"Now, Ava, this will be a little cold."

She nodded, and the gel was cold.

He pressed the device against her stomach. Then he moved it around and she stared at the screen, not seeing anything until he got it in the right position, and there was her little baby. "Still early. I reckon you're three months along, roughly. We can get a definite estimation for when you're due when you come back. I want to do a follow-up check as my notes state you had an X-ray and at the time, you said you weren't pregnant."

"Will that hurt the baby?" she asked.

"I don't want you to worry too much right now. Let's take it one day at a time." He smiled at her.

The rest of the appointment went by in a blur. She went back to the reception to organize another visit. In her hand, she held the photo that showed she was indeed pregnant.

She was going to have Smokey's baby.

The same man she'd been trying to avoid.

They were going to have a child together.

There was a cab waiting for her outside of the hospital. She sat in the back in a bit of a daze. Arriving at home, she closed and locked the door. She went straight to the kitchen and opened the fridge. She hadn't drunk any beer or wine since her accident, but she'd purchased a couple of bottles of each a few days ago. Staring at the alcohol, she put a hand to her stomach.

She was going to have a baby. All she'd ever wanted was a child.

Now she was going to get her dream and the father was a man she couldn't trust.

Tears filled her eyes, but she reached into the fridge, and one by one, she pulled the alcohol out and threw it in the trash. She wasn't going to drink anything that would harm her baby.

Once her fridge was empty, she put both hands on her stomach. She'd noticed a slight thickening of her waistline but had figured that was all the chocolate ice cream. "I'm going to take care of you, sweetheart. Just you and me. One day, we'll figure everything out."

Leaving town was now out of the question. She didn't want to talk to Smokey, but he was the dad and he needed to know she was pregnant. Sitting down at the dining room table, she stared at the ultrasound picture. She'd get another one on her next visit.

Getting to her feet, she folded the paperwork the doctor had given her, stating she was pregnant. She made a single note on the back, telling Smokey she was. She found an envelope, and then she went to her car.

She hadn't driven it in so long. Once she was behind the wheel, she ran her hands across it and smiled. No more cabs. She turned over the ignition and pulled out of the driveway.

Driving into town, she went to the post office first. She knew the address of the clubhouse and was sure it would get there very soon. Smokey would have the letter on his desk the next day. She wondered when he'd actually read it.

Ignoring the guilt that flooded her body at the lack of personal touch, she stepped out of the post office and went to her bakery.

She hadn't been inside the building in so long. The realtor had a set of keys to the place so she wouldn't have to be present when people were looking around. There hadn't been any interest though.

As she stepped through the building, she looked around. She hadn't wanted to come because this place held a lot of memories for her. This was her achievement. Now, without furniture, it was so dead and vacant.

Tucking her hair behind her ear, she made her way into the back office. The catalogs were still there, so she picked up the phone. Within two hours, she had all the equipment on order, due to arrive within three days. She made sure stock was also ordered.

With a baby on the way, she was going to have to hire some help.

She sat back.

Only one person. She'd hire one person and see if she could train them. Whoever she got to work with, they would have to get along. She refused to have a working environment when she couldn't stand the person.

With that settled, she made the phone call to the realtor to bring back her keys. She wasn't going to be selling.

Smokey hadn't gotten the letter yet, but when he did, he'd come to her.

Ava ended the day feeling focused. She left the shop and came to a stop when she saw Smokey across the street.

He climbed off his bike, and she noticed people had stopped to watch. She hated feeling like a spectacle.

"Why are you here?" she asked. I'm pregnant with your baby, and a few months ago I'd have given anything to be this way. Now, I feel so lost and so broken. Why did you have to do that to me?

She didn't speak any word of what was going on inside her head. She wanted to. There was a lot she wanted to yell at him.

Like the good woman she was, she kept it all locked up inside. Nothing good would come from screaming at him.

"I come here every single night before I go to your house."

"Why?"

"I want to see if you've opened it. Are you opening it?"

She should tell him in person that she was pregnant. He was right here, but Ava didn't want to witness his reaction.

Smokey had surprised her more than once, and him finding out they were going to be parents, well, she didn't want to see that revelation.

"Yes," she said. "I've organized everything."

"Good. That's good."

"It's just to see how everything is. You know. I may not have any customers." She shrugged.

"Your food is the best, Ava. They'd all be fools for not coming. I can guarantee they do."

"No." She shook her head. "I don't want you forcing people to come to my shop. If my food is as good as you say, then they'll come, regardless."

"How have you been?" he asked.

Tell him.

"Fine. You?" She wanted to tell him, but she was afraid.

The news was good for her. She wanted to have a baby. If Smokey didn't and he asked her to get rid of it, he'd break her heart even more. After everything, she was holding on by a thread. Once he read the news in his clubhouse, in his own time, she'd have to deal with the fallout.

They had never discussed the future or children, or anything.

She tucked some hair behind her ear. This was one of the many reasons she hated short hair.

Smokey's nostrils flared as she did this.

"I better go. Don't come to my house tonight," she said. "I know you're always there. Stay home. Go back to the clubhouse."

"I miss you."

She smiled. "You know what, I miss you too, but I miss what I didn't really know."

Smokey took a step toward her, and she backed away.

"I won't hurt you. I promise."

"You won't intentionally hurt me, Smokey, but there are a lot of ways to deliver pain. They don't have to be an actual physical blow." She couldn't look at him.

"I will make this right."

She chanced a glance at him and saw the way he looked at her. "Some things can't be made right. I'm sorry, Smokey." She took another step back. "I need to head back home." She was getting hungry, and well, the longer she stood with him, the more the guilt of not telling him ate away at her.

There was so much she wanted to say to him.

"You'll always be mine," he said.

This made her pause and look back at him. There was no reason to say anything else.

She walked to her car, climbed inside, and resisted the temptation to look back at him. Would he be watching her? She drove all the way home, hearing the sound of his bike as he followed her.

Smokey hadn't listened to her.

She arrived at home a few seconds before Smokey's bike pulled opposite her house.

Continuing to ignore him, she went inside and locked the door. Resting her back against it for a few seconds, she put a hand to her chest. "I can do this."

She removed her jacket and went straight to the kitchen. Ava didn't allow herself to think. She took ingredients out of the fridge and started to prepare herself a meal.

A nice stir fry.

She'd purchased some tofu the other day at the grocery store. She'd had this craving for it. Now as she prepared it, her mouth watered as she fried it in a small amount of oil until it was crispy on each side. It smelled delicious and she wanted to eat it instantly, but it would burn her mouth. She had to show restraint.

How would Smokey react when he finally read the letter? Would he be happy?

She'd know soon enough.

****

Smokey drank down the strong espresso, closing his eyes as he wished for the caffeine to work.

"You've got to stop doing this," Hunter said.

"I'm doing what needs to be done."

"You're going to get yourself killed for a woman who doesn't want you."

He dropped the glass and smashed his fist against

Hunter's face. The brother didn't take the hit, throwing a punch to his stomach. He grunted, but the pain was better than feeling nothing at all. Smokey threw another hit, tossing Hunter sideways until he collapsed on a table. The impact smashed the table.

Feminine screams filled the air. He cracked his knuckles. Hunter came at him.

"Enough!" Brick said.

Smokey grabbed Brick and shoved him out of the way. Anger flooded his gaze, and he wanted to kill everyone in sight.

Ava loved him. She just didn't want him. The pain of that knowledge, the anger and hatred at himself, manifested. The club came at him. Each man taking him on. They landed a few blows, but he went for a full-scale attack.

The women were moved out of harm's way. Chairs and tables pushed as he fought. Kinky was one of the worst sons of bitches around. He came at him, wrapping his arms around Smokey, holding him still.

"This is not the way, brother."

"Let me the fuck go."

Kinky wasn't letting him go.

Ugly Beast came through the door. "Let him go," he said, stepping up close.

"You want your ass beat?" Smokey asked.

The brothers stepped back as he faced off with Ugly Beast. "You think this is going to make you feel good?" Ugly Beast asked. "Taking us on one by one?"

"I don't need you all to be pussies. I can take you on. Let's make it an orgy." Smokey knew he was being a dick. He needed to feel the pain that his club could dish out.

Ugly Beast stood there. "Then come at me." He held his hands open. "Go ahead. Take me. Hit me."

The fight had left Ugly Beast. There was no tension in his shoulders. No indication the man would even fight.

It was useless.

Smokey hated Ugly Beast at that moment. "One day, Ugly, you and me."

"It's never going to happen. You'll realize you're fucking up. When that happens, I'll still be here."

He wiped at his face and saw blood ran from his nose. Pushing Ugly Beast out of the way, he limped toward his office.

"This won't win her back," Ugly Beast said.

Smokey paused and glanced back at him. "Nothing is going to win her back. She's lost to me." With that, he turned away and went straight to his office, closing the door. Collapsing in the chair, he grabbed some tissues and wiped under his nose. The blood kept on coming. The nose wasn't broken. Pity.

He threw the tissue into the trash and saw the pile of mail on his desk. He usually ignored the mail, leaving Hunter or Brick to open it.

Staring at the pile, he lifted the letters, and one by one, he put each letter on the desk. There was some bill or other. When he came to a different-looking letter with his name on the front, just Smokey, he paused.

It had Ava's handwriting.

Turning it over, he quickly tore into it and reached inside. A single letter and a picture. He looked at the image. It reminded him a little of the baby picture Abriana had shown around when she was pregnant.

What the fuck?

He opened up the piece of paper to see they were blood test results. Scanning over them, he saw the marking for pregnant. He flicked the letter over and spun it around as the writing was upside down.

Smokey,

I'm pregnant. I don't want or expect anything from you. I didn't plan this, and it's news to me as well.

Ava.

What the ever-loving fuck?

That was it.

She had seen him yesterday. He'd been outside her house all fucking night, and she'd sent him a letter. It wasn't even a detailed letter. This was basic.

Getting to his feet, he stormed out of his office. The men and women were putting the room back to rights with the few pieces of furniture he hadn't destroyed. The rest was being taken out.

He stared at the mess and it hit him.

He was going to be a father.

Ava had told him in a letter but ... he was going to be a dad. Responsible for another human being. Not that was any different from the club, but a boy or girl of his own flesh and blood.

"You okay, Smokey?" Swallow asked, coming toward him.

He looked at the woman who worked as a porn star for them in the shack.

"I'm going to be a dad."

This had the entire room pausing. The air felt still. No one moved a muscle. If this was a movie, it would be like everyone had pressed pause. What were they waiting for?

He lifted up the picture. "I'm ... a dad. I'm going to be a dad." Holy shit, he was going to be responsible for a little baby. The revelations kept on happening, repeating themselves, and each time he thought about it, the fear began to build.

A baby was a huge deal.

"Congratulations," Hunter said.

The brothers came around to congratulate him.

"Ava told you in a letter?" Big Dick asked.

Smokey stared down at the image and the paperwork. Why hadn't she told him when she saw him? Was this just another sign from her that they were well and truly over?

"Yeah, she wrote to me."

"Dude, that shit is cold," Elijah said.

"At least she told you," Ugly Beast said. "She didn't have to."

"That's why she was at the bakery. She's opening it back up. She's not going to leave." The anger he'd had moments ago evaporated. A kid. He'd forgotten about the risk he'd taken in coming inside her.

A baby. He'd knocked her up.

It hadn't been his intention to get her pregnant, but now that she was, he was so fucking happy. They were going to have a baby.

"I'm going to be a daddy," he said.

The club erupted in cheers.

Smokey apologized to each of the brothers. He shouldn't have attacked them, but Hunter's words had rung in his head, and it had set him off. When it came to Ava, he didn't know what to do to win her back. She was the only person he wanted, and yet, she was lost to him. At least that was how it had felt.

With a baby, he had a chance. She was bound to him in some way.

"I've got to go."

No one stopped him as he left the clubhouse. He got on his bike, shoving the paperwork in his pocket.

Smokey arrived at her house in record time, and much to his surprise, she wasn't inside.

His next stop was the bakery.

The town was busy once again, but he noticed the bakery still wasn't open, however, he saw the lights on inside.

After parking his bike across the street, he walked across the road and knocked on the window. Ava was wiping down one of the counters. She hesitated.

He pulled out the ultrasound picture and slammed it against the glass. "We need to talk."

This got her moving.

She unlocked the door, stepping back for him to enter. She closed and locked the door behind him.

The scent of lemon was heavy in the air, and he watched as she walked around the counter.

"You've fixed the place up good. When do you start?" he asked.

"You want to talk about my work?"

"No, I want to talk about this, but I figured we could build to it."

She smiled. "I start tomorrow. I'm going to look at hiring someone for when I'm ready to give birth."

"You're not leaving?" he asked.

"It seems wrong to leave now." She put a hand to her stomach. "I don't want any trouble, Smokey. I can take care of myself, and I don't see this baby as a punishment. I see it as a blessing." She smiled, and how he'd missed it.

He watched her, trying to memorize it.

Seeing her smile was fucking everything to him.

"I understand if you don't want to have anything to do with our child."

"I want to be involved."

"You do?"

He chuckled. "What makes you think I don't?"

"We never talked about kids or a future. I figured

you wouldn't be interested in having a baby with me."

He put his hands on his hips. "I was a little pissed that you sent me this letter instead of telling me. You knew yesterday when we talked. Why didn't you tell me?"

She tucked her short hair behind her ear. Another reminder that he'd fucked up. Until she grew the length back, he was going to be forever reminded of what he'd done wrong with her.

"I didn't know how you'd react. I was scared that you'd be angry or that you might ask me to get rid of it." She put her hand protectively over her stomach. "I love our child already. I don't want to—"

"No," he said. "I would never ask you to get rid of our child. I want to be part of their world. Boy or girl."

"I don't want us to get back together," she said.

He nodded. "Fine."

"I know this is going to be hard."

He shook his head. "It doesn't have to be. One day, Ava, you will realize how sorry I am. How much I love you."

"No, don't say stuff like that. I don't want you to say that."

"It's true."

Tears fell down her cheeks. He wanted to take her into his arms and promise her it was going to be okay.

She shook her head and looked up toward the ceiling. "I don't want to cry anymore. After everything that has happened, you can't tell me you love me. With what happened, it's not that easy."

"I know." He tried to speak gently with her. From now on, he would never raise his voice, never speak harshly to her. The club would come first, but she would take priority. "I don't expect you to trust me. I will earn it back." He looked down at the picture again. "Please, let me be involved. I want to get to know my kid. I'd love to share this experience with you."

She smiled. "Okay. I have another ultrasound in a couple of weeks. This one will determine how far along I actually am, and when they believe I'll be giving birth. You're invited to come."

"Can I take you?" he asked.

She shook her head. "No, I think it best I meet you at the hospital. The appointment's at ten o'clock."

"I'll be there. Can I ... can I touch you?" He looked at her stomach.

"There's not a lot to feel, but if you want to, then yes." She stayed perfectly still and he closed the distance between them.

Slowly, he cupped her stomach, staring into her eyes. There was a slight swelling.

"Can you feel it?" he asked. "The baby?"

"I don't know. Sometimes I think so. I don't know if it's too soon for a baby to be felt." She laughed. "It's kind of surreal, you know? All of this. I've wanted a baby for so long."

"You have?"

"Yeah. Derek didn't want one."

"Your ex is an asshole. You're going to make an amazing mother."

"I hope so." She laughed.

She looked at him, and the last few months evaporated. He stared into her eyes, and she had the same expression on her face. Full of love, hope. He wanted it. Craved it. How had he taken this for granted before?

Ava looked away first. The mood was broken.

"If there's ever anything you need, call me, okay? I will be here. I want to offer you protection as well."

"It's fine, Smokey. I've got it handled. A lot of women handle pregnancy without a man or a woman around. I can handle it."

"I don't want you to."

"It's not your choice." She pulled away. "I need to get back to work."

"I do love you, Ava. I will make you realize I'm not just saying it."

"I think it's time you go."

Chapter Fifteen

The bakery started out slowly when she finally reopened. At first, people just walked on by the shop, until it was like they eventually realized she was officially reopened. The moment they did, people came in and out. The atmosphere wasn't the same as before. When she first opened, people talked and welcomed her to town, offered to help or gave her hints and tips of the kind of customers she'd like. Who to stay away from.

This was different but at least it was business.

By lunchtime, she was exhausted and nearly sold out. She did make sure she had a backup supply of cookies and muffins.

No one had responded to her ad for a bakery assistant she'd placed in the paper and in several shops. She hoped someone would respond locally, otherwise, she'd have to look further out.

When Raven, Brick, and Kinky entered her shop, she tensed up. No one else was inside and she folded her arms. "I need to ask you to leave." She wouldn't look at them.

"We're not here to cause trouble."

"I've very politely put up a sign asking that no member of the MC comes inside my shop. I'd appreciate it if you leave." She'd written out the sign and hated herself for doing it. The memory of how they'd entered, the attack, being dragged to the club's basement… It had been too much.

She wasn't a strong woman and had no way of fighting them off. They were the ones with all the control.

"We heard about the baby," Raven said. "We wanted to offer you congratulations and our sincerest apologies."

Ava looked up. "I don't accept them. You can't get away with doing what you want when you want to. Not with me. I was your friend, and that was how you treated me. I've got nothing more to say to you. Now, if you want to have baked goods, then send someone else in. I don't want any of you, nor Smokey, in my shop. Ever again."

Her hands clenched into tight fists.

Raven nodded. "We understand."

They each left the shop, and once they had, she breathed a little easier. Was it easy? Her heart raced, and she rushed to the shop door, flicking the lock into place and turning the sign to say she was closed.

She immediately went to her office, closing the door, dropping down into her chair, covering her face with her hands, and sobbing. The tears fell hard and fast. Uncontrollably. Each time she thought she was getting a little better, something would happen to make her realize she wasn't getting anywhere.

Staying in Fort Clover was going to be hard enough. Seeing them every day. Allowing her child to go to the clubhouse. She needed to be able to be around them again. Until then, she was going to have to be strong.

She grabbed some tissues, wiping her nose and taking some fresh ones for her eyes. She composed herself before heading back out.

Opening the shop up once again, she waited for customers to come in. By three o'clock, she was sold out and about to close shop when a dark brunette rushed inside, knocking her over.

"Crap, shit, crap, I'm so sorry," she said. "I know you don't stay open too late because let's face it, your baked goods are the bomb, but I didn't mean to run you over like that."

Ava chuckled. The woman helped her up. She vaguely recognized her but didn't know her name.

"It's quite all right. I was about to close up. I don't have anything to offer you."

"Oh, that's okay. I'm vegan. I don't eat anything with animal products in."

"Okay," Ava said.

"I was wondering if you still had a job opening?" she asked.

"What's your name."

"Oh, it's Harlow Erickson. I'm nineteen years old, and I would really love to work here."

Ava frowned and looked at Harlow. The woman was beautiful. She had thick, gorgeous, brown hair. Her arms were decorated in ink.

"Crap, I messed up. I left it too late, didn't I?" Harlow asked.

"It's not that. Honestly. You're the first person to apply."

"Does that mean I have the job?" Harlow asked.

"You're a vegan."

"So?"

"I bake with non-vegan products. Butter, eggs, cheeses, meat."

"I can still serve, right?" Harlow asked. "You bake. I serve. I don't mind. I just don't want to eat it." She smiled.

Ava found her charming in a strange way.

"Er, I'm not sure how this is going to work. You see, I'm pregnant."

"Congratulations. I totally love babies." Harlow rubbed at her stomach. "I bet she or he is going to be a cutie."

Ava laughed, she just couldn't help herself. "Are you like this all the time?"

"Oh, you mean, hyper, talk too much, and generally weird? Yeah, I'm like it all the time." She shrugged. "The curse of living with six brothers who are all assholes. They're not, but you get the drill. Believe me, you have to learn to stand out."

"I really don't know."

"Please, I won't let it interfere with selling. I'd like to learn as much as I can so I can also implement some of the skills within my own baking."

"You bake?" Ava asked.

"Yeah. I happen to love being in the kitchen. My mom went a little bitchy when I told her I was vegan. She refused to cook for me, so I fed myself until she realized I can eat as good as anyone else."

Ava was intrigued.

"You're curious."

"I don't know how you can bake without, you know, milk, cream, eggs, butter."

Harlow laughed. "A lot of people think that way. I've adapted. Believe me. I'm happier for it."

"You're hired," Ava said. She didn't even know why she said it. Asking for a vegan to work with her seemed like the biggest mistake of her life. She had never considered baking anything for a vegan.

Harlow let out a scream. "Hell, yes, I'm so excited. You're the best, Ava." Before she knew what was happening, she was pulled into the young woman's arms. "I will be the best assistant you've ever had. I promise." Next, she was kissed on the cheek.

Her enthusiasm was infectious.

"I've got to clean up."

"How about I start today? I love to clean. I can clean anything. Honestly."

"Okay, why not."

For the next two hours, she showed Harlow

around the small shop, teaching her how to clean certain items, washing everything down, keeping it sanitary. All the while, Harlow filled in the silent spots, talking about everything and nothing. She'd never known a woman to talk so much.

By the time they were finished, Ava was so tired, but Harlow looked wired.

"Do you want to have dinner with me at the diner?" Harlow asked.

"You can eat at the diner?"

"Yep. It's not hard to do."

"But, your diet?"

Harlow blew out a raspberry. "It's not important. I know what I can eat. Come on, my treat for making me have a really awesome day."

Ava smiled. "Sure. I'd love to."

They walked together toward the diner. She followed behind Harlow who found a seat for them in the crowded diner.

"Can I ask you something?" Ava asked.

"Sure thing."

"Did Smokey put you up to this?"

"The MC dude?"

"Yeah."

Harlow frowned. "Put me up to what?"

"Coming and asking for a job. Trying to be my friend."

"Oh, no, absolutely not. I know Smokey, but we're not close." She wrinkled her nose. "One of my brothers is a member of the club."

Ava froze. "He is? Who?"

"He goes by Big Dick. He's the eldest son. Believe it or not, his real name is George." Harlow rolled her eyes. "Is that a problem? I saw the MC sign thing, but I'm not part of the club. I rarely see my brother. He stops by for the occasional holiday, but other than that, we rarely see him."

"It's fine. Just a surprise."

Harlow shrugged. "He looks scary with all of his tattoos and muscles and stuff, but he's a giant softie."

Their food came out.

"And you don't know Smokey?"

"I know him. Said a few words to him when I was a kid. Nothing else. Why?"

"I didn't know if he'd put you up to coming and seeing me, and you know…"

"Is Smokey the baby daddy?"

Ava cringed.

Harlow chuckled. "Oh, my, I didn't even think that old bastard had any feelings. The way people talk to him, it's like he's a robot or something. Holy shit. So he does walk and talk like a man?"

Ava forced a smile, but she felt her cheeks start to ache from the action.

"I'm sorry. That wasn't polite of me to say so, was it?"

"It's fine."

Harlow looked past her shoulder. "Speak of the devil and he appears."

Ava glanced behind her to see Smokey, Brick, Big Dick, Kinky, and a couple of the other brothers enter the diner.

Silence fell on the room for all of five seconds before everything started up.

Ava spun around and sat, looking at Harlow.

"He does know he's the baby daddy, right?"

"He knows."

"Is this a good thing?"

Ava shrugged and tensed up as Smokey put his hand on the back of her chair.

"What are you doing here, squirt?" Big Dick asked.

"I'm eating, or going to be eating with my new boss, asshole. You can carry on. We don't need you here," Harlow said.

Big Dick laughed.

"New boss?" Smokey asked.

"I hired her." Ava didn't dare look at him.

"Yep, I'm the new blushing assistant at Ava's. I'm so excited."

"You know she's a vegan, right?" Big Dick asked.

"Yes, she knows," Harlow said before she got a chance to respond. "It's not a big deal."

"It is. She bakes actual food."

"Vegan cooking is actual food. Ugh, you're such a jerk face. Fuck off."

"I'll tell Mom about your language."

"It would actually require you to be around to tell Mom. I'm surprised you even know what I look like." Harlow covered her face. "You're so embarrassing. Please, go away."

Big Dick laughed. "Hi, Ava."

"Hi," she said but didn't look at them.

No one spoke, and the silence between them became awkward.

"We're getting a table," Smokey said. "How are you feeling?"

"Good. We're going to enjoy some food, and then I'm heading home."

"I can take you," he said.

She shook her head. "I drove my car. I can take myself home. Thank you, though."

"Anything you need, Ava." He reached out as if to touch her.

Ava tensed up.

His hand clenched, and he turned away, walking past her table. The rest of his men followed.

"That looked uncomfortable. Was the baby consensual?" Harlow asked and then winced. "I might also warn you, I don't have much in the way of a filter. I say what I think. I hope that's not going to be a problem."

"It's not a problem, and with me and Smokey, it's complicated."

"He didn't force himself on you, did he?"

"No, of course not. Conceiving this baby was … wonderful."

"Good, I started to worry there."

She really needed to change the subject. "So, no filter."

"I say it like it is. It's why I lost my last job at the bank. I have no tact. I try to." She shrugged.

"Is this from living with a lot of brothers?"

"Nah, I think this one is just who I am. I can't change it." Harlow shrugged. "My mom says I'm never going to find a man who wants to go out with a woman who's always talking and saying shit they don't want to hear."

"What do you think?"

"My mom has been happily married to my dad for nearly thirty years. She says a lot of stuff, and he's still around. It can't be that bad. That earned me a nice whack around the back of the head." Harlow laughed. "My family is wonderful. We're the classic dysfunctional family."

"It sounds perfect," Ava said.

****

Smokey arrived at the appointment early with a bouquet of flowers. It was corny, he knew, but it was the best the florist had to offer. He'd talked to Abriana about the best way to win his woman back.

She'd said to give it time and attention.

Flowers were good. As were chocolate and food.

He stared around the parking lot. Ava had texted him five minutes ago to say she was leaving.

Leaning against his car, he waited for her.

The past couple of weeks had been slow. Big Dick and Hunter were still gathering as much information on the Twisted Bastards MC as they could. The few details he did have, he'd acted on. Creed owned two strip clubs and a brothel. Calling in a few favors from Carlos Santigo, he'd gotten all three places shut down and nice big fine for the trouble.

Smokey intended to take every single little bit of pleasure Creed found and make the bastard pay.

Slowly and painfully, he planned to bring the fucker down into the dirt, and then he'd crush them. Until he could accomplish his goal, he was content to tear the fucker apart.

Ava arrived twenty minutes later. She pulled up several cars away from him.

With the bouquet in hand, he walked toward her.

She looked up as he approached the car. "Good morning," he said.

Ava looked pale. Under her eyes was dark as if she hadn't gotten a lot of sleep the night before.

"Hey," she said.

"These are for you."

"They're beautiful. You really didn't have to get them for me."

"You're carrying my child. It's the least I could do." The flowers weren't as big of a hit as he'd hoped.

Later today, he had a necklace due for delivery at her house. Would that work any better?

"I saw them and wanted to get them for you."

"I appreciate them, Smokey. Thank you." She laid them gently in the backseat. "Are you ready?"

"As I'll ever be."

She walked beside him, and he wanted to touch her. Sleeping was the worst for him. All night, he stayed outside her house, and it was in the morning he slept, fitfully. He'd gotten used to her being in his bed.

"What do you think to … you know, the baby?" she asked.

"I can't wait to meet our guy or girl. I don't care what the sex is. Have you felt it move yet?" he asked.

"Not yet. I don't think. Sometimes I think I do, but then I can't be sure if it's wind. Crap, I can't believe I said that. That's so embarrassing."

"Our kid is making you fart. I can't wait to tell them that at their wedding."

Ava burst out laughing. "They're not even here yet and already you want to marry them off."

"I'm planning ahead, you know?"

She snorted. "You're so bad."

"And you like it." They got to the entrance of the hospital and Ava paused.

"Wow," she said. "It was so easy to forget."

"Ava?"

"No," she said. "I don't want to talk about it. Let's just get this appointment over with."

"I didn't mean to upset you," he said.

"I'm not upset."

She paused, looked at him, and then turned away. He wanted to stop her, but instead, he followed her toward what he assumed was the pregnancy ward. They entered a room with a lot of heavily pregnant women, plenty of kids walking around. Men looking like they wanted to escape.

Ava signed herself in at the reception and took a seat. He sat beside her.

The room was quiet apart from random whispers of *quiet*, *behave*, and *do something*.

Ava rested her hands on her thighs. The dress she wore molded to her tits and waist, but flared out at the hips, hiding her stomach.

Smokey put his hand on top of hers, knowing she wouldn't want to cause a scene.

Her hand shook beneath his, and he hated that he'd done this to them.

"You know, this wasn't on the top of my list of experiences," he said.

"No, I don't imagine it was."

He chuckled. "The club dominates everything. I never thought of having kids of my own."

"Did you ever want them?" she asked.

"I didn't even think about it. Not once. The club came first, and I'd have to trust a woman to want kids, which I never did."

"And you still don't trust me."

He squeezed her hand as she tried to pull away. "I trust you, Ava. I fucked up. I made a mistake, but I promise you I won't make that mistake again."

"Smokey, this really isn't the time."

"When are we ever going to get time?" he asked. "We've got a baby on the way."

She turned toward him. "You think I don't know that? I do, but talking about this in front of a room full of strangers isn't the time or place."

Smokey held her hand. "Let me make it up to you."

Ava tilted her head to the side. "You hurt me in so many ways, Smokey. You told them to. You packed my bag and was prepared to kill me." He looked at her, but she turned away. "That's not going to change with this baby."

He brought her fingers up to his lips and kissed her knuckles. "I love you, Ava. One day, you will see it too."

She opened her mouth as if to dispute him, but she didn't get a chance to as her name was called.

Holding her hand, he locked their fingers together, and they walked into the room. The doctor shook his hand, but he saw the hesitation, and he expected it. He hadn't removed his leather cut, and most people were put off by the club.

"Are you ready, Ava?" the doctor asked.

"Yes, this is my … the baby's father. Doctor McCarthy, I'd like you to meet Smokey."

He took note of the doctor's firm handshake. He gave as good as he got. There was no way he intended to be intimidated by the older man.

"It's a pleasure to meet you. Shall we get started? We're going to see how far along you are and if we can determine sex. Would you like to know?" he asked.

Ava shook her head. "I mean, unless you want to know?" She looked toward him.

"I'm happy with whatever you want to know."

She offered him a smile. "Then I just want to make sure my baby's healthy. Can we do that?"

"Of course, we can. This is a process though. Your baby still has some growing to do."

Ava nodded.

Smokey took the seat beside her as they prepared her. Ava lifted up her dress, she'd worn a small pair of loose shorts underneath that weren't visible on the outside, and he stared at her stomach. He noticed a slight roundness to her abdomen but nothing to indicate she was pregnant.

"It's a little cold, like last time."

Gel was squirted on her stomach, and then the doctor had some kind of probe. Anticipation ate away at him as the tip of the probe was placed on her stomach. He wanted to know if his baby was okay, but more importantly, mommy too.

"Ah, there we go. Let me get a few little measurements."

Smokey tuned him out as he looked at the screen. He couldn't make much out, but then the doctor turned the volume up, and sure enough, he could hear his son or daughter's heartbeat.

"Oh, my," Ava said. "That's the most precious sound in the world."

"Isn't it?" The doctor did some more dates and numbers. "You're about three months along, Ava. So, we're looking at a New Year baby, give or take. We'll know more details as the months go along. I couldn't determine sex yet, but these things take time."

Smokey listened as the doctor gave her a list of instructions. She had to rest, eat healthy, avoid certain foods. The list was endless.

"Intercourse is allowed," the doctor said.

"That's not necessary. We're not together."

The doctor looked at him, and his face stayed blank, not giving anything away. "Well, in case you both change your mind. You're allowed to have sex. It's one of the most asked questions couples with their first pregnancy ask me."

"Is that all?" Ava asked.

"Yes. I've given you the leaflets, and I think everything is all set. You can collect your images from reception and book your next appointment. As always, Ms. Sinclaire, it's a pleasure to see you."

Smokey shook the doctor's hand and turned to

leave.

At the reception desk, Ava was given the pictures and she booked another appointment.

Smokey took the picture from her and flicked it open to see their baby. Their child. He had no idea what it was. There wasn't even a clear picture. It was so small.

Hearing the heartbeat, now that had been precious.

They exited the hospital together, and he took her hand, leading her to the car. "Have lunch with me?"

"I don't think that's a good idea."

"We've both just heard our baby's heartbeat for the first time. Don't you want to enjoy that?"

Ava nibbled on her lip.

"I promise to be on my best behavior. It's nearly lunchtime. Come on, Ava, let me take care of you."

"I can eat," she said. "Meet you at the diner?"

"I'll follow you."

He wasn't letting her out of his sight. One bad move and she'd run. Ava smiled at him and climbed into her car. He rushed to his own, pulling out of the parking lot and following her.

His cell phone rang and he saw it was the clubhouse.

"What's up?" he asked.

"I wanted to see how your first baby daddy experience was going?" Hunter asked.

"All good so far." Ava was driving slowly, and he stayed close behind her. "I'm heading into town to get some lunch."

"Er, Smokey, we got a tip. Creed's been spotted in town with a couple of boys."

"Shit, fuck, shit." He clenched his hands around the steering wheel. There was nothing he could do about it now. "I can't do this. I wanted to take Ava out to lunch. Gather a few of the boys up and come into town. A show of force."

"Okay, will do. Also, we've got a few problems at the shack."

"Where it rains it pours. What could be the fucking problem at the shack?" he asked. He didn't see why there had to be a problem. A bunch of people fucked for the camera. Not a whole lot of drama or death.

"It would appear someone has given the actors bad food. Vomit and shit are all over the place. We've had to close the place down. I've got a cleaning crew working on it. Billy the cameraman doesn't understand it as they don't have any food on set. They don't even celebrate a good clean wrap. His words, not mine."

"You think someone poisoned them?" Smokey asked.

"It would make sense. We hit out at Creed, he's going to hit out at us."

They earned a good living off those porn films alone. The dirtier the men and women were willing to go, the higher the paycheck.

"I want everyone tested. I want to know why they were sick. Then I want to know what they were sick with."

"Already on it. Until we know what went on, it's shut down. Also, Santigo called, he's got another run."

"We did one for him less than a month ago."

"I know, but it's up to you to handle that business," Hunter said.

"Fuck, fine. I'll deal with it. Make sure you send a check to the hospital for Ava's medical bills. I don't want her to worry about anything."

"The woman's loaded."

"I'm taking care of it." He wanted to contribute more to this than his sperm. He honestly didn't know what kind of dad he was going to be.

Chapter Sixteen

"Your baby's a cutie," Harlow said.

Ava laughed. "You can't tell all of that from a picture."

"I can't tell, but you know I'm blessed with being able to read people." Harlow took the ultrasound photo and touched it. "Yep, he's going to be a cutie, and all the girls are going to swoon."

Ava took the photo back. "Not that I disagree, because I don't, but I really hope you're right. Not that it matters if he's not a cutie. I just want him to be happy and healthy." Ava touched her stomach. It was starting to show a more roundness. The sickness was still part of her daily life as well. The mornings sucked big time, and each time she stared down at the toilet bowl with no one to rub her back as she vomited, it only served to remind her she was all alone.

"Hey, where did you go?" Harlow asked, shaking her hand back and forth in front of her face.

"I didn't go anywhere." She snorted. "Don't worry. I'm still very much here."

"What made you sad?"

Ava shrugged. "A lot of things."

"Does this have to do with the baby daddy?" Harlow asked.

"A little."

"What is the deal with you guys? Don't get me wrong, I heard all the gossip. How the town believed you'd been blacklisted and all that fun stuff, but you're still here. Anyone blacklisted by the Bastards don't tend to stick around for long, and it doesn't look to me like there's much of a problem with him."

Ava waited. Harlow had a tendency to keep on talking. She just ran on and on and on. She didn't mind it. Harlow filled in the silence that only enforced the truth of how lonely and isolated she felt. There were times she could pretend her life wasn't empty, but this wasn't one of those times.

"Have you even seen the way Smokey acts around you?"

Ava heard the oven beeping in the background and shook her head before answering. "No, I don't."

Harlow moved to the doorway. They didn't have any customers yet.

Going to the oven, she checked over the cookies and was somewhat impressed. Harlow had asked her to attempt a vegan cookie recipe. She had tried it, and now she was surprised. The next true test would be in the tasting.

"It's okay. I keep an eye on everything for the two of us. Smokey can't take his eyes off you. He's like a lost little puppy. I'm not joking about this. If you watched him, you'd know he's obsessed with you."

Ava snorted. "I know for a fact that's not true."

"Why?"

She thought about the bruises, the beating. The aches she still got in her hand. The doctor had said that was all normal, but she couldn't help but feel something was missing from her life. Even though Harlow had a brother in the Hell's Bastards MC, she couldn't bring herself to talk to her about it. It didn't feel right. What happened between her and Smokey, along with the club, was secret. She wasn't going to abuse Smokey's trust even though he'd completely obliterated hers.

"Does this have to do with all the bruises you got? Is Smokey beating you?"

"Of course not."

"No, I just follow her around like a lost little puppy," Smokey said, making them both jump as he suddenly appeared behind Harlow, who had turned deathly white.

"Did you read the sign?" Harlow asked, her voice rising.

Ava tried not to laugh, but the look on her new friend's face was just priceless.

"I figured I could come and see Ava. I wanted to know if you'd like to go out to lunch?" Smokey asked.

"I can't leave the shop."

"Why not?" Both Smokey and Harlow asked.

She smiled. "Because this is still my shop and I still have to be here for the lunch rush."

"You saw me handle it just fine yesterday. I can do this, Ava. Please, let me show you."

Harlow was a hard worker. No doubt about it. She served beautifully. Her customers adored her.

"If you're sure. I just figured you'd want more … practice."

"No, I've got this. People love your food. Go and have some yourself. Hopefully, it will make you smile, unlike some people around here."

Ava glanced at Smokey. She didn't want to make a scene. "Would you like me to bring you anything back?"

"Sure. I'd like that. You know what I don't eat," Harlow said, winking at her. She stepped further into the room, putting herself away from Smokey. "Can I try one of these?" She pointed at the new chocolate chips.

"Sure."

Harlow took one, and Ava waited, watching the woman take a bite.

"Oh, fuck me, that's so good."

Ava burst out laughing. "Really?"

"Yeah, you have got to sell these. Wow. Can I take another?"

"Yes. Put them in a basket as a taster, please," she said.

"Why?"

"I want to see what other people think of them before I offer them up for sale."

"You don't need to do that. They're that good, but I will do as you ask, boss."

Ava nodded. She turned to grab her bag, but Smokey stopped her.

"I'm paying. You don't need to worry about anything."

She'd hoped to stall. For some imaginary problem to light up and cause some issues. Nothing.

She followed behind Smokey, leaving the sanctity of the bakery behind her.

He only had his bike and the idea of riding that thing would give her the perfect excuse to cut this lunch short.

Smokey didn't go to the bike. He turned down the street and they headed toward the diner.

It was just before lunchtime, so as they arrived, there were plenty of seats to take. He waited for her to take a seat before he sat down.

She glanced around the diner. There were a few customers, but not many. She had no doubt it wouldn't be long before it completely filled up and people were struggling to get seats.

"How have you been?" Smokey asked.

"Good. You?"

"Good."

She reached out for the menu and started to glance over each item when she noticed Smokey was just watching her. "You're not going to look?"

"I know what I want to order."

"Oh, I haven't been here that often. I tend to cook

for myself. Do you know what's good here?"

"I do. Do you want me to order for you?"

"Yes, please." She'd scanned part of the menu, and it was like her mind had decided to not understand anything in front of her. The words were all clear. No problem there, it was everything else.

The waitress approached, carrying her notepad and pen, along with a big smile.

"Smokey, so good to see you here."

"Hi, Olive. You okay?"

"I can't complain. You know how it is. Busy man, busy life. What can I get you two?" Olive asked.

"We'll take your burger house special with plenty of fries. Make sure to do one of your veggie burgers to go for Harlow. You know what she's like."

Olive wrote it down. "Coming right up. Harlow's will be ready if you give me a five-minute warning of when you're leaving."

"Great," Smokey said.

"I'll be back."

"Burger house specials?"

"They're really good."

Ava nodded. This was so awkward. She'd never felt this way when they'd been dating. She had no idea what the problem was.

"Please, don't be nervous around me."

Smokey's hands were on the table. The tips of his fingers relaxed together.

"I'm fine. I'm a little surprised about your visit, but I'm fine."

"Do you think if you keep saying that you might believe it?"

Ava chuckled. "Look, this is hard, and I'm trying."

"I know."

She put her hand on her stomach. "Harlow thinks our baby is going to be a cutie. She also thinks it might be a he."

"Boy or girl, our baby is going to be a looker."

"You think?"

"If they're anything like their mother, then yes."

"Smokey, don't. I know I'm not a looker or anything. Please, don't insult me like that."

He reached out, taking her hand. She hated how nice that felt. His touch surrounding her, making her feel so many different emotions. None of them had anything to do with hate or shame.

She … missed him.

Damn it. She missed him so much.

Ava pulled her hand away.

"I know that asshole ex of yours did a number on you. What I said that … day. I lied. Everything I said about you was a lie."

"We don't have to do this."

"We do. We're going to have a baby together, and fuck me, Ava, I'm going to need all the help I can get. You think I don't know how messed up I am? What I did? What I caused?"

Ava felt her tears well.

"I took a lifetime of betrayal and I assumed you were exactly the same. That's on me. I fucked up big time."

"I really don't want to talk about this." Being out in the open, talking to him about that kind of pain, she wouldn't be able to contain her emotions for too long.

He sighed.

Olive saved them from more pain as she brought out their food. She'd never been more grateful for an interruption.

The moment the plates were in front of her, she

understood why it was the house special. Food was everywhere. Burgers with two, or did she count three burgers? Lots of lettuce, tomato, cheese, and sauce leaked out of the sides. It looked like a precarious leaning tower. That wasn't all. Macaroni and cheese was also on the plate, with a large order of fries.

Smokey didn't reach for his food though. He took her hand, running his thumb across her knuckles. "I know sorry isn't going to cut it but one day soon, we're going to have to have that talk."

Ava forced herself to look at him. "I know, but I don't want to have that talk in a diner with people present."

He agreed. "Enjoy."

With their conversation, her appetite had waned. The amount of food was too much to send back.

Picking up her fork, she scooped up some macaroni and took a bite. It was so good. Completely unhealthy food, but it was so good, and strangely enough, exactly what she craved. She didn't know how it happened, but she had finished her food in record time. The fries, macaroni, and burgers were all gone, while Smokey still had some food on his plate.

"I didn't realize I was so hungry."

Smokey chuckled. "I love a woman with an appetite."

"That was so good." She rubbed at her lips with a napkin, not that there were any leftovers to wipe away. She leaned back and put a hand to her stomach.

"Good?"

"Really, really good." She smiled as he finished off his food.

"Do you want dessert?"

"No. Absolutely not. I don't even know how I'm going to be able to move when I head back to the shop."

Smokey chuckled. "It feels good to feed you."

Ava didn't say anything.

Olive came back to fill his coffee. The scent wasn't making her queasy, but she settled on some iced tea to help her. The fruitier the better.

"So how is everything going with Harlow?" he asked.

Ava was slightly surprised by the change in conversation, but she welcomed it. They would have the *real* talk soon, but until then, she was happy to play it safe.

"She's doing really good. I adore her."

"Big Dick says she does nothing but talk and can be an irritating bitch." Smokey winced.

Ava shrugged. "I love that about her. I don't have to fill in the blanks. I'm not a very talkative person anymore."

"That's my fault," he said.

"Look, Smokey, I'm just … my head is full with a lot of things going on. It's not always about you. I hope you understand that." She tried to smile. It was always about him, but she didn't want to talk about it.

There was no way he wanted or needed to hear how she stayed up all night thinking about the women he was screwing. He didn't need to know how she hoped one day she could forget all about what happened. Nor did he need to know how she wished he loved her. He said he did, but she didn't believe it.

"How is the club?" she asked.

"We're doing good." He sat up and leaned forward. "Actually, I wanted to let you know I won't be around much next week. I've got to take care of some club business in the city. I was wondering when I came back if you'd be interested in doing some baby shopping."

"Baby shopping?" she asked.

"You know, a stroller, crib, breastfeeding stuff."

Her cheeks heated. "You've been thinking about this?"

"I … figured it would be nice to know what we want to do. Breastfeeding is good for the baby, or so I've read."

She laughed. "I was going to breastfeed."

"Good. Good."

Ava glanced down at the time and saw how late it was getting. "I really need to be getting back."

"Right, of course." He signaled the waitress for them to start finishing Harlow's order.

Smokey paid, refusing to let her.

He walked her back to the bakery. She held Harlow's food. It was awkward as she waited.

She looked at Smokey, and he leaned in close only to take a step back. "I'll see you when I get back."

She didn't say anything, instead, watching him go.

****

"How's Ava?" Raven asked.

Smokey turned to her, but he didn't want to talk. "Fine."

"Look, I know you hate me."

"No, Raven. You're wrong. I don't hate you. I can't hate you."

"After what I did?"

Smokey checked to see the loading dock before he gave her his full attention. "You can try to take the blame for what went down, but it's not on you. It's on me. I'm the one who told you to do what you did. You can't blame yourself. I'm sorry Ava won't talk to you."

Raven quickly looked away, but he saw the pain in her eyes. She thought she wasn't easy to read, but he knew.

"I miss her," Raven said. "I haven't been good at making friends. Since it all happened, Abriana won't have me around either. I lost the two friends I thought I had."

He didn't say anything as it was once again, all his fault.

"How is the pregnancy?"

"Good. The baby appears healthy."

"Will you both be getting back together?"

"Raven, I really don't want to talk about it." The last of product was unloaded and Smokey stepped forward, shaking the mafia man's hand. A brown envelope was given to him, and he took it, turning on his heel and leaving.

His men were already on their bikes, and Raven was to the left, straddling hers. She refused to stay at home.

Now he understood why. If Abriana wasn't seeing her, nor Ava, Raven didn't have anyone else. She didn't have anything outside of the club.

Once they were out from the drop-off, they took to the open road. Forty minutes later, they arrived at an abandoned warehouse.

He, Raven, and Hunter, walked inside.

Carlos Santigo was waiting for them, a large bag by his side. He hung up his cell phone as they entered. "In record time."

"If you plan to stitch us up, you better know I'll take you down with me. I've played this dance before."

"Drago said you'd be a pain and completely untrustworthy."

"You people broke my trust."

"You people." Carlos glanced over them, lingering on Raven. "You have a woman here. Is she some kind of gift?"

"Fuck you, asshole," Raven said.

Smokey chuckled. "A gift. I don't owe you shit."

Carlos continued to look at Raven.

"What's the matter? Can't stand a woman being here?"

"I can. It's just … unusual."

Raven snorted. "Why don't you try to pretend your women have brains for themselves? You'll be pleasantly surprised. What the fuck are we doing dealing with this asshole?"

"You were there at the drop?" Carlos asked.

Raven rounded Smokey and took a step toward Carlos. "My ass sat on my bike, riding your product across the city, hotshot. Believe me, I can do a hell of a lot more than that."

One of Carlos's guards reached out as if to touch her, and Raven reacted. She slammed her elbow against the man's face, dropping him.

Within seconds, guns were raised and Smokey had enough entertainment. Any other time in his life, he would've allowed Raven to have her fun, but he had a woman waiting for him back home.

She's not waiting for you.

Fuck.

Just another reminder of what he'd lost.

Ava wasn't waiting for him, but he wanted her.

Pulling Raven behind him, he pointed his gun at Carlos. "We didn't cause this."

Carlos smiled and signaled for his men to lower their weapons. "Here is your payment. It's a pleasure doing business with you." He turned on his heel and walked away.

Smokey checked over the money, seeing it was all there.

He was going to have to get Ugly Beast to call Drago. He was growing tired of the whiplash Carlos was causing.

"I'm sorry," Raven said.

"Don't apologize. The guy is a fucking asshole." Smokey divided the cash between them all. They'd bring it back together at the clubhouse, equal it out, and then they'd be on their way.

They left the warehouse, climbed onto their bikes, and took to the road, riding well into the deep of night, only arriving back at the clubhouse when the sun had started to come up.

The guys were waiting at church. The money was distributed, and with nothing else to discuss, they all went their separate ways.

Straddling his bike, he only had to wait a few seconds before Ugly Beast came out, putting a hand on his bike.

Smokey stared at his friend, shocked he would even dare to touch his bike.

"I don't think it's a good idea you going out," Ugly Beast said.

"Get your fucking hands off my bike. I'm going to go and see my woman."

"Smokey, you've been without sleep for nearly forty-eight hours. You're not going to be any good to us nearly dead."

"I'll rest when I want to. You're riding to Abriana. Why can I go to Ava?"

Ugly Beast winced. "Because my wife is going to let me into my house and snuggle up close to her. Ava's not going to let you through the front door."

Smokey snorted. "I can't believe you just said *snuggle*. All the guys are going to hear about it. You're not living it down."

"Damn it, Smokey, I'm not kidding."

"And you think I am? I'm going to my woman. I haven't seen her and I want to. Get the fuck off me. I mean it." He glared at Ugly Beast, ready to beat the shit out of the guy if he continued to get in his way.

"I'm following behind you."

Smokey rolled his eyes, but he didn't give Ugly Beast a chance to catch up with him.

He rode all the way to her house, breaking every single speed limit. By the time he arrived, it was close to eight o'clock, and he was so fucking tired.

Rather than linger on his bike, he parked in her driveway.

Ugly Beast had caught up, and he wasn't too far behind.

Ignoring him, he walked right up to Ava's door and knocked.

She didn't have to take him in.

He wouldn't blame her for pushing his ass out.

Ava opened the door.

Her blonde locks were down. The shortness of them hit him in the gut.

"Smokey?" She looked, pale and he noticed perspiration on her brow.

"Is everything okay?"

"I … I had to see you. I've just come back from a run. Ugly Beast is following my ass, and I really want to beat the living crap out of him. Can I … crash here?"

"You want to sleep in my house?" she asked.

This was a big mistake. He should apologize for interrupting, but instead, he nodded. He should turn away.

"Sure. Of course." Ava stepped back and she surprised him by letting him inside her house.

She'd changed the locks, and he had no choice

but to destroy the key he'd taken weeks ago, or was it months ago now? No, it was months ago.

The time with Ava blended all together.

Ava closed and locked the door. He was tempted to give Ugly Beast the finger, but it wasn't appropriate.

She rubbed at her temple. "Er, do you want to … I don't know, go for a shower? Change?"

"I could use a shower."

His stomach chose that moment to growl.

"If you go and shower. I'll make you some food."

"Ava, are you okay?" He noticed she swayed a bit, and then her hand went to her mouth.

She dashed past him and he followed her. She bent over the kitchen sink and threw up.

He wrapped her hair in his fist and he missed the length.

Your fault.

All of this is your fault.

Smokey held her hair out of the way as she continued to vomit.

"I'm so sorry about this," she said, seconds later. She cleaned up the mess and he kept her hair pinned back. She washed her mouth out standing up, and he had no choice but to let her go.

"How long have you had to deal with that?" he asked.

"I've been enjoying the sickness for a few weeks now." She shrugged. "The curse of being pregnant. I'll do myself some dry toast and all will be fine. You go and shower. I'll make you some breakfast."

"You don't have to do that."

"Go, Smokey. I got this. I've been throwing up, feeding myself, and working at the bakery without any help. I can keep on doing it."

"Just because you've been doing it doesn't make

it right."

She folded her arms. "I'm happy to keep on doing it. Please, go and shower."

He hesitated but her stance spoke volumes, and he had no choice but to do as she asked.

Smokey remembered where the shower was. He also found some of his clothes still in the drawer where he'd left them last time. Why hadn't she thrown them out?

He took the fastest shower, rinsing off the days of grime and sweat from being out on the road. He was so fucking tired, but being in Ava's house, he'd become wired.

She was in the kitchen making him some food.

Clean and refreshed, he changed into some clothes and made his way downstairs. He hung his jacket up beside her coat and held the smelly clothes in his fist.

Ava was frying him some breakfast as he entered. She finished putting the eggs into the pan and turned toward him. "I'll take them."

She grabbed the clothes and stepped back, disappearing to her laundry room. He'd forgotten how much he missed this place.

Ava came back. "Have a seat."

She was no longer in her pajamas, having changed into a pair of sweatpants and a shirt with lots of holes in it. Her hair was tied up at the back of her neck.

To him, she still looked like the sexiest woman in the world. He wanted to tell her so but kept it to himself.

"I hope you enjoy breakfast." She put out a plate full of tomatoes, sausage, bacon, eggs, and lots of toast.

He glanced over at her plate. She had a single slice of dried toast. She hadn't even spread it with butter.

"I don't like this," he said.

"I'm fine. It's why I can enjoy a really good

lunch." She nibbled at her toast and he saw she drank a glass of water.

"You're really content to eat just that?"

"It settles my stomach." She patted her abdomen. "I'm hoping one day he or she will let me eat something more substantial. I like to start my day with a good meal."

"This is really good." He felt guilty for being able to eat, but he shoveled the food in, thankful for something good. On the road, he'd eaten his fair share of greasy diner food, and not all of it was good.

Ava finished her toast and water. "I've got to head out to the bakery. I'll be back later tonight." She reached into her pocket. "If you'd lock up and hand me back the key."

"Ava, you're going to trust me with this?"

"I don't have a choice. I could kick you out, but that seems mean. Besides, you're my baby's daddy. I'm not going to be mean." She forced a smile. "I hope you feel better."

Smokey wanted to say something to get her to stay, to talk to him, but once again, he drew a blank. He had nothing good to say and Ava, she needed her space.

The moment he heard the door close, her entire house felt so empty, and he hated it. He finished his breakfast. Cleaned the dishes and wiped down her kitchen. He walked upstairs, and rather than use the spare bedroom, he didn't even look at it. He went straight to her room. Lying down on her bed, he breathed her in, and for a few short hours, he could pretend she was right there with him.

Chapter Seventeen

"I don't need anything too big," Ava said, several days later.

She stood in the baby store with Smokey. They had yet to settle on a single crib. She'd already started to decorate the spare bedroom in her spare time. When her baby arrived, she wanted to be ready. Being a busy businesswoman, she knew how little time she'd have when it finally arrived.

"It's not that big. What if we have a large baby? You're going to want room for them to grow."

"How big do you think this baby is going to be?" she asked, laughing.

"I don't know." He reached out as if to touch her stomach and held himself back.

They stood in a store with all kinds of couples around them.

"Do you … do you want to touch it?" she asked.

He looked into her eyes and shrugged.

She chuckled. Ava didn't give herself time to regret her decision. Reaching for his hand, she placed it on her stomach. The last few days, the weather had been changing between cold and hot. Today was one of the last days of the warm weather and by the end of the week, a snowstorm had been forecast.

Ava tensed up as Smokey's hand curled around her protruding stomach.

"See. It's not so big right now."

Smokey stared into her eyes.

The world faded away.

"Can I help you pick something out?" the sales assistant asked.

"Fuck off." Smokey growled at the man to make him leave.

She gasped and found it amusing as the man quickly rushed off as if he was being chased by some kind of monster.

The world came back in full focus and Smokey cursed.

"You didn't need to do that."

"Do you have any idea how many times I've wanted to touch you?"

His words brought the image of him touching her all over. She wasn't disgusted or hurt. Her body came to life.

"If you want to, all you need to do is ask."

"I fucked up, Ava, big time."

She stepped away.

"I don't want to have to ask to touch you." He came toward her, resting his palm on her shoulder. "There are days all I can think about is touching you. Holding you in my arms."

Most nights, she woke up feeling the same way. She didn't tell him that though. "We need to make a decision on the crib and everything, Smokey."

He sighed.

They made their way around the store and finally, Ava saw the perfect one. It was an oak crib. Cushions lined the sides and it looked perfect.

Smokey organized everything. The furniture, unfortunately, didn't come pre-made. Boxes would arrive, which acquired assembly.

They sat down at a café, ordered some lunch, and Smokey smiled at her.

"What?"

"I'll build everything. You don't have a problem. We'll pick a room and get everything set up."

"I already have a room designed."

"You do?" he asked.

"Yes." She told him about the spare bedroom. "Didn't you see it when you slept there?"

"I used your sofa. It didn't seem right going upstairs."

"Oh, okay." Their food arrived. She'd settled on a salad bagel while Smokey went with cheese fries.

She took a bite of her food, feeling the hunger hit her hard.

They didn't talk, enjoying their food, and then Smokey paid the bill.

Once outside, Smokey held her hand as they walked toward the car. He opened the door and he settled her inside. Smokey surprised her when he took the seatbelt out of her hand and slid it into place.

"I can do that."

"I know. I don't want you to."

She smiled. She loved how attentive he'd become.

Ava truly believed she could become addicted to his touches.

He drove them back to her house, the radio filling the silence between them. It didn't feel awkward though. Ava relaxed, staring out of the window. Her bakery was closed for the first time in weeks. Ever since she hired Harlow, she'd been opening it more and more. The young woman fascinated her.

The way she talked all the time and shared her views on recipes. They talked nonstop about cooking. She loved her.

For the first time, she'd found a similar like-minded soul.

Back at her home, she glanced at Smokey. "Do you want to come in?" she asked. "I can show you what I've done with the bedroom."

Smokey was already unbuckling his seatbelt.

After climbing out of the car, she followed him into the house. He didn't have a key. He'd mailed it back through her letterbox after he let himself out and locked the house.

He was like an entirely different person. Sometimes, she wasn't entirely sure which part of him was real or not.

Smokey closed the door behind him. She slipped off her shoes, put her jacket and bag on the hook by the door, and went to the stairs.

He'd done the same and started to follow her up.

Opening the bedroom door, she stepped inside.

She'd stopped painting several days ago and there was no lingering smell because she'd kept the window open the entire time. Even as the weather had gotten cold, she'd simply donned a sweater.

"What do you think?" she asked.

She'd gone for neutral colors. A sunshine yellow that made her think of lemons. She'd found some little heart glow-in-the-dark stars that she'd put on the ceiling. The walls were plain as she couldn't draw at all.

"I'd love to have some pictures on the wall, you know. I thought about a tree, but I think plain works for now." She had a small chest of drawers that she'd struggled to assemble but she'd got it working. Abriana had asked Ugly Beast to come, and he'd tightened up the screws and attached it to the wall so it didn't move.

She could bake and cook, but decorating or assembling wasn't in her repertoire.

Clasping her hands together, she turned to look at Smokey and waited.

He touched the walls, saying nothing.

Did he hate it?

It was her house. She could decorate however she wanted to, but it was really important to her that he like it.

"You hate it?"

"No."

"What?" she asked.

"It looks amazing. I wish you'd let me do this for you. I don't like the thought of you decorating anything without me here."

She went to him, touching his arm. "It's fine. I don't mind doing some painting. It gave me something to do." She'd been thinking about him, wondering what he was doing, imagining all the women who wanted him.

There were plenty of women at the club who would love to be with him.

"What don't you like about it?" she asked.

If he really didn't like it, she'd change it for him. They were both having a baby after all. They weren't together, but that didn't mean she couldn't compromise.

She knew how to do it all.

"It just hit me. We're going to have a baby."

Ava frowned. "It has only just hit you?"

"You know what I mean. Sure, I saw the ultrasound image and everything, but this is real. There is no backing out of this. We've made a baby, and one day soon, we're going to be able to hold it."

He put his hand on her stomach and she covered his with hers. "I know what you mean. Some days, I find it all a little surreal, but I love it. I really do. I want this baby so much."

Smokey cupped her cheek and brought her in close. Her heart started to race and heat flooded her pussy. Need consumed her. She glanced down at his lips.

Would it hurt to have one little kiss?

Ava watched him.

Kiss him.

Sucking the corner of her lip into her mouth, she

resisted the temptation.

Each second that passed, she convinced herself to step back and create some distance. She did neither.

She took a step close to him. Her body flush against his.

"Ava?"

She covered his mouth with the tips of her fingers. "Don't."

Gripping the back of his neck, she pulled him close, pressing her lips against his. Smokey let go of her stomach and he sank his fingers into her hair. With the other hand, he grasped her back, drawing her close.

The evidence of his arousal pressed against her swollen stomach.

In the back of her mind, she kept screaming at herself to stop. It wasn't fair.

What wasn't fair was the loneliness. The pain. Wishing he was close but hating him all at the same time. She hated how they'd turned out.

Each day, she grew bigger with their child, and she felt this distance between them. Smokey had hurt her once, and it wouldn't take him long to hurt her again. He'd done so last time so easily.

Forgive him.

She couldn't just forgive him.

He hadn't trusted her.

He'd pushed her aside.

Ava screamed in her mind for it to shut up. She didn't care that he'd hurt her. All she cared about were the feelings he inspired at that moment. The way he touched her.

She pushed him back until he was against the wall.

Tugging at his shirt, she eased it up and over his head, throwing it to the side.

Smokey did the same, tearing her shirt open so the buttons flew all over the place. She'd pick them up later.

For now, she wanted his hands all over her.

He cupped her tits, pressing them together, and she moaned. He flicked the catch of her bra, and it fell open. She helped him take it off her. Ava threw it to the floor, and Smokey held beneath her breasts, lifting them up.

She watched him as he leaned in close and slid his tongue across one of her nipples. She cried out.

"No, don't close your eyes. Look at me. Know it's me doing this to you."

Ava couldn't look away as his tongue danced across her nipples. He held them so close together for each touch. They were so sensitive, she cried out for more.

"Please, Smokey."

"Tell me what you need. Just say the words and it's yours."

She shouldn't say it. All it made her was a weak woman. She didn't want to be a doormat, but his tongue. The very essence of him, she couldn't deny him.

"You, Smokey, please, I need you. Fuck me."

He released a growl but didn't take his time removing her clothes. They all fell in a heap on the floor. His hands were everywhere. Touching her face, down her body, cupping her pussy.

When his fingers delved between her slit, she couldn't take that kind of pleasure. His name was a mantra on her lips.

"You have no idea how many times I've thought about you. How I've craved for this very moment."

She had a rough idea because she'd been feeling it too. Even when she hated herself for yearning for him.

This man hadn't trusted her. He'd been the cause of her pain, and yet, as he took her to the floor, she couldn't think of a single word to say to tell him to stop.

He slammed his lips down on hers, and she cupped his face, never wanting him to let go.

Smokey broke the kiss. His lips created a path of intense pleasure as he glided down to her neck. He had some stubble, and the roughness of it made her melt. The slight pain mixed with the pleasure was almost too much for her.

Down he went, lavishing her tits with equal attention. Sucking on them deeply before he let them go with a plop. He captured her hands, keeping them locked at her side. His lips trailed down her stomach, and he took his time, kissing her rounded bump.

Her pussy was already soaked, so when he got between her thighs, she spread herself open to him. All sense left her as his lips finally touched her, and she knew what heaven was like once again.

****

This wasn't their beginning.

Smokey knew that.

Even as he knew she would hate herself in a few short hours, he couldn't bring himself to stop. Ava wanted this. She'd begged for this, and he'd be the biggest asshole in denying her.

Watching her regret this would cause him pain, but he'd live with it. What Ava wanted, he'd give her.

Staring at her pretty, swollen cunt, his mouth watered. He slid his tongue between her slit and touched her clit, caressing down toward her hole and circling her entrance. Ever so slightly, he pressed against her, nearly penetrating, but he held himself back, going to her clit.

Smokey sucked her into his mouth, and he groaned, hearing her gasp. Glancing up her body, he found her arching.

He still had a hold of her hands, keeping them locked at her side. She wasn't fighting him, and he loved having her at his mercy. He let her clit go and went back to her opening. Around and around he circled, tantalizing her. Giving a promise of what was to come.

"Please." Her moan echoed around the walls.

Her desperation was clear to him.

Pushing his tongue slowly inside her, he made her wait, letting her feel him fill her. What he was going to do with his tongue, and she'd be hungry for more.

He let go of her hands and cupped her ass, lifting her up against his mouth. Smokey got her into a position so her ass was on his open palm and his other hand was free to explore her pussy.

Sliding a finger into her cunt, he dipped in and out, getting himself nice and slick before moving back down to tease across her anus.

She was already so soaking wet that some of her pre-cum had leaked down the crack.

He bit down on her clit and took her hard into his mouth at the same time he pressed against her back entrance.

"Yes, please, yes," she said.

Ava took his thumb as he rode her higher toward her orgasm. She thrust against his face, danced on his thumb, and when she came, he swallowed her release, loving every second as she spasmed on his thumb.

He allowed her to ride that wave of pleasure, her body finally letting go, and she rested on the floor. Removing his hands, he crawled up her body, licking his lips.

"Tell me you want this," he said.

It was one thing to give her an orgasm, but quite another thing to take more.

"Yes, Smokey. I want you."

"Say it," he said.

He wasn't going to go any further until she told him exactly what she wanted.

She licked her lips. Her body was flush and glowing from the pregnancy and post-orgasm.

"Fuck me. I want to feel you inside me."

Ava had already removed his clothes when he'd taken off hers. There was no need for a condom seeing as she was already pregnant.

Smokey gripped his cock. He was rock-hard, pre-cum leaking out of the tip as he placed it against her pussy.

At first, he slid between her creamy slit, getting himself nice and wet before he went to her entrance.

He stared into her eyes, not wanting to look anywhere else but at the woman he loved. The woman he'd fucking hurt. The same woman he was intent on winning back. He wasn't a quitter. There was no way he was going to let her go.

She belonged to him.

Heart and soul.

Her body as well.

Smokey knew he wouldn't be sated until she finally gave every single part of herself to him, and he'd die making it up to her. He'd never stop trying to be the man she deserved.

Inch by inch, he sank inside her tight, hot pussy. She was so wet, and with each thrust forward, it felt like he was coming home. He'd never experienced this before in his life.

Closing his eyes, he loved every second of it until he was balls deep within her walls. She pulsed around him as she still had aftershocks of her orgasm.

He pressed his face against her neck, allowing

him a few seconds to bask in the tight feel of her. She was all he wanted.

At that moment, Smokey hated himself more for what he did. He'd really fucked up when it came to Ava. There was a chance they would never be together, and he couldn't even stand the thought of being close to her without having her.

Opening his eyes, he stared into hers. "Tell me if you want me to stop."

Ava reached for his ass and held him to her. "I want this, Smokey."

Locking their fingers together, he pressed them on either side of her head, keeping her in place as he slowly began to rock back and forth inside her. He started slowly, not going too deep but riding her pussy the way it needed to be, heightening her pleasure.

He shoved her hands above her head and gripped one knee, moving it to just the right angle over his hip so he could get as deep as possible. He did the same with the other.

His thrusts sped up, becoming pounds as he fucked her, going to the hilt within her, owning her. Working her pussy until she cried his name and he felt her come. Little ripples of pleasure rushed through him as her heat surrounded him, tightening, contracting, making him ache.

Smokey didn't want it to stop, but he knew there was no way he was going to make this last.

Slamming his lips down on hers, he took the kiss he'd been wanting, and she moaned his name, arching up toward his touch. He growled as his release filled her.

He wanted to get as deep within her as possible, but nothing seemed good enough. The pleasure was next level, and as he filled her, she came apart beneath him. Her moans filled the room as he held her.

This was what he'd been missing so much. Being close to her.

Wrapping his arms around her, he pressed his face against her neck, breathing her in, remembering the delicious scent of her.

He couldn't get enough. As with all things, time wasn't on his side.

Ava's hands ran along his back, and he just sensed the ticking of time.

He lifted himself up and stared down into her eyes, smiling at her. She gave him such a sweet smile that he'd cherish always.

"Please, don't hate this," he said.

"I don't. I know I wanted it."

"But you're having second thoughts?"

Tears filled her eyes, and she shook her head. Her lips pressed firmly together almost as if she couldn't stand the thought of talking.

"Tell me, Ava."

"Why did you do it, Smokey? Why did you put me through that?"

The break in her voice undid him.

"I've only known betrayal."

"From everyone else. Not from me. I was good to you. I loved you."

He heard the past tense, but he refused to believe it. Even as her words broke apart his entire world, he stared into her eyes, refusing to allow himself to back down.

"I can make you love me again."

She laughed. "Smokey, you hurt me."

"I know. You think I don't hate myself for what I did to you? You think I don't wake up wondering where the hell you are, wishing you were in my bed, and knowing I did this? I can't stand the thought of being away from you, Ava."

"We're a mess, Smokey. We're supposed to be having a baby, and now we've had sex." She pressed a hand to her forehead.

"Don't overthink it. This means we've still got something between us. This means we have hope."

"But I don't want to have hope." The tears fell from her eyes. She looked utterly heartbroken. "I want to have a life filled with love and devotion. I don't want to be second best. I just got out of a marriage where I wasn't even that. I was used for everything he could get and tossed aside like I was a piece of trash, and it was all my fault. I can't do that again. I won't."

"I won't do that to you."

"Smokey, you've always said the club comes first. It will always come first. I'm not going to compete with that. We'll share this baby and maybe friendship with time, but I don't think we should even consider having anything else between us. It would hurt way too much."

He wanted to deny it. To tell her she was making a big mistake, but she wasn't.

He'd done this.

Slowly, he eased out of her, but he didn't run off. Smokey picked her up in his arms and carried her toward the bathroom. From there, he ran a bath. He had no intention of joining her. All he wanted to do was give her some pleasure and to show her what she meant to him.

With Ava, he was going to have to prove he'd be there always. Ugly Beast was able to prove it with Abriana. He didn't see why he couldn't have the same thing with Ava. Time. It was all he needed.

Helping her into the bath, he grabbed soap and a sponge, lathering it up.

"Smokey, you don't need to do this."

He put the sponge to her body and began to wash her. "I do. It's what I want to do." He ran the sponge all over her body, taking care of her the best way he knew how. After her body was clean, he took care of her hair, rubbing the shampoo in, washing it all out, then the conditioner.

This was why Ava was different. He wanted to do this with her. To take care of her. To love her. He'd never taken the time to truly care for any other woman, but Ava was different. She would always be so to him.

One day, he hoped she realized how much.

Chapter Eighteen

"Man, this storm is freaky," Harlow said.

Ava agreed, walking from behind the counter to see about eight inches of snow already on the ground, and it was getting thicker fast. "I didn't even know a storm was forecast."

"Yep." Harlow folded her arms. "I'm not going to lie to you, but I really want to go and build a snowman."

She chuckled. "When you get home?"

"Totally." She sighed. "My brothers all say I'm a big kid at heart. It's true. I don't see the reason to completely grow up just yet."

"Of course not. Growing up is for losers." Ava offered her friend a smile. Over the past several weeks, she'd gotten close to Harlow. The other woman was such a sweetheart. She'd even had a couple of sleepovers with Harlow. The woman could talk, and it was nice to have the company. Of course, Smokey still stayed outside for as long as he could. The nights were getting colder, and she wasn't a bitch. The need to make him suffer lessened when he was in real danger, liking dying of the intense cold.

She had no choice but to open her door and let him in. She'd given him extra blankets and a pillow.

Ava never stuck around to hear him making up the bed downstairs. Ever since their ... one sexual encounter, they hadn't spoken about it, nor had there been a repeat. The furniture for the baby had arrived and was waiting to be assembled. Smokey had been too busy with club stuff to have the time to do it.

She'd taken out the instructions, but even she'd struggled to make sense of them. All of that would be saved for Smokey.

"Not that I think you're a loser."

Ava laughed. "I know I'm a loser, but I'm proud of it."

"See, nothing wrong with being proud of your loserness." Harlow groaned. "One of my brothers is going to turn up. Mom will moan incessantly until they do what she wants."

"And that's a bad thing?"

"I don't want you to see me as a little girl having to be escorted home by her brother. It will probably be Big Dick. Asshole that he is."

Ava walked away from the window. The snow was starting to cause her some concern. "You adore your brothers. Each unbearable one."

"Now that is completely true," Harlow said. "I wouldn't want anything to happen to them. I don't know if they like me."

"You're family. Of course they do."

"You never talk about your family," Harlow said. "Do you have a close relative nearby?"

"My parents died some time ago, actually. No other relatives. I know they wanted more kids, but it never happened."

"Oh, crap, I'm so sorry."

Ava smiled at the woman, knowing deep in her heart Harlow would never hurt her, at least not intentionally.

"I know. That's life. It's hard to get used to. There are times I wish they were still alive." She put a hand on her ever-increasing bump. "Like with this one. I wish Mom could give me advice. I have no idea what I'm doing, and I'm terrified I'm going to raise a serial killer."

"I wouldn't worry about that. You're going to be an incredible mom. If he turns out to be a serial killer, blame his dad."

Rather than be offended, Ava found herself laughing. "That's a good one."

"It's what I'm here for." Harlow looked out of the window and made a yuck sound. "What did I tell you. Big Dick. I don't even know why she bothers to phone him."

"He's still her son."

"Yeah, but he's also club. I don't think Mom wanted him to join. He did so anyway. I can't remember the rest, but there was a big fight between them all."

"He's here."

"Come on, Harlow, I've got to take you home. Mom's orders."

"Oh, so the big, bad biker gets to take me home."

Big Dick rolled his eyes. "You're going home, baby."

"No. I happen to be working."

He turned toward her. "I know you don't want me in here, but I've got to do what my mom said."

"I removed the sign," Ava said.

"You did?"

Ava nodded. "Yes, you can stop sending in your prospects without their leather cuts." She turned away, refusing to meet his eyes.

"I'll let everyone know."

She'd stared at the sign one morning and rather than leave it up, she'd torn it down. This was a business, and she had to treat it like one. Not allowing any MC men or women, well, it was bad for business. She wished for her shop to thrive, and that was exactly what she did.

"You know about that, huh?" Big Dick asked.

Ava shrugged. She hadn't suspected until one of the prospects had walked across the street and before leaving, put on his leather cut, showing who he was. At first, she'd been pissed, and then she'd found it funny.

Clearly, her baked goods were popular.

"You can go," Ava said, looking toward Harlow.

"I don't feel comfortable leaving you."

"I'm fine. I'm going to close up and head on home. We haven't had many customers today. I'm all set."

"I don't like the thought of you driving in the snow," Big Dick said.

"You don't have to worry about me. I'll be perfectly fine. Go and take Harlow home. I wouldn't want anything bad to happen to her."

Harlow sighed. "I'll grab my stuff."

She left them alone.

"How is she doing?" Big Dick asked.

"Fine. Why?"

"Harlow has … trouble. I don't know why or what it is. She was never good at making friends growing up. She's found life difficult at times."

"I think she's wonderful," Ava said. "And she's always got a job here."

Harlow returned, pulling on a jacket. "I'm here. You will call me the moment you get home. Promise me."

"I promise."

Ava gave her a tight hug. "Go and warm yourself up."

"I don't like leaving you."

"I'm a loser grownup. I can handle it."

Harlow still hesitated, and Ava waved her and her concern off. Once the door was shut, she locked it, flicking the sign to Closed. There weren't many people around. The thought of going back home to loneliness didn't appeal, but being here wasn't going to change that.

She packed away all the cookies and cakes, trying to preserve them for as long as she could. She cleaned every single surface. Being thorough.

With nothing else to do, she had no choice but to start making her way home.

The cold was already starting to seep into the shop.

After grabbing her bag and jacket, she pulled it on. The moment she stepped outside, the cold flooded her, making her gasp. She was a lot happier to have settled for boots rather than some inappropriate heel.

She locked up the shop and quickly walked to her car. After letting herself in, she turned over the ignition, trying to get as much warmth as she could. The window wipers were next, moving off the fallen snow.

It was no good. The cold was just too much. She had to get home.

Slowly, she put it into gear and took her time as she navigated out of her parking space and drove in the direction of home.

Within a matter of minutes, it was snowing harder than before. She struggled to see.

Ava wasn't too far from home, when all of a sudden, she must have hit a block of ice. She wasn't going too fast, but the car spun. She let out a little scream, and she tried to press the brake. Panic filled her, making her actions jerky as the car seemed to pull hard, and then flipped, landing in a ditch.

The seatbelt held her in place, but with the snow falling, her fear gathered.

She'd somehow managed to end on her side in a ditch. The odds weren't in her favor.

She covered her face as tears fell. Panic rose even higher.

"I can do this."

She needed to call someone. Glancing around her car, she noticed the engine had also died and the cold was intense.

She swiped at her cheeks. There was no way she was going to get out of this alive.

Her baby chose that moment to start to move, and another kind of fear rushed over her. There was no way she could lose this baby. The very thought of it filled her with dread.

"I need a cell phone." She looked around the car and saw her bag must have fallen during the accident because it was in the furthest corner away from her. "Oh, come on. This isn't fair."

With a sudden pain in her abdomen, Ava put a hand to her stomach. "No. No. No." She wasn't going to lose this child. That fear alone stopped her from releasing the seatbelt.

Any movement could affect the baby.

The cold made her shudder. Her breath coming out as a puff of smoke the moment it left her mouth.

"We're going to be okay."

Smokey would come and hang out at her house. When she didn't invite him in, he'd get suspicious, and then, he'd come and find them. Until then, she had to find a way to stay warm and hope the snow stopped so it didn't cover the entire car.

Helplessness filled her. This wasn't good. Her cell phone was too far away for her to reach.

Ava moved her hand toward the seatbelt, determined to do something rather than wait. Just as she was about to press the catch to release it, pain floored her.

She screamed and cried.

"No. No. No. No. No." The last one she screamed long and hard. "You're not going to die, and you're not coming out."

She pressed her hands to her stomach and began

to deeply breathe, trying to find whatever she could to relax her and the baby. "I've got you, baby. I've got you."

Stupid snowstorm.

And when it had happened that morning, she'd found it to be the most beautiful.

****

Smokey was working through the pile of bills when he got the call. Big Dick's number lit up his screen.

"What's up?" Smokey asked.

"Give me the damn phone," a woman said.

"Get off it, or I swear, Harlow, I'll give you a fucking wedgie."

Smokey frowned. Checking the number, he saw it was Big Dick. "I don't have time for games."

He wanted to get the paperwork done so he could go and keep an eye on Ava. She allowed him inside her house, and for the most part, he stayed on the sofa. Before she woke up, though, he allowed himself a good half an hour of watching her sleep.

There was nothing stalkery about it. If they were together, he'd get to see her sleeping. At least, that was what he told himself.

"Damn it, Harlow."

"Ouch. He pinched me. Mom!"

Smokey rubbed at his temple as he heard the squabbling of siblings. What made it worse, both of them were adults and behaving that way. If they were still children, he'd see a good enough reason for it.

"Big Dick, get to the point."

"It's Ava," he said.

Smokey tensed up. "What about her?"

"She drove home in the snow," Harlow said.

"Give me that." There was a smacking sound and a groan. "Holy fuck, Harlow, you punched my nose."

"Look, I know you have feelings for her, but I've got a bad feeling. Ava told me she'd call me the moment she got home. I haven't heard from her. That was three hours ago. I think something bad has happened. Her cell phone just keeps ringing, and it's bad out there."

Smokey was already on his feet. "I'll go and check her out."

He hung up the phone before anyone else could speak. The thought of something bad happening to his woman scared him.

Rushing out of his office, he passed Hunter, Kinky, Brick, and Raven.

"Ava's missing. Harlow thinks she's gotten caught in the snow." He didn't need to say anything more as he left the clubhouse.

Smokey hesitated at the vehicles. He looked at the bike.

Kinky was already in the truck. Smokey ran to the passenger seat as Hunter, Brick, and Raven joined him.

The snow was a pain in the ass, but the truck was designed for this. Smokey stared out of the windows, not liking the snowfall. In a few hours, Ava could have been injured or died of the cold. Anything could have happened.

His knee bounced, and he wanted to run on ahead to make sure she was fine. He couldn't help but hope that she'd fallen asleep somewhere.

Kinky arrived at her house and Smokey knew she wasn't there.

"Her car's not there," he said.

Without waiting for instruction, Kinky had already put the truck into gear and was heading in the general direction.

"Keep it slow. She could be anywhere."

Smokey typed in her number.

It rang.

And rang.

Then went to voicemail.

Hanging up, he cursed. There was no sign of her.

"Stop," he said.

Kinky brought the truck to a stop.

Smokey climbed out, feeling the cold instantly.

He pressed on Ava's number and waited. It rang in his ear but then he heard something else.

A ringtone.

The line went dead.

He dialed it again and followed the sound.

Kinky, Brick, Raven, and Hunter got out of the truck and followed him.

"Are you hearing this?" he asked.

They all agreed, and Smokey went across the road. As he glanced over the edge, he saw the car. It was nearly covered in snow, but the two wheels were still visible.

He didn't think, just reacted. The way it fell, it hadn't gotten too deep near her doors.

With some force, he found the door handle and yanked it open.

Kinky and Hunter helped him to open the door, and there was Ava. Her teeth were chattering.

"Smokey," she said.

"Fuck. I'm here." He bent down, looking in the car, trying to find something that would help him ease her out.

She let out a scream as her hands went to her stomach.

"What's wrong?" he asked.

"I don't know. I think there's something wrong with the baby." She whimpered. "I can't lose it,

Smokey."

"You won't," he said. He couldn't allow her to lose it. That baby was one of the only connections he had to her. If they didn't share a kid, they had nothing. There was no way he could allow that to happen.

"I've got Hunter, Kinky, Brick, and Raven with me, baby. I know after everything, you don't like them, but they're going to help me get you out. Okay?"

She whimpered but agreed. "I'm so cold."

Smokey looked at the car. They couldn't lift it up.

"I'm going to slide in. Take her weight as I release the belt. Then all of you are going to work together. We're going to carry her to the truck and then we're getting her to the hospital."

"Maybe we should call for an ambulance," Raven said. "If we move her, what if she has another injury?"

Smokey growled. "We don't have time."

She'd been out in the cold for far too long. He didn't want to risk Ava or the baby's life. He had to get her out of there and hold her.

Smokey removed his jacket. "Wrap this around her the moment she's out."

He looked into the car. He didn't know if it was a saving grace that she was on her side on the ground. There was no easy way to do this. Either option put her at risk. If he moved her and she had an injury, this could cause more damage. If he left her here, she could freeze to death. That wasn't an option. Slowly and carefully, he climbed into the car. Ava had pushed the chair back, and he was able to fit in front of her with the steering wheel jammed into his back. He got himself into a position, which meant he was able to look into Ava's eyes.

"You're going to wrap your arms around me and I'm going to pull you out."

"Smokey, I could hurt you."

"I'm going to hold you. I've got you. I've got this, Ava. Do you trust me?"

She nodded. Not a single hesitation.

He wanted to puff out his chest, but instead, he made sure he was braced and ready to take her weight. He was not going to fuck this up.

"I'm so scared," she said.

"Me too. I'm going to get you out of this. Are you ready?"

She nodded. Her teeth chattered as he reached out for the belt buckle. Staring into Ava's eyes, he clicked the button and she wrapped her arms around him.

Instant cold hit him.

She screamed in pain and he wrapped his arms around her, trying to soothe her.

Kinky, Hunter, Raven, and Brick were there.

With their help and taking their time, they were able to help her out of the car.

Smokey crawled out and was sure to grab her bag as he did.

After following his guys to the truck, he climbed in the back and moved Hunter out of the way, who'd been talking to Ava, trying to soothe her.

He cupped her face. "I'm right here, Ava. I'm right here." He took her hand as the car started.

"You came for me," she said. "I knew you would."

"Of course, I did. I wouldn't leave you. I will always come for you. You know that."

She nodded. "I do. It hurts."

"We're getting you to the hospital, okay? The doctor will fix everything."

"I don't want to lose this baby."

"We won't." He put his hand gently to her stomach, not sure if he was hurting her or not.

"I really want to be a mother."

"And you will be. I'm not going to lose either of you." He pressed his face against hers, rubbing his cheek on hers, trying to do anything to give her the warmth she needed. The cold was starting to affect him. "I love you both, Ava."

She began to cry, and he held her.

"Nothing will happen. I've got you. I will always get you."

She gripped his arm. Her hold was tight, and he did nothing more than wrap her in his arms, keeping her safe and exactly where she was meant to be.

Chapter Nineteen

"I'm not sick," Ava said two days later.

She still lay in a hospital bed, wearing a gown with machines hooked up to her. It had been touch-and-go for a short time. The cold had affected her and they needed to warm her up. Also, her baby was being observed every single day.

"I know," Smokey said.

He changed the flowers that had begun to wilt in her room.

Not once had he left her side.

"Have you gone home once?"

"Nope."

"Why not?" she asked.

Smokey tossed the wilted flowers into the trash can and then turned toward her. "Simple, I wasn't going to leave you alone. I held you, Ava. You were sobbing. Brokenhearted. You thought you were losing our baby. You weren't. Our baby is just fine." He put his hand on her stomach and she covered his with hers.

"I'm so glad. And you found me."

"I wasn't going to give up. When Harlow told me, I never felt fear like it. With what I've seen and done, you wouldn't look at me for the monster I've been, Ava. Knowing you were out there and that you could die, I felt real fear. I never want to experience it again."

"You can't be in the room when I give birth," Ava said. "It's just as scary. Men have passed out."

"I'm going to be here."

"You are?"

"Yes."

"Like, in the room?"

"Yes."

"I find that hard to believe."

"I helped create this life. The least I could do is be with its baby momma while our child is being born into this world." He let go of her stomach and took her hand.

"When I get out of here, we're going to need to talk about you assembling the crib and all that stuff you were determined to buy."

"I'm there. Whenever you need me, I'm there." He kissed her hand.

Ava smiled at him. "This is nice."

The sound of a throat clearing drew her attention to the door. Harlow stood there with bloodshot eyes and a teddy bear.

"Hey," Ava said.

Harlow rushed into the room and threw herself at Ava. She was careful to miss her stomach as the woman wrapped her arms around her. "Don't ever fucking frighten me like that again. I nearly lost ten years of my life worrying about you. My parents kept on saying don't worry, but I just knew I should. I know you, and you wouldn't allow me to keep worrying."

Ava ran her fingers down the woman's hair. "It's fine. I'm safe."

"It's not fine. Damn it. Nothing can happen to you."

"Nothing did happen to her," Big Dick said.

Ava looked toward the other man.

"I'm sorry. She was nagging and Smokey said you were allowed visitors, and well, we're all here."

"All?" Ava asked, glancing over at Smokey.

"The club is here. Ugly Beast and Abriana want to come as well."

Harlow still hadn't let her go.

"Raven. Brick. Hunter. Kinky. All of the others."

"Oh," Ava said. "They didn't need to come."

"They did," Smokey said. "They're worried about you."

Ava wasn't sure if he was telling the full truth. She'd started to become close to the club when everything had turned ugly. Since that day, other than Abriana and Smokey, she never talked to anyone else. Big Dick being the exception in the past few days.

Harlow pulled back and Ava drew her attention to the woman, who was crying.

"Please, don't cry."

"I should have made you come home with me."

"No. I wouldn't have accepted. This isn't your fault. Don't blame yourself. The doctors have already said I'm doing fine. I'm healthy. The baby is healthy."

"But you're still here."

"I was out in the cold for a long time. They're doing everything to make sure I'm perfectly fine."

Harlow kissed her forehead.

"Come on, Harlow. Let's get you a hot chocolate."

"I'm staying."

"Now."

Ava chuckled. "I've got a few other visitors to see. Go and have something to drink." She saw the worry in Harlow's eyes, and the darkness surrounding them. "You're a good friend, Harlow. Thank you for not giving up on me."

Harlow nodded and got to her feet. She hesitated, and Smokey held his hand up. "I'm not going anywhere."

The other woman left, and Ava sighed.

"I think that woman has a crush on you," Smokey said.

"No, she doesn't. She's just a really good friend." Harlow didn't have any sexual feelings for her. She was a woman who didn't hold back in expressing her emotions. It was one of the many reasons Ava adored her. She found it refreshing to be around someone who didn't hold back.

"I can tell the club to leave," Smokey said. "They wouldn't be offended."

"It's fine. I can see them."

She wasn't exactly sure if she was ready to see them. Not after they'd all stood by and allowed her to be hurt.

Sitting up, she settled the blanket around her and took a sip of her water. Abriana and Ugly Beast were the first to come to her room, with a wriggling Bella. She smiled as Abriana came in with a packet of grapes and some flowers. She gave her a hug, being careful with her.

They both wished her well.

After them, a couple of the prospects and some patched-in members she didn't really know well enough. She recognized them.

Each member came with some flowers and more food. One by one, her room filled up until it was a floral scent.

Ava glanced over at Smokey, who hadn't moved from her bedside. "Did you put them up to this?"

"No. My men don't always do what I tell them to."

"How can you be the club president if they don't follow every single one of your orders?"

"They follow the ones that matter." He gave her hand a squeeze, and she looked up to see Hunter there.

"How are you doing, Ava?" he asked.

"I've been better, but it could have been so much worse. Thank you for helping me."

"Don't mention it. We've missed you around the clubhouse. After everything, we've all felt your loss."

Ava pressed her lips together. She'd missed the

clubhouse. "Thank you. But … I'm not ready. Not yet." She didn't know if she'd ever be ready.

"Well, we're all hoping you get well soon. You're the only person we know who can keep this man on his toes."

Smokey chuckled.

Ava joined in.

Hunter had already put down his flowers.

"The nurses are going to ask me to leave," Ava said. "This has to be some kind of health hazard."

"Let them try," Smokey said.

When Brick, Kinky, and Raven came into the room, all three held flowers in their hands, and Raven also had a teddy bear. It was a small one, but from where Ava sat, it was cute.

Ava couldn't help but tense up.

All three had been the ones to bring her to the clubhouse. She'd experienced so much pain from Raven.

"We're so sorry," Raven said.

"None of our apologies will ever excuse our behavior," Kinky said.

"We were glad to help. We don't want anything to happen to you," Brick said.

They put the flowers near the door.

She noticed they didn't come too close into the room.

Slowly, Ava began to relax.

"Hopefully, one day, you will be able to forgive us," Kinky said.

"We will protect you, Ava. With our lives. All of us." This came from Brick.

"No, that's completely unnecessary. I don't want that at all." She didn't want them putting their lives at risk or thinking they should just because of her.

"I think it's time for you to go," Smokey said.

Kinky and Brick left.

Raven still held the bear in her hand.

Ava forced herself to look the other woman in the eye.

Raven's brow was creased. She hesitated. "I've … everything in my life I've done, it has all been justified. Doing it for the club, for my life, to survive. I've never been in the wrong." Raven pressed her lips together. "I will always beg for your forgiveness, Ava, but I will never expect it. I messed up. I should have argued. I should have questioned because looking back, I spent time with you. I knew you. I knew what you were capable of, and it wasn't this level of deception, and I am sorry for that." She stepped forward and placed the teddy bear on the bed. "I'm so glad you're safe and well."

Ava watched Raven leave.

She didn't call her back even as her throat felt like it was on fire from trying to control the tears.

"She means well," Smokey said.

"I know."

"I didn't ask any of them to do this."

Ava glanced over at him. "But?"

"But I'm so glad they did. You mean everything to me, Ava. I've got a lot to make up for. I know that."

"Can we not talk about it?" she asked.

"I think we should. It has to come out, Ava."

"You really want to know how lonely my life feels?" She tried to keep the tears at bay, but they seemed to have a mind of their own and fell down her cheeks. She swiped at them. "After the crap that happened with Derek, I had no one. My parents were dead. I had no friends. No hope. I came here to start a new life. I wasn't looking for you or the club. When I found you, and my feelings for you began, I started to have hope, Smokey. I wanted to be by your side. I adored your club. I was falling in love with you and with them. I get that you don't come alone. You've got your own little family. I get that it's … not legal. You've got secrets to protect. I accepted that. When you did what you did, you shattered all my illusions. The club wasn't my friend. They were putting up with me because I was the woman you were fucking."

Smokey knelt on the floor beside her bed. "No."

"Yes. You know it."

"Ava, you started out as being the woman I was fucking, but slowly, you changed in their eyes. You became more." He kissed her hand.

"If I did, someone would have stuck up for me. That never happened."

"We fucked up big time, Ava. Me more than anyone else. They do as I say."

Ava laughed. "Even though you told me a few hours ago that they do what they want?"

"It's crazy, I know, but when it comes to the club's security, I'm the one they turn to. If I had reason to doubt you, they would follow it. I had no reason. I told them that. Give us a chance, Ava."

Ava sighed. "Can we just agree to think about it? We've been doing really good so far, don't you think?"

"We have, but I want more."

"You're being greedy."

"When it comes to you, all I ever want to be is greedy. I can't get enough of you. That's never going to change."

Ava stared down at their hands, which were locked together. His touch made her feel alive, and she'd tried to fight it for so long, but it was no good. This was how he made her feel.

"What about the other women?" she asked.

"There are no other women."

"The club women."

"What about them?" he asked.

"They're available to you all the time."

"No. They're for the club, Ava. I haven't touched another woman since you were in my life. I can't even stand to think of another woman." He kissed her hands. "There's no one else. If you want them gone, say the word, and I will kick them to the curb. You won't be popular with the boys, but I don't care about them. Whatever you want, name it."

Ava stared at him and shook her head. "No. I don't want you to get rid of the women." She didn't want them around him, but they were there for the brothers.

"Just say what you want."

"Nothing. I want to see where this goes."

He leaned down and kissed her lips. "I'm yours. I'm always yours."

She really hoped that was true, but then she was worried to even give herself chance to hope.

****

"You don't understand a word of it, do you?" Ava asked.

Smokey lowered the instructions and glared at her. "They said it was a simple assembly."

"And it is supposed to be."

"Are they written in Latin? That's not even a language anymore."

"I think it still is for botany. I'm not sure."

"Well, unless these are instructions on how to build a rose garden, they're no good." Smokey flipped the instructions over and started to look at the pictures.

"Do you think we should call the store?"

"No. I can do this. The guy said it was an easy job."

Ava held her hands up in surrender. "How many

cribs have you put together?"

"This is my first one."

"So you don't have any children elsewhere that I should know about?"

Smokey glanced at her. "Are you trying to figure out if I've got something to hide?"

She tucked her hair behind her ear. It had started to grow out again, but it wasn't as long as he liked it.

The coveralls she wore seemed to emphasize her bump as the fabric stretched across her stomach.

"We don't really know a lot about each other, and seeing as we're going to be sharing a child, don't you think we should know some things? You know a lot about me."

"True. I didn't know everything until I got to know you."

"Then tell me some stuff," she said. "I promise I won't tell."

"I trust you."

"Makes a change." She offered him a smile, and he fucking loved it. He'd give anything to see that teasing look in her eyes.

"I don't have any kids. Anywhere. I've been with a lot of the club women."

She wrinkled her nose. "I didn't mean that kind of sharing."

"I know what you mean." He sighed. "I don't have a whole lot to share, to be honest, Ava. The club has been in my blood for a long time, and any life I had before that, it doesn't fucking matter."

"No siblings or anything?"

"Nothing. I have no family to offer you. Just me and the club."

"That's not a bad offer, Smokey."

"I don't know. You deserve to have a big family.

I want to give you that."

Silence fell between them.

He continued to look at the pictures, rearranging the pieces to make up the crib into different orders.

It wasn't working. The paper had to be wrong.

"Are you thirsty?" she asked.

"I could do with a drink."

"I'll be right back."

She got to her feet and left the room. With her out of the room, he reached into his back pocket. He'd gone shopping during the days she was in the hospital. He pulled out the gold band with a string of diamonds across the top. The ring had cost a fortune, but he wanted to spend every single penny he had on his woman.

Asking her to marry him wasn't going to be easy. He didn't have the right words of what to say to her.

Pocketing the ring, he went back to the list of instructions that made no sense to him. Life at the clubhouse had settled down and he'd been able to find the time to come and finally build the furniture for his kid's arrival. The shack was back up and running. The sickness bug going around was simply that. No drugs. No cause to believe something untoward had happened. Carlos had already told him they weren't going to have some product for a couple of months as they were dealing with some legal heat breathing down their neck. When it came to Creed of the Twisted Bastards MC, he was keeping his distance. Smokey had been able to close several of the fucker's businesses and it had caused him to retreat.

There was no sign of them.

He had no doubt Creed and all the Bastards would come out of the woodwork at some point. Until then, he was basking in the few weeks of peace he had to win his woman back.

Ava returned with a steaming mug of coffee and a warm hot chocolate for her.

"Does the smell affect you?" he asked.

"It's fine. I can deal with it."

"You don't have to deal with it."

Ava lowered herself into a chair that he'd brought up. "It's fine, babe, drink it."

Smokey paused and glanced at her. She'd gone a bright shade of red. "Ignore me. I don't know where that had come from." She pressed her lips together. "I'm not myself right now."

"You don't have to apologize. I liked it." He sipped the hot liquid. *You're a fucking pussy.*

Just because his woman had called him babe. He was on cloud nine.

Totally pussy-whipped and what was more, he didn't fucking care either.

"Are you going to concede?" she asked.

Smokey pulled out his cell phone and dialed Kinky's number, waiting for the man to answer. He didn't have to wait long.

The feminine moan in the background alerted him to the fact his man wasn't alone. He rolled his eyes and put it on speakerphone.

"Yes, fuck yes. Pound my pussy. Oh, it feels so good. Don't stop. I love it. I've got to have it. Fuck me. Fuck me. Fuck me."

"What is it, boss?" Kinky asked.

"I need your help, but you sound busy."

"Oh, he is, Smokey. Tell him to fuck me real good."

Ava got up and walked out of the room.

"When you're done, come to Ava's house. I need your help," he said, hanging up.

Getting to his feet, he put the cup on the floor and

found Ava in her bedroom. She stood beside the window, staring out at the garden. The snow was still thick, but most of the roads had been cleared. They were due another snowstorm, and Ava had already agreed to let him stay close to her.

"That wasn't anything," he said. He'd never justified anything to anyone. This was a whole new experience for him.

Ava smiled, but it didn't quite reach her eyes. "I get it."

"No, I don't think you do." He stepped toward her.

"Smokey, we don't have to have this conversation."

He moved behind her, wrapping his arms around her thickening waist. Each day, he struggled to hold her close, not that he got a chance to, but he took every opportunity he could. Resting his hands on her stomach, he pressed his face against hers. "I haven't been with anyone."

"I believe you."

"Then what's the problem?"

"Nothing. I don't have a problem."

"I wasn't there."

She groaned. "Please, Smokey, stop."

"Tell me what I can do to fix this. To fix us."

Ava turned in his arms. "I'm not angry about what I just heard, okay. I know you're not there, and that woman was well, she was…"

"Aroused?"

Ava's lips pressed together as she nodded. "Yes, and hearing that…" She covered her face. "This is so embarrassing."

"Talk to me."

"I found it arousing too. There, I've said it. I

found her getting fucked arousing. As I listened to her getting it, I wanted it, but I didn't want any other man to give it to me. Okay? I don't even know what's wrong with me." She laughed, a cold, hard sound. "I thought I didn't like sex. That I was made wrong. It was boring and I hated it. Sure, porn looked good, but that was all fake. Reading about it in books, again, that could be the author's fantasy, making it all lies. Then, I met you."

"And?" he asked.

"I realized everything I ever knew was a big, fat lie. I like sex a lot. I love having it. I enjoyed your cock and I loved being yours. I loved having you as mine. I wanted it all and then ... ugh, then *that* happened." She flicked her hair as she said it. "And it made a mess of absolutely everything. I can't have you because you couldn't even trust me enough to let me in. You believed the worst, and I've got to be strong. Do you have any idea how fucked up that is? I want you, but I can't have you."

He cupped her face. "Who says I can't have you? Who says you can't have me?"

"You hurt me in every single possible way. I can't allow myself to fall for you. It wouldn't be fair. I won't do it."

"But you love me, Ava. I know you do, and I'm doing everything I can to make it up to you. I will never betray your trust again. You can love me. You can have faith in me."

He slammed his lips down on hers, tasting her.

Ava grabbed his arms, and he groaned as her hands moved down his body, working toward his dick. She rubbed his length, going up and down.

He peeled the straps down over her arms of her coveralls. The item of clothing had never looked so sexy as it did on this woman.

Smokey worked it down past her bump, and he shoved them to the floor. She stepped out of them. He didn't have the patience with her panties and he tore them off, snapping them in two.

Next, he had her shirt off and the catch of her bra open. He bent her over the bed, sliding a hand between her wet, creamy slit.

She was so aroused, and he groaned, feeling her heat. His cock tented in his jeans.

Letting go of her pussy, he tugged his jeans open, easing out his cock as he did. Starting from the base up to the tip, pre-cum leaked out.

He placed the head at her entrance, eased inside her a couple of inches, grabbed her hips, and slammed to the hilt.

Their cries of pleasure mingled together, echoing off the walls. He closed his eyes, basking in the tight heat of her cunt. It wasn't enough for him.

Opening his eyes, he grabbed her ass and spread her cheeks wide, staring at her pretty asshole and cock-filled cunt.

He pulled out of her, until only the tip was inside, and then drove in deep. Smokey leaned over and trailed out some of his saliva, coating her anus, and he pushed his thumb through, getting her nice and slick.

With the tip of his thumb at her asshole, he pressed inside, and she whimpered. Her ass gave way, letting him in.

Smokey used his free hand to reach between them to stroke her clit, bringing her close to the edge of release.

Her ass tightened around his thumb as her pussy did the same on his dick.

He didn't stop, working in and out of her, teasing her clit. Ava came, her tight muscles clamping down on him. His name spilled from her lips. A constant tease.

Once he was satisfied that she'd come hard enough, he grabbed her hips and pounded inside her cunt. He'd already spoken to the doctor about having sex with her. It was safe, and he loved it, taking what he wanted, filling her pussy over and over. He kept her ass cheeks spread so he could see everything. As he thrust into her one final time, he came with a grunt, flooding her womb with more of his cum.

They were both panting by the time it was over.

"Ava, if that is what you need, then all you've got to do is say so." He pressed a kiss to the base of her back.

Chapter Twenty

Ava rubbed at her stomach.

The days and weeks were merging together, and she was well into her second trimester. Smokey was with her for all the appointments, and the doctor had even offered to tell them the sex.

They'd both agreed to wait to find out the truth.

"Are you okay?" Harlow asked, coming into the back of the bakery.

"Yeah, I'm fine." She rubbed the back of her neck.

"You don't seem fine." Harlow folded her arms.

She glanced over at the other woman and sighed. "It just feels like it has been a really long couple of months is all."

"I can imagine. You're carrying around another person, and of course you've got Smokey on your case. I don't imagine being around him is easy."

Ava chuckled. "He's okay."

Harlow grabbed one of the chairs and slid it over to her. "What's up?"

"I don't know. I think I'm just worried about the baby and everything, you know?"

"No, I don't really. This isn't about the baby, though, is it? This is about something else."

Ava sighed. "It's not important."

"What are friends for if they don't share? Have you ever thought that maybe you're overthinking everything?"

Ava put her hands on her shoulders and gave a little stretch. "I know I am."

"Then try me. I may be young, but I know a hell of a lot of things. I love to research answers. Come on."

Ava licked her lips. "Fine. If you must know the

truth…" She stopped and tucked some hair behind her ear. "I think I'm still in love with Smokey."

"That's not a revelation. Anyone can see that."

"No, you don't understand. I promised myself I would never fall for him. Ever again." She closed her eyes and rubbed at them. "I know this sounds crazy, but he hurt me, and I … I don't have a good track record with men. I suck, to be honest with you."

"And you don't want to suck anymore?" Harlow asked.

"I had an awful marriage. By the end, when I caught him cheating, I was so happy to get out of it. I wanted nothing from him. I didn't care about him."

"And Smokey?"

"I … I didn't want to love him. It didn't even start out as love. It was sex. That's what we offered each other. Sex. No complications. No strings. Just sex."

"But?"

"But I fell in love with him. I know he's a little rough around the edges and he's not for everyone, but I liked him, and it wasn't so hard to fall in love with him either. He makes me happy. Then he … he destroyed that part of me, or at least I thought he did." She shook her head. "I wasn't going to love a man who couldn't love me. Who thought so little of me."

"And now?" Harlow asked.

"Now, we've got a baby on the way, and I want to hate him, but it's like he knows I'm weak. He's breaking down the walls I put up, wanting to hate him."

"Have you ever considered that you might still be in love with him?" Harlow asked. "No matter how hard you try to fight it. You still love him and maybe always will."

"What if he breaks my heart again? What if he does something even worse this time?" She couldn't tell

Harlow about the attack or how he was prepared to kill her. Those secrets would stay with her.

Big Dick may be a club member and Harlow was his sister, but Ava didn't know what she knew of the club and their dealings.

"Have you ever thought about forgiving him?" Harlow asked. "Forgiving someone doesn't make you weak at all, Ava."

"I … he hurt me."

"And when I see him and the way he looks at you, that man is in love with you. He will do anything for you."

"What if it's all a trick?"

"It's not."

Ava laughed. "You're so young."

Harlow shrugged. "I may be young, but I also know people, and I do understand them. Don't write me off."

"I'm not. I'm sorry."

"How do you feel when you're around him?" Harlow asked.

Ava paused and thought about the question and her feelings for Smokey. "When I don't think of what happened, he makes me feel so alive. So happy."

Harlow took her hands. "I know I'm young, and I don't know anything. Here is what I do know. Life is way too short for you to hold any hatred. Forgiving can be empowering. I'm not saying to forget. Of course, remember. I'm sure Smokey will never forget what he did. That doesn't mean he's not living with his own regrets. He loves you in his way. Talk to him."

Ava nodded. They'd tried to talk. Each time they did, it always ended up with sex, which she didn't mind. They were able to communicate through sex.

There were even a few times he'd joined her

afterward, holding her. She loved falling asleep in his arms. There was no better feeling in the world.

Harlow stayed with her and helped her clean up the bakery before heading home. Smokey was already waiting for her as she put the lock into place.

"Hello, gorgeous," he said.

Ava stepped into his arms and pressed a kiss to his lips. "I missed you."

Smokey stared at her for several minutes before he shook out of whatever surprise she'd caused him.

He held out his hand and she took it. They walked together toward his car. He hadn't been riding his bike since he'd been driving her to and from work.

"You don't have to keep doing this. I can drive."

"I like taking you to work." He held the door of the car for her.

"Don't you miss riding your bike?"

"I can ride my bike any time. Don't worry about me."

He helped her with her seat belt. It was these little intimacies that she was starting to really enjoy and get used to.

Smokey helped her inside and rounded the car to climb behind the wheel. She was silent as they drove toward her house. More snow had started to fall as they arrived at her house. Ava stared at her front door.

The silence in the car wasn't awkward, but Ava felt something else. A new connection.

"Are you okay?" Smokey asked.

Ava glanced over at him. "I forgive you."

"Ava?"

"I … I don't want to keep on hating you or pushing you away. We're going to have a baby. I don't know if we'll ever be back to where we were, but I do know I don't want to keep on feeling this way." She forced herself to look into his eyes. "I hope … we can build a future together. Do you think that is possible?"

"Yes."

"You didn't even hesitate. Are you not going to think it over?"

"I don't have anything to think about. I know what I want." He reached out, cupping her cheek. "I want you, Ava. I'm not good at this stuff. I've never been great at it. With you, I want to try."

"Then we'll try," Ava said. "If you want to, that is."

"Yes."

She smiled. "I don't know what else to say."

"You don't need to say anything else." He stroked her cheek. "Let's get you inside. I don't want you catching a cold."

****

"Ava, I love you and I'm glad we're trying. I want to marry you," Smokey said.

"I don't get it. Are you asking her or stating that you want to?" Ugly Beast asked.

"I hate you right now."

"Hate me. You're not the one who has to sit and listen to his prez stumble over some quick and easy words."

"You're supposed to be helping me."

"I am. We're on a stakeout of the Twisted Bastards MC due to an anonymous tip. I didn't know that would mean I'd have to list to your endless list of shit proposals."

Smokey wasn't exactly happy about talking to his sergeant at arms about this either. He originally planned to do the stakeout with Raven, but with how new his relationship was with Ava, he didn't want to mess that up. This required a woman's touch. There was no way he was asking Abriana or Harlow since both women would go to Ava immediately.

He'd been tempted to ask her to marry him when she'd forgiven him in the car. That had been two weeks ago. He still hadn't asked.

He didn't know what was wrong with him because he wanted to marry this woman. She was his old lady in every single way that counted.

"You're supposed to be able to help me. You're married."

Ugly Beast laughed. "Do you even remember how I got married?"

Smokey sighed. "I arranged it. It was purely a business deal, but you and Abriana are going strong. You could help."

"I can't tell you how to marry a woman, Smokey. I didn't even know how to marry Abriana and be a good husband. It takes time and effort."

"You're not even tempted by any of the other women, are you?"

"Hell, no. If you're worried other women are going to have your attention, you're doing this all wrong and should just be a co-parent or whatever that is."

Smokey tapped his fingers on the steering wheel. He wanted to try again with his proposal, but he'd put Ugly Beast through a lot already.

"What's it like to watch the birthing process?"

"Holy shit, have I turned into your bitch now?"

"I'm still the boss and can whoop your ass. Don't start."

Ugly Beast ran a hand down his face. "We're not girlfriends. We shouldn't be sharing this shit."

"I know. I get it, but … Ava's getting bigger and well, she will drop soon, won't she?" Smokey asked. "I want to be in the room with her, but I've heard of some guys fainting. Is it the blood?"

Ugly Beast turned toward him. "We're really doing this?"

"I want to know."

"Dude, your woman's pussy is only so big and that thing has got to stretch to pop a kid out."

Smokey winced.

"Yeah, it's magical and all that. I held Abriana's hand. The screams alone are enough. She's going to be in pain. A lot of pain. You can't stop it. You can't make the doctors do anything if it's too late. You're helpless." Ugly Beast spun back around to face outside. "It's a lot to take in. It's not easy. With Abriana, I struggled. I wanted to kill every single fucking asshole in the room because they couldn't take the pain away."

"So, I'm not going to enjoy the birthing process."

"No. You're going to hate yourself and everyone around you. Then you're going to hear this scream and it's going to be an amazing sound. Your son or daughter is going to unleash in the world and you want to protect and love it for the rest of your life."

A smile played on Ugly Beast's lips, and for the first time in his life, Smokey was envious.

Ugly Beast had experienced love and having a child. Smokey wanted to have that as well.

"You'll find in time, you'll become anything and everything for your child and your woman, Smokey. We've got movement," Ugly Beast said.

Focusing back on the road, Smokey watched as three Twisted Bastards MC left the bar that they'd been at. Three girls were under their arms, all laughing.

Rather than follow them down the street in the car, he and Ugly Beast climbed out.

Keeping a distance, he put his hand on his gun, ready to strike at a moment's notice.

No one paid them any attention as they walked down an abandoned alley. He heard the men demand the women get on their knees, ready to take cock. Smokey wasn't ready to see any of the men's cocks, but he waited until they were vulnerable enough.

It wasn't long before their pants were around their ankles and the women were sucking at them.

"Showtime's over," Smokey said. He pointed the gun at the bastard's head while Ugly Beast came up behind him.

The women screamed at the sight of the guns, and they ran in the opposite direction. Ugly Beast laughed. "Well, well, well, I was out for some takeout and look what I find."

"Fuck you," the one on the right said.

Smokey took aim and fired in the fucker's thigh. He went down.

Ugly Beast tutted as the other two went to help their friend. "Don't move. Your dicks are still swinging free and I'm very trigger happy right now."

"What the fuck do you want?" the one he'd shot asked.

"What's Creed up to?" This was a long shot. Most men wouldn't give up shit on their president, but seeing as none of the men he'd caught with their pants down had any patch other than a member's one, they might value their lives more than their club.

"I don't know, man."

Smokey stared at the man. "Seeing as you don't know anything, you're free to go."

The man looked at him. There was something about him that rubbed Smokey the wrong way. He started down the alley, pants around his ankles, dripping blood, and he didn't even bother to look out for the men he was with.

Taking aim, he fired, shooting him in the back of the head. The man went down without issue.

Smokey spun around. "You're all going to end up like that." He smiled at each of them. "Now tell me, what's Creed up to?"

He waited as both men looked at each other. The one nearest Ugly Beast started to talk. He listened to the information provided.

The moment the man had nothing to say and begged for his life, he shot the one who hadn't spoken in the head, and Ugly Beast pounded the shit out of the rat. Even though they weren't part of the Twisted Bastards, a rat was a rat, and they had to be wiped off the face of the earth.

Once Ugly Beast was done, he picked the man up, and they walked back to the car, dumping him in the trunk.

"Do you believe what they said?" Ugly Beast asked.

Smokey spun the wheel, heading them right back to Twisted territory. He parked several miles from the clubhouse. Ugly Beast got out and pulled the beat-up member, dumping him on the ground.

"I don't care if it's right or not. The fact is they know about Ava. I've got to protect her."

Creed planned to kill Ava. That was what he'd been told tonight. His woman was in danger from being with him. He wasn't going to allow her to be hurt because of him.

"I want around-the-clock protection on her."

"Smokey, I know what they said, but you don't think they're bullshitting you, do you?" Ugly Beast asked.

"No."

"Come on. We know those pussies don't have a

whole lot of power in the club. Creed would be fucking crazy to allow anyone in on his plan. Especially ones who blab so easily."

"Would you willingly risk it with Abriana?" Smokey asked.

"No."

"Then don't assume I will. Ava's too important."

"This woman has got you twisted up, and you can't figure out how to ask her to marry you. Don't you think that is a little fucked up?"

Smokey gripped the steering wheel tighter. "We're not talking about this shit anymore. You had your chance to help me. That's over."

"I'm here if you change your mind. Remember, I'm in a successful marriage."

"Like you said, one I organized. You didn't do shit."

Ugly Beast glared at him and Smokey smiled.

They arrived at the clubhouse with everyone present so he could give them a rundown of what went on tonight.

"I want volunteers," Smokey said. "To help me protect Ava."

"You really think Creed will come after her?" Raven asked. "She's a woman and has nothing to do with the club."

"He did the first time. Look what I did. I imagine the next time, he'll take her out."

Raven sighed. "I'm in. I'll protect her."

"You don't have to do that."

"I helped Creed last time, didn't I? She won't come around the club and even though she has opened up the bakery to us once again, I can't bring myself to go inside. Not after what I did. I can protect her. There's nothing else I can do to make this right, but I can kick anyone who thinks they can get close."

Smokey thanked her. One by one, all of his men agreed to take turns protecting Ava. This was his club, his family.

After ending church, he climbed on his bike and rode to Ava's house.

She hadn't given him a key yet, but the moment he climbed off his bike, she'd opened the front door.

"Welcome home," she said.

He smiled, pulling her into his arms. "This is the best wake-up call a man could ask for." He pressed his lips to her, wanting to hold her and to never let her go.

"Whoa, what's wrong, Smokey?"

He tightened his hold on her. "I'm just glad to see you."

"And I'm glad to see you, but this is something more. Come on, stop holding back. Tell me what's the matter."

Smokey pulled away and stared into her eyes. She was so beautiful. So sweet.

"I … you trust me?"

"Yes, of course."

"From this day forward, you're going to have one or more of the guys tagging along."

Ava groaned. "I know I'm getting close to dropping, but we've got time."

Smokey put his hand on her stomach, crouching down to kiss her. "It's not about our baby arriving too soon. This is about something more."

"What is it?"

He ran fingers through his hair. "I don't want to scare you."

"You are scaring me. I can't go around not knowing what's bothering you. Tell me, Smokey. Now." She spoke softly.

"I've got reason to believe Creed isn't done. He's going to try to take you from me."

"Take me?"

"Yeah. He's going to try to hurt you."

"That's not possible. I'm safe."

"You'll be even safer with one of my guys with you. I'll feel happier you're living normally with one of my guys."

Ava rubbed the back of her head and stepped back.

He didn't like having any space between them.

"Are you sure?"

"I'm positive."

"I'm no one," she said. "Why would this man want me?"

"Because you're the love of my life, and he knows it."

"Smokey, come on."

"No. I can't. It's the truth. You don't believe me, but I've loved you long before I found out you were pregnant. I fucked up once. I'm not going to do it again. I refuse to do it again." He stepped toward her, cupping her face. "I'm in love with you. Creed knows it. He's going to try to take you from me. I can't let that happen."

"I thought I was done with the crying part."

"I know it's going to take time for you to believe me, and I've got all the time in the world." He pressed a kiss to her lips. "But don't put your own life on the line. Let me take care of you. Let me keep you safe."

"Fine. You can … do that. If it will make you feel better."

"It will. It really will." He pulled her into his arms, dreading the thought of anything happening to her.

He loved this woman more than anything, and one day soon, he was determined for her to wear his ring.

Chapter Twenty-One

"She's just going to sit there?" Harlow asked.

"Yep. Just like all the others."

It had been over a month since Smokey had arrived home and told her his fear of this man Creed.

She glanced over at Raven and quickly averted her gaze. So far, every single day, she'd had a new MC member either sit in her bakery, escort her to the grocery store, and pretty much was a bodyguard to her every waking move.

The only time she was left alone was when Smokey arrived to take over. Having someone breathing down her neck twenty-four seven was proving to be exhausting.

Her pregnancy was also causing her some difficulty as she neared her due date. She was supposed to give birth in the New Year. Christmas was right around the corner, but she had a feeling this baby was going to come sooner. She hoped it did because it was driving her crazy. The constant need to pee. The uncomfortable movement.

Smokey loved spending the time feeling their baby move. He believed they were going to have a son because of how many times he kicked. Ava wasn't sure. So long as their baby was happy and healthy, she didn't care.

"Don't you think it's weird? She doesn't do anything," Harlow said.

"I can hear you."

Raven didn't move her head. She continued to look out the window. Ava sighed. She had offered Raven a hot beverage, and the woman had accepted.

It seemed odd to her now that she'd once been friends with this woman. She did miss the closeness. She doubted she'd ever be close to Raven again.

"So, you can hear. Can you do magic tricks?"

Raven turned toward her. "Who are you?"

"That's rude," Ava said.

"Oh, come on, is that all you've got?" Harlow asked.

"You think you can take me on in insults?"

"I lived with plenty of brothers. Big Dick being one of them. I've heard it all, babe."

Raven snorted.

"Enough," Ava said. "You two might want to verbally spar, but I still have a business to run." She picked up a discarded napkin, and as she stood up, a shooting pain went right through her back. Wincing, she rubbed at the spot.

Harlow and Raven were at her side.

She looked at Raven's hands on her, and she instantly withdrew.

"Are you okay?" Raven asked.

"I'm fine. Just another part of being pregnant I'm not going to miss." She stepped away from their comforting hands and threw the napkin in the trash. She rubbed at her stomach and back.

"You really should go home and rest," Harlow said. "I can handle this here."

"I'm fine."

"No, you're not. You're hurting, and you're tired. I love your company. You know this, but I know enough that I can keep this place running smoothly."

The doctor had advised her to take it easy.

She spent most of her day on her ass, which she hated. Ava had always liked moving around, doing something with her hands. She couldn't stand sitting around and not accomplishing anything.

When the pain didn't lessen, she went to her

chair, aware of Raven's gaze following her.

"I'm fine," she said, sitting down.

"Do you want me to take you home?"

"No. I can get through a day." She took several deep breaths until the pain abated somewhat.

Ava forced a smile to her face. "Thank you."

"For what?"

"For caring."

Raven nodded. "I … I never wanted to hurt you. The club comes first. I thought … you know what I thought."

"I know."

"I'm sorry."

Ava nodded.

She looked at Raven, wanting to say so many different things to her. Screaming was high on her list, but she settled on silence.

Raven's arms were folded and as Ava looked at her, really stared at her friend, she realized how vulnerable Raven actually looked.

She wanted to protect her. This was an odd feeling. She continued to rub the base of her back. Forgiveness. Did she truly forgive Raven for everything she'd done? That was a whole lot to give at that moment.

The baby, Smokey, the club, she didn't want to live her life in fear, but she also didn't want people to feel constantly guilty when they were around each other.

"Raven," she said.

The woman turned her head toward her.

Ava was about to say something as the front door was slammed open, the glass breaking from the force of the impact.

Raven was up and Ava watched as she started to fight the first man that came at her.

Three men wearing black masks filled the store.

Ava stood as one came toward her. She held her hands into fists. There was no way she was terrifying. Swollen stomach, probably her entire body as well, threatening this man, but she'd do anything to protect her baby.

Harlow was suddenly there, throwing her foot in the air, taking him off guard as she swiped him in the face.

"Ava, run," Harlow said.

She wanted to argue, but instead, she took off, trying to go for the office, but she didn't get far as someone caught her hair, yanking her back.

The impact hitting a hard body winded her, and the pain worsened.

"You're about to have a lot of fun," he said, whispering the words against her ear. He wrapped his fingers around her neck and dragged her out of the shop and into the black van waiting for them.

She was thrown into the back and she pushed her hair out of the way, looking up to find Raven unconscious on the floor. There was no sign of Harlow, and fear gripped her at the thought of what could have happened to her friend.

"Raven?"

She crawled to her friend, touching her face, then her neck, feeling for a pulse. When she found one, she nearly cried out with relief. There was no way her friend could be dead.

Fear lodged in her throat as she moved to cradle Raven's head in her lap. She ran her fingers through the woman's hair.

"I've got you." She closed her eyes as another bolt of pain worked its way up her spine.

Breathing deeply, she continued to whimper as they went over some potholes. Each jar of the van causing more pain.

She didn't know how long they'd been driving for before Raven began to wake up.

"Fuck, ouch, fuck," Raven said, wincing.

Ava stroked her hair. "You're awake. You're fine, I hope."

Raven opened her eyes and she watched as the other woman became aware of her surroundings. "Where are we?"

"I don't know."

She didn't sit up.

Ava stayed, running her fingers through her hair.

"One of them got me good."

"I was dragged in here," she said, sniffling. "Harlow's not here."

"She'll be okay," Raven said.

She sat up with a groan, sitting on the opposite side of the van. "Smokey's going to kill me for this."

"Do you know who we've been taken by?" Ava asked.

"The Twisted Bastards. They weren't wearing leather cuts, but they're the only ones after you and they are pissed at us for shutting down several of their operations."

"Smokey warned me."

"You were his top priority."

"The club comes first."

Raven laughed. "They all say the club comes first, but we all know they think with their dick." Raven closed her eyes, frowning. "I don't mean anything bad by that."

Ava smiled. "It's fine."

"What I meant to say was Smokey loves you. I'm not talking the sweet kind of romance either. I'm talking the full-on die-for-you kind of love. I never thought I'd see him fall hard for a woman. I'm glad he has."

Ava smiled. "I love him so much. There are times I can't even think of being without him, and I'm so jealous of the women at the club."

"He'd get rid of them in a heartbeat if that's what you wanted."

"He told me, but he warned me the guys would hate me."

Raven laughed. "Yeah, they would. They would totally be pissed about it."

Ava's hands continued to shake.

"We'll make it out of here," Raven said.

"How can you be so sure?"

"I know Smokey. I know the town. He'll be alerted in no time what happened. Harlow's involved, so we know Big Dick will be all over it. He has the ability to find anyone. We'll be fine, Ava. We've just got to make it through."

The truck came to a stop.

"Don't do anything stupid," Ava said.

"Like what, like charge at them?"

Raven got into a position as if to attack, but Ava reached out.

"Don't. Don't make them angry." She didn't want Raven to get hurt.

Raven settled down, taking a seat.

Ava breathed a sigh of relief.

They had to get through this.

The truck's back doors opened, and men rushed in, grabbing them. Raven didn't fight them, but she struggled in their arms.

Ava didn't have the energy nor the strength to fight.

The hand holding her was tight, and she gritted her teeth, putting a hand to her stomach as they entered a large warehouse. There were a few boxes in the corner, and Ava tried to figure out where they could be.

The sound of applause made her stop. She turned toward it and saw the man who'd turned her entire world upside down by taking pictures outside of a bank.

Creed. He wasn't in a business suit anymore. The leather cut with the logo was a clear indication of who he was and what he belonged to.

"It was about time you got here. I was starting to worry."

"Well, if it's not little pussy Creed," Raven said. "You're going to take more pictures, you fucking prick?"

Raven was shoved forward, and she went down on the floor, being kicked in the back for her troubles.

Ava gritted her teeth.

Creed reached down, grabbing Raven's hair and pulling her to her feet. She didn't scream.

"How did that go for you? From what I saw, Ava got a nice face pounding for the trouble."

"Fuck you," Raven said.

Creed glanced toward her. "I've always wondered what made Smokey tick. I never thought I'd live to see the day that person is a woman. Tell me, Raven, what will you do to make sure I don't have my men touch her? Fuck her up? Rape her?" Creed asked.

Ava's heart started to race.

The grip on her arm tightened and she whimpered.

Raven spun toward her. "Don't you fucking touch her."

"Answer now," Creed said.

"I'll do anything. You know that."

Creed smiled, and fear rushed up Ava's spine as she looked at him.

"I thought you might say that."

Ava was pulled across the room and dumped into a chair. More pain rushed through her body, and she wrapped an arm around her stomach protectively.

Smokey had to come and get them.

Whatever was about to happen, it was going to be bad. She knew it in her gut.

Creed moved to her side and he snapped his fingers. One man stood forward.

"Then you're going to fight for her. Every punch and blow you get will help save her."

"No," Ava said. "You can't do this."

"Shut up, Ava," Raven said.

"Let's see what you're made of, Raven, and just how long you last. The moment you fall, Ava's all mine."

Raven turned toward Creed. "So, it's true then, you always want what Smokey has. His town, his club, his turf, his woman. The list keeps adding up. Scared to be an original?"

Ava tried to take in air as Creed wrapped his fingers around her throat, cutting off circulation.

She couldn't breathe.

"Stop it. Stop it."

Seconds passed.

She was going to faint.

He let her go and she took in several deep breaths of air.

"Fucker, she's pregnant."

"Which will make losing them both all the more fun. Now, let's see you earn back her life."

Raven stared at her, and Ava shook her head even as tears came to her eyes.

She rubbed her stomach as Raven spun and faced off with the first man who came. Ava couldn't stand it as Raven fought. Several blows were landed on Raven's body, but the woman didn't fall.

After a few minutes, she managed to connect with the man's balls, sending him to the floor, where she punched him in the face.

It wasn't over.

Ava watched helplessly as the woman fought for her. Some of the men were harder than others and Raven continued to fight even when bones had to have broken. One of the men grabbed her arm and twisted it, and Ava screamed right along with her as it popped right out.

She wanted to protect her, but Raven wouldn't stop.

Even with only one arm, she kept on fighting.

Blood covered her face, and she saw some dripping onto the floor. Ava couldn't stand it.

After all this time, Raven was fighting for them both, and all Ava wanted to do was tell her to stop.

****

Smokey stood with Carlos as he got the call.

Harlow's voice sounded cracked as she sobbed at him.

"They took Ava and Raven." Harlow cried out. "I think I'm dying."

The line went dead.

Big Dick was close and he looked at his prez. Without another word, he was out of the warehouse. They weren't too far from Fort Clover.

"What's going on?" Carlos asked.

Smokey looked at the man.

So far, in the last few months, he'd proven to be nothing like his predecessor. "I think my woman and Raven have been taken. I'll have to rearrange this meeting."

He didn't linger, going to his bike as Big Dick took off. He didn't blame the man. Big Dick had told him that his parents wanted him to keep an eye on Harlow. They discovered she worked for his woman, and parents could be so judgmental. They didn't like any of their kids working for the MC.

At his back, Kinky, Hunter, and Brick followed.

He used his speed, pulling himself in front of Big Dick. They arrived in town in record time. The door of the bakery was completely smashed, and his heart raced as he stepped inside. Harlow rested against the front of the counter, her hand near her stomach. She looked pale.

Big Dick was by her side, moving her hand.

A piece of glass had been thrust into her stomach. "You know, this really hurts," Harlow said.

"What the hell happened?" Smokey asked.

"It as an ambush. They came for Ava. Raven fought them, but there were three of them. I tried to help. They took them." Harlow groaned. "I think Ava's going to give birth. Her back was hurting her, and I think that's the first sign." Her voice started to fade, and Big Dick picked Harlow up.

She passed out.

"I've got to go," Big Dick said.

"Get her to the hospital. The club will handle all medical costs."

Big Dick was out of the door. Elijah had already made it to town with one of the cars, and Smokey watched as they drove off.

Glancing around the bakery, he knew Creed had taken his woman. There was no doubt in his mind.

"I'll gather the boys," Hunter said.

"It won't be enough time. Creed will be anywhere, and Big Dick's got to take care of his sister."

"Club comes first," Hunter said.

"Family comes first. Harlow's a young kid, and she's ... my woman's friend. I'm not going to find Ava and tell her that I let her friend die." He ran a hand down his face, aware of people watching him.

Smokey watched as Carlos arrived on the scene. He climbed out of his car with several soldiers in tow.

"What the fuck are you doing here?" Smokey asked.

"You need help, and seeing as I can offer you that help, I want to."

"This club is nothing to you. My woman is my responsibility."

"Call it an investment. If you try to retrieve both women and some of you die, it's a poor investment for me. I don't get the same standard I've become accustomed to."

Smokey laughed. "You're talking bullshit."

"I'm helping, Smokey. We can work together or apart. That's up to you." Carlos adjusted his cuffs. "Seeing as I already have intel on where Creed may be holding those women, and Ava is close to giving birth, I'd say you don't have much choice. My men are available right now. You'd have to organize your men. One of the women could die in the process."

"I fucking hate you right now."

"Hate me all you want. You know I speak the truth."

He still hated him for it.

"Fine."

"Good." Carlos clicked his fingers and a laptop was given to him. "Here is your last known location of Creed."

"You had this on you the entire time?"

"Creed and the Twisted Bastards MC are enemies of ours as well. You never stay one step ahead unless you know your enemy's next move. This is where we last located. Where would he take them."

Smokey looked at the map and clicked on the keyboard, bringing it in closer.

The place Creed was last seen was a motel, but he would be too stupid to take Ava and Raven there.

Smokey looked around and knew exactly where he'd go.

"There," he said.

"That's where he is."

Carlos closed the laptop and left.

"Call the boys," he said, turning to Hunter.

"You need me with you."

"I need you to grab our men in case this goes south fucking quickly. Do it. I can't have anything happen to Ava."

Hunter nodded.

"The rest of you, you're with me."

He went to his bike, straddling the machine, purring it to life, and took off, heading toward the warehouse where Ava was.

If anything had happened to his woman, he wouldn't fucking hesitate. He'd kill the bastard. There was no way he was going to be able to live.

With his men at his back, and Carlos and his men trailing behind him, Smokey tried to focus on finding his woman. On loving her. Never letting a moment pass him by when she didn't know the truth.

He gripped his handlebars, trying not to let his emotions get the better of him. He was always in control. Right now, he felt close to exploding. He itched to kill Creed. To watch the life extinguish from him.

As he rode hard, the time passed too fucking slow. He was already breaking speed limits, and as he got closer to his destination, his need to hurt Creed increased. He wanted to annihilate him. To watch him fucking burn.

Ava's sweet smile. Her kisses. The way she held him. It all flashed through his mind.

He was coming for her.

As he got near the warehouse, the smart thing to do would be to stop and sneak upon them. Smokey didn't have time for that. He continued to drive past the part he would normally park to attack. He rode straight into the gates, pulling out his gun and firing at the single guard he saw waiting.

One by one, his men joined him, as did the cars.

Smokey didn't wait.

His woman was in that warehouse. She needed him.

Holding his gun firmly in his hand, he shot at two men coming toward him.

His brothers joined him as they advanced into the warehouse. More men wearing the Twisted Bastards insignia came forward.

He fired. Some going for the head, others for the leg.

Ava's scream filled the air.

Panic rushed through him as he advanced into the warehouse, aware of Carlos joining him. There were club men everywhere.

Fire rushed through his shoulder as he took a bullet. He ignored the pain, firing.

Trusting his men and Carlos to keep the bullets off his back, he charged forward and came to a stop where he saw Creed holding a gun to Ava's head.

She held her stomach and he spotted a bruise forming on her cheek.

"Hello, Smokey."

"You should have left her alone."

"What kind of fun would that have been? You wouldn't have come to claim her?" Creed licked her cheek and Ava screamed.

The sound was full of pain.

"Raven did provide me with some entertainment, but she was no match for my men." Creed glanced toward Smokey's left.

He knew Raven was on the floor. He'd caught sight of the puddle of blood.

Smokey didn't know if she was dead or not, but Creed's life had only minutes left to it.

Creed leaned down. "He's wondering if he can kill me. How you will see him if he kills me right here. Will you be able to love a killer, Ava? Or will you turn your back on him like everyone else in the world?"

Ava turned to look at Creed. "I don't care if he kills you." She looked toward him. "He made me watch as Raven took each punch, each beating. He deserves to die."

That was all Smokey needed.

Aiming at Creed's head, he shot a single bullet, and it went straight through his head.

Ava let out a cry, moving out of Creed's hold.

Carlos came forward as Ava screamed.

Smokey watched as liquid fell between her thighs, coating the floor. He went to his woman.

"The baby's coming, Smokey." She sobbed.

"I've got you."

He glanced over at Carlos, who had picked up Raven.

"She's got a pulse, but it's faint. I will take her to the hospital."

"If anything happens to her—" Smokey said.

"Nothing will happen to her."

Smokey knew that sound. He knew what Carlos was thinking and feeling.

"You don't get to have her," he said.

Carlos didn't say a word. He turned on his heel, and Smokey went to put that shit to right, but Ava screamed and he watched as she began to turn red.

"Our baby's coming. I'm not in the hospital and it's coming."

"We need to get her to the hospital," Ugly Beast said.

Ava chose that moment to scream again. He grabbed her hands as she spread her legs.

"Check," Smokey said.

"Dude, I'm not checking."

"I need to know if I can get her to the hospital. You're the only one who knows what you're looking for."

"Dude, that requires me looking at your woman's … parts."

"Do it," Smokey yelled as his woman screamed some more.

Ugly Beast looked like he wanted to kill him.

He did as asked.

Ugly Beast lifted up Ava's skirt and quickly pushed it down. "Oh, yeah, that baby is coming."

Ava shook her head. "No. No. No. No. It can't come here. There's so much blood. I watched Raven fight for me." She sobbed. "I never got to tell her that I forgive her. I saw what they did, Smokey."

"Raven is going to be okay. What we've got to do now is focus on you."

Kinky, Hunter, Brick, Elijah, and Demon were there.

"Let's get this out of the way." He pointed at the body behind him as he removed his leather cut. "You're not going to make it to the hospital, but we'll take you there as soon as we can." He looked at Ugly Beast. "You're going to help deliver."

"What? Fuck no. I don't know how to do that shit."

Smokey was already taking out his cell phone, dialing Ava's doctor.

"It hurts. I need to push."

The doctor answered, and Smokey quickly brought him up to speed.

"You need to bring her into the hospital."

"Not happening. She's having this baby right here. Right now. We'll bring her to you as soon as it's safe for us to move her."

Ava chose that moment to scream.

The next few minutes were the most surreal of Smokey's life. With the doctor instructing, Ugly Beast helped them to give birth to his son.

Chapter Twenty-Two

"It's good to see you awake," Ava said.

Raven groaned. "Thanks."

The woman looked so damn small in the hospital bed.

"Can you ask Smokey when I get out of here? I can't stand hospitals."

"I know." Ava wanted to get closer. "Thank you."

Raven opened the one eye that wasn't badly swollen. "For what?"

"For protecting me and Umberto."

Raven groaned. "Umberto? Why the fuck would you call your kid that?"

"Smokey told me it was important. Ugly Beast helped to bring him into the world. I don't think he'd like the name Raven, but if I have a little girl, I'm going to call her that." She smiled at the other woman. "Thank you. You didn't have to do that."

"I did."

"No, you really didn't." She got to her feet and moved a little close to the bed. Her son made a little moaning sound that caught at her heart. "I forgive you, Raven. Don't ever put yourself in danger for me again."

"I care about you, Ava. It wasn't out of guilt that I did what I did. You're Smokey's woman, and you're one of my friends. I fucked up. I wasn't a good friend."

"Then let's agree from this day forward, what happened in that basement, stays in it. You and I, we're good. We're friends again."

Tears fell from Raven's eyes, but the woman didn't sob or show any other indication that she was crying. "I'd like that."

"Would you like to see him?"

Raven nodded.

Ava chuckled. "He's such a big boy."

"I love kids," Raven said.

"I've seen the way you are with Bella. You're good with kids."

"How's Harlow?" Raven asked.

"She's fine. She lost a lot of blood, but the glass didn't hit any major arteries," Ava said. She'd already gone to see Harlow. The other woman was in good spirits. Her parents were angry, but Harlow wouldn't hear a bad word said about her or the club. She was due to go home tomorrow. She was already talking about returning to work.

The sound of a voice clearing had her turning to see Smokey standing in the doorway.

"I'm sorry I failed you," Raven said. "I will hand in my leather cut."

"Don't talk so fucking stupid." Smokey entered the room, coming to her side. "I'm not here to take your cut from you, Raven. I came to thank you."

"Thank me?"

"I didn't expect you to win being ambushed. You saved Ava and my son the best way you could. I'm not going to hold it against you, being taken. That could have happened to anyone."

"I tried so hard," Raven said.

Smokey went to take her hand, but one of them was crushed and the other had been broken.

He put his hand gently on her cheek. "You did, and I'm so proud of you. Your place at the club will never be in question. The guys are all proud of you."

"Which one of you had to carry my ass out?" Raven asked.

"That would have been me," Carlos said.

Ava turned to see Carlos. The other man's arms were folded, and Smokey had told her who he was and what he did. In fact, over the past couple of days since giving birth in the warehouse, Smokey had shared a lot about the club. More than she thought he ever would.

"Why are you here?" Smokey asked.

"To see how she's doing. She was in pretty bad shape."

"We can take care of our own," Smokey said.

Carlos smiled. "Until next time. I hope you continue to recover."

Ava looked at Carlos then at Raven.

They didn't leave until after Carlos, and Raven was exhausted. She passed Kinky who sat outside the door reading a book.

He offered her a smile, and she returned it.

Umberto was getting quite heavy in her arms. Smokey, seeing her struggling, took his son in one arm, holding him close, and with the other, he wrapped his arm around her waist.

"What was that all about?" she asked, as they took the elevator.

"What was what?"

"You didn't see that?" Ava asked.

"What?"

"The way Carlos looked at Raven?"

Smokey shook his head.

"You totally did see it. Don't even deny it."

"I saw it, but it can never happen."

The elevator opened up and they stepped out, making their way toward the exit. Ava was already planning a gift basket to bring back to Raven. "Why not?"

"Simple, Carlos is mafia. He has to marry a very sweet, virginal woman from his own kind."

Ava frowned and shook her head. "That doesn't seem right."

"Right or not, that's what has to happen. It's their rules."

"Rules are stupid."

Smokey leaned into the car to put Umberto into the car seat. Ava climbed in to strap him in.

Her breasts felt heavy, so he would be hungry soon.

"Have I turned you into a rebel?" Smokey asked. "Since when does my woman think rules are stupid?"

She laughed. "You know what I mean." She shrugged. "They are."

"I don't know if I like this new woman."

He cupped her cheek, running his thumb across her lip. "Marry me."

Ava gasped. "What?"

"Marry me. I'm in love with you, Ava, and I believe you're in love with me too. I want to have the world with you. I know I can't offer you a normal life, but I can offer you one filled with lots of love. You'll never want for anything."

She couldn't believe what she was hearing.

He wanted to marry her.

He loved her.

She loved him so much.

"I don't want anything else. I only want you. I love you. Yes."

"Yes?"

"Yes, I'll marry you."

She watched as he patted down his leather cut, then his jeans before holding out a ring.

"You bought a ring?"

"I've been wanting to ask you to marry me for some time."

This did surprise her.

"I love you, Ava. I've been wanting to make you

mine. The guys think I'm pussy-whipped. I tried to practice how to ask you to marry me."

She cupped his cheek, leaning over Umberto to kiss him. "This is perfect."

"I'll never treat you like your ex did."

She laughed. "I should hope not."

He slid the ring onto her finger, and it was the perfect fit.

Smokey couldn't offer her normal or easy, but she didn't want that. She'd fallen in love with the President of the Hell's Bastards MC. She didn't want any other kind of life.

Epilogue

Ava laughed at the scowl on Raven's face. Her long black hair was pulled back into a ponytail with a few strands falling around her face. The bruises had long gone, and she'd been doing some physical therapy for her leg and hand.

Most of the damage had been healed with time, however, Raven had also been living with Abriana, and that woman had bought her dresses. It was why they were at the Fort Clover summer picnic, and she looked like she wanted to commit murder.

Ava sat with Umberto resting against her stomach. She lay on her side, watching her friend. Harlow had already made her excuses to leave. Raven's bad mood had gotten to her, and she'd headed off somewhere.

"You find this funny?"

"Who wouldn't?"

Ava ran fingers through her hair. It had started to grow out again. She had thought about having it cut, but Smokey loved the length.

Speaking of her husband, she glanced over to see him talking with Carlos. The mafia man seemed to be spending a lot more time in town, which pissed Smokey off.

Raven didn't look toward him, and Ava wondered if the other woman even realized she had an admirer.

Smokey shook Carlos's hand and then made his way to their picnic mat. He sat next to Ava's head and she rested on his thigh.

He stroked his fingers through her hair.

"You're looking pretty, Raven."

She glared at Smokey, got to her feet, and

stormed off.

"You did that on purpose?"

"What? I said just the right thing that would piss her off and make her walk off? I didn't mean to."

"You're lying." Ava sat up, putting a hand on Umberto's stomach.

Smokey reached out, stroking his son's head.

The club surrounded them, and she felt at peace just by being near them. In the last few months, she'd gotten over her anxiety when it came to stepping foot into the club. She spent a great deal of time there.

The memories, no matter how painful, were all in the past, and she was determined to move on.

Raven struggled.

Smokey had told her many times how she woke up the clubhouse screaming. Sometimes, Ava was there and she'd go to her, offering her comfort.

"What were you and Carlos talking about?" Ava asked.

"He's purchased a house in town."

"He has?"

"Yes."

"And you're happy with that?"

"I'm not happy with any of it. I don't want him near Raven nor in town. One problem at a time."

"Have you heard who has replaced Creed?" she asked. That name left a bitter taste in her mouth.

"No. They're still arguing for leadership. I'll deal with whatever comes. You know me. No more talk of shop or business." He pulled her close, resting his face against her neck. "Where do you want to go on your honeymoon?"

"I thought we couldn't go."

"I've already organized it. Hunter can handle things. If things fuck up, I'm a phone call away. Harlow

SMOKEY

can handle everything at the bakery. I want to take you and Umberto somewhere."

Ava smiled as she glanced behind her. "I only ever want to be where you are. You pick a place, and I know I'll love it."

Smokey gripped the back of her neck and slammed his lips down on hers.

She had finally found what she'd longed for.

Her soulmate.

The End

www.samcrescent.com

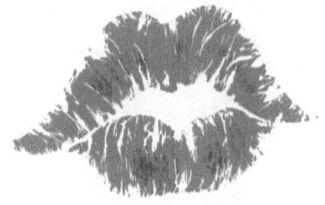

EVERNIGHT PUBLISHING ®

www.evernightpublishing.com

www.ingramcontent.com/pod-product-compliance
Lightning Source LLC
Chambersburg PA
CBHW031547240626
47153CB00002B/417